Praise for

T H O S E G I R L S

////////////////////////

"Saft has captured **the darker side of female friendship** and the redemption of forgiveness. Hand to fans of **edgy chick lit**."

—BOOKLIST

"In this debut novel, Saft gives readers a look at the **complicated relationships** between high school girlfriends. The female characters she crafts are **complex**."

—SLJ

"I read *Those Girls* the way you accidentally binge-watch a great TV show—I always had to know what happened next. Lauren Saft's debut novel is **smart**, **funny**, and **raw**, and I can't wait for more people to read it so we can talk about it."

—*New York Times* bestselling author SARAH MLYNOWSKI

"*Those Girls* spills over with secrets, backbiting, and messy, messy love. Saft doesn't back away from the **ugly truths** or the **beautiful complexities** of female friendships. She simply tells it **exactly like it is**."

—SIOBHAN VIVIAN, author of *The List*

THOSE GIRLS

LAUREN SAFT

POPPY

LITTLE, BROWN AND COMPANY

NEW YORK   BOSTON

Poppy

Hachette Book Group
1290 Avenue of the Americas, New York, NY 10104
Visit us at lb-teens.com

Poppy is an imprint of Little, Brown and Company.
The Poppy name and logo are trademarks of Hachette Book Group, Inc.

The publisher is not responsible for websites (or their content)
that are not owned by the publisher.

First Paperback Edition: May 2016
First published in hardcover in June 2015 by Little, Brown and Company

Library of Congress Cataloging-in-Publication Data

Saft, Lauren.
Those girls : a novel / by Lauren Saft. — First edition.
pages cm
"Poppy."
Summary: Eleventh grade at Greencliff, an all-girl school near Philadelphia, is momentous for long-term best friends Alex, Mollie, and Veronica, as the secrets they are keeping from each other about boyfriends, eating disorders, and more begin to undermine their relationships.
ISBN 978-0-316-40366-5 (hc) — ISBN 978-0-316-26016-9 (pb) —
ISBN 978-0-316-40367-2 (ebook)   [1. Best friends—Fiction.
2. Friendship—Fiction.   3. Conduct of life—Fiction.
4. Dating (Social customs)—Fiction.   5. High schools—Fiction.
6. Schools—Fiction.   7. Bands (Music)—Fiction.]   I. Title.
PZ7.S1293Tho 2015   [Fic]—dc23   2014009416

10 9 8 7 6 5 4 3 2 1

RRD-C

Printed in the United States of America

To Maggie, Laura, and Liz,
for being my biggest supporters, my best friends,
and the reason I will always know the difference
between these girls and those

Part 1

BACK TO SCHOOL

ALEXANDRA HOLBROOK

Same shit, new year. The first day of eleventh grade. Mollie called at the ass crack of dawn to ask if I'd pick her up for school. Was a really sunny day, September—my favorite time of year. Everything, everyone, is so fresh and unsoiled: new books, new shoes, a new haircut, like summer is some sort of master cleanse reset button. I figured Mollie's request for a pre-school rendezvous was to orchestrate a united front against Veronica, who would surely come bouncing in with her usual tales of European slutcapades that neither of us was impressed by anymore.

When I pulled into her driveway, Mollie was already waiting for me. Mollie, my best friend since kindergarten. I don't totally remember how we became best friends or when we decided to call ourselves such, but the fact that Mollie Finn and Alex Holbrook are best friends is pretty much the only absolute truth that I (and the rest of Greencliff) know to count on. I have no memory of a time when this wasn't the case.

We've done everything together. Besides both being lifers at the esteemed Harwin School for Girls, we took tennis, gymnastics, and horseback riding lessons. Brought each other on family vacations, to religious functions, and to holiday dinners. We even had our first kiss on the same night, at the same time (not with each other, obviously).

At school, people actually get up and move over if one of us walks into a room and there isn't a seat next to the other one. Without even being asked. It's just understood that we are supposed to be next to each other. All the time. Alex-and-Mollie, one compound word, rolled off the collective Greencliff tongue like Romeo-and-Juliet or Sodom-and-Gomorrah.

We brought Veronica in when she came to Harwin in fifth grade. I liked her first—Mollie thought she was snobby. I liked that Veronica was tall (like me) and that she did dumb things like run around naked (which was cuter when we were ten) and make up words to songs, and that she would talk to anyone about anything and seemed to be just completely missing the embarrassment gene, which I sometimes felt was the only one I possessed. Mollie started dating Brian O'Connell in seventh grade, so I started going over to Veronica's house after school instead of hers. We'd swim in her pool and try on her mom's clothes and make amateur music videos. We'd do stuff that Mollie would be too regimented and self-conscious to do. Stuff that Mollie might try to do with someone else but couldn't with me, because I knew her too well. I'd see the awkwardness in her eyes; I'd see her scrutinizing herself from the outside, judging herself, wondering what she looked like, who was watching, what they thought, and if they thought she looked dumb or fat or like she was trying too hard. She'd see me seeing her looking like she was trying to look like she was having fun. And then no one would be having any fun.

Anyway, then we got to high school, and Mollie and Veronica (not me) started getting invited to the senior parties. They hooked up with older guys and were the "hot freshmen," and that's how Veronica officially became our third. We'd auditioned other ones here and there over the years, like Jessica Sawyer (lived too far away), Liz Masterson (had a really strict mom), and Emily Canter (kleptomaniac), but Veronica was just the one that stuck.

But through all the guest stars, Mollie and I never drifted. We never fought (out loud) or disagreed or veered from our self-proclaimed title of best friends. Even if we weren't sure why we chose each other anymore, of all the other best friends we could have chosen, what we knew was that it was working for us, and it made us feel protected and powerful in the fickle and volatile Greencliff private school battleground. Our best-friendship was our life raft—I imagine the army employs the buddy system for similar reasons. It was our job to make sure the other was never left behind. Even when I stopped going to Mollie's house after school, I'd call her at night and we'd talk about Veronica or Brian or our parents or how we were so lucky to have each other, someone else who truly understood what it was to hate everything.

She stood in her driveway now, planted next to her mailbox like a lawn ornament, arms crossed, biting her thumbnail, tapping her snakeskin ballet flats.

"Can we stop at a drug store?" she groaned, slamming the door of my antique Volvo.

"Sure. Why?" But I already knew why.

"I need to take a Plan B."

"Again?" I said, exhaling my morning Marlboro Light, backing out of her cul-de-sac. "You do realize that Plan B is not actually a recognized form of birth control."

"The condom broke. Fuck you."

I rolled my eyes. Mollie was always having some sort of pregnancy or STD or UTI crisis—in my opinion a convoluted way to keep her active sex life a relevant topic of conversation.

"You really want to take it again? You puked for, like, twenty-four hours straight last time."

"Better to puke today than every day for the next nine months."

She pulled her silky blond hair into a ponytail, opened her mouth, and applied eyeliner in my rearview mirror, which meant that she was expecting to see her boyfriend, the glorious and notorious Sam Fuchs, at some point midday. No one wore eyeliner to an all-girls school unless they were expecting an unexpected visit from a boy.

"You're probably not even ovulating. People try for like years to get pregnant and can't. All odds and Sam's roid-raged, THC-saturated sperm considered, I very seriously doubt that you managed to conceive last night."

"This morning…" She snickered.

I knew she wanted me to ask how she managed that, but I refused to take the bait. Mollie was having sex. I was not. And she felt the need to remind me of this on a daily basis. Because, for the first time, we were not in the same place at the same time, and she seemed to revel in that.

I had news of my own for her for once. News I'd been

putting off sharing for weeks but knew I'd eventually have to tell her. I figured now was the perfect time to slip it—while she was busy in her own vortex of self-obsession.

"By the way," I choked out as we turned into the parking lot, "I'm doing something kind of random."

She looked at me cross-eyed. "Uh, what?"

"I'm trying out for a band."

She laughed. "You're joking? When?"

"Wednesday."

As we pulled into the suburban shopping center, silver, white, and navy SUVs pulled in and out of the spots around us. Greencliff moms with frosted ponytails wearing full-body Lululemon armor bounced in and out of the CVS and Starbucks and tanning salon holding toddlers and lattes, pushing strollers and fingering their smartphones. Dads puttered around the parking lot in business suits, clutching paper coffee cups, noses buried in *Inquirer*s and *Wall Street Journal*s on their way downtown into Philadelphia. Greencliff was already abuzz, and dew hadn't even burned off the asphalt yet.

"I need to do something different," I said as I shifted into park. "I'm kind of bored. Aren't you bored?"

"What kind of band? A metal band, an R&B girl group, a marching band, perhaps?" She glared at me cockeyed and scrunched her slopey freckled little nose.

I chose to ignore her snark and pretend her questions were supportive and genuine. "Remember my old piano teacher?" I chewed my cuticles to avoid her glare. "Mrs. Farber, with the cankles?"

She nodded, eyes still skeptical and accusatory.

"Apparently, her son's band needs a keyboard player. She thought of me. Random, but what the hell, right? All we do is sit around and drink and smoke and talk shit, it'll be nice to do something, make something, for a change..."

"So you've known you're gonna do this and you *just* mentioned it? Does Veronica know?"

"No, I sort of forgot."

I lied. For a number of reasons.

Mollie twirled her golden ponytail around her finger and threw those stupid Tory Burch flats up on my dashboard.

"Since when do you forget to mention shit? You mention when you're out of conditioner. You mention when your foot itches, and when your mom buys a new brand of hummus. But whatever, you're joining a band. Sweet. All these years, who knew you were such a repressed emo-rocker chick?"

I shrugged and watched the cars on Franklin Avenue whip by. I knew this was how she'd react. Mollie didn't like change, surprises, or deviations from her status quo, but I was not going to be intimidated out of my decision this time just to soothe the beast. I was going to do something I wanted to do, without her approval, for once. Damn it.

"Anyway"—she rummaged through her backpack; I couldn't tell what she was looking for—"can we deal with my fucking unborn child, so I can participate in your future coke binges and backstage orgies?"

I cracked a smile, maybe released a short nasal exhale that resembled the beginnings of a laugh. "One day you really are going to get pregnant with a little demon Fuchs baby and no one is going to believe you. You're the girl who cried pregnancy."

"That's not even funny. If you were having sex, you would understand how not funny that actually is."

"You're right. Subjecting a child to being a 'Fucks' for the rest of his life is not a laughing matter at all."

"It's F-uuuu-chs. Like fuck-YOU-chs."

We laughed, and she dabbed her running eyeliner with her knuckle. "Want anything?"

"Diet Coke."

I waited in the car and lit another cigarette while she ran into CVS. I turned up the radio, grabbed the wheel with locked elbows, swiveled my neck, and car-danced to some horrible pop song, as I like to do sometimes.

My phone vibrated somewhere, and I reached down through the mess of books, papers, wrappers, snacks, and mangled packs of cigarettes in my bag to find it.

It was a text from Drew: **Not even 9 am and I just saw someone get punched in the nuts. This place is disturbed. I miss summer. Sesh after school?**

I wanted more than anything to tell him to fuck the *after* and to come meet me right now. I then had a short fantasy about the two of us ditching class and driving to the stream in the Meadowfields. We'd go swimming in our underwear and have long, heated discussions about the decline of the music industry and how much we hated everyone in and everything about our blond-haired, blue-eyed popped collar of a town. We'd talk until it got dark and go swimming again. Our slippery, naked skin would find each other's under the water; we'd lock glowing eyes in the wet moonlight and realize how happy we made each other. He'd kiss me, and I'd look knowingly into his eyes before I kissed him back. I'd wrap myself around him, and he'd carry me out of the water, and we'd make slow, throbbing, Harlequin love on a smooth, flat rock under some sort of weeping tree. Afterward, he'd tell me how long he'd wanted to do that, and I'd smile coyly, knowing that after that moment we would be together forever.

I texted back: **I feel your pain. I'm currently waiting in the CVS parking lot to assist Mollie with another contraception crisis. I'll call you after practice. Good luck, soldier.**

I'd known Drew almost as long as I'd known Mollie. He lived down the street, and when we were little, we played Chutes and Ladders in his tree house and went sledding on snow days. He goes to Crawford, the brother school to Harwin, and somehow we'd successfully made it through the awkwardness of middle school with our platonic friendship still intact. We enjoyed watching our friends hook up and break up from the sidelines, where we were free to mock, judge, and ridicule the romantic follies of our misguided, hormone-ridden peers; it was all very *what fools these mortals be.* We thought we were so much better off, out in my driveway smoking weed, laughing at poor, abused Mollie and Veronica and their latest ventures in sex and delusion.

I turned up the radio.

"Nice moves," Mollie said, tumbling back into the car.

"Nice dead baby."

Mollie stuck out her tongue and snorted at me.

MOLLIE FINN

I should have known that junior year would be interesting, considering it began with me puking in the fucking senior parking lot. Which, now that I think about it, Alex always managed to park in despite the fact that she wasn't a senior.

I tried to put aside Alex's whole *I'm joining a band* thing, which was shady for a shitload of reasons, and just focus on not vomiting as we drove into school. Alex and I were lifers at Harwin, meaning we'd been there since kindergarten—together. The same fucking school every fucking day surrounded by all fucking girls, for twelve fucking years—no wonder we were so wound up. We drove, for the millionth fucking time, through the wrought iron gates into the mouth of the ominous crimson towers of the Victorian institution for the young women of tomorrow. Though Greencliff was an innocuous suburban town—big houses; big lawns; shutters; fences; trees that were green in the spring, gold in the fall—Harwin looked like a psych ward or some fascist medieval finishing school where girls walked with books on their heads and drank Earl Grey in silence with their ankles crossed. But that was just the foreboding veneer meant to impress and intimidate Waspy trophy wives already worried about their four-year-old daughters' future piercings and subpar SAT scores. The outside was dark and imposing, but the halls were bright with a team of underpaid, poorly kept, spinster teachers and gum-cracking, foulmouthed wenches like me and Alex and Veronica. Nothing to be scared of, really. With all the girl power and sparkly posters and pep rallies, it really felt more like a cheer camp or a sorority house than a school.

It was the first day, so green and gray balloons bounced from all the doorways and lampposts. Little whores-in-training in crisp plaid kilts hugged and compared class schedules and tan lines. The Plan B started to kick in. I rolled down the window and laid my head back, hoping my nausea might be assuaged by a breeze or the valor of the cherry blossoms or some shit like that, but no such luck. As soon as Alex jerked her jalopy into park, I flung the squeaking door almost off its hinges and leaned out as far as I could to puke Diet Coke all over the hot asphalt.

Alex ran around the car to check the damage. She knelt down and petted the top of my head like a puppy's. "Aw... Molls—thanks for not getting any in the car."

I gave her a watery-eyed smile and slowly rolled out of the vehicle, as its clammy, smoky signature smell was not helping my situation.

Alex perched on the hood to chat with some senior girls, totally unmoved by their obvious displeasure with her presence in their hard-earned parking lot. They asked what was wrong with me. I told them I was sick, but they seemed suspicious.

They probably knew. Bitches were just jealous. I get it. I was violently purging the unborn child of the hottest guy in their grade; I'd be mad at me, too.

I watched Alex talk to the seniors, all her clothes hanging off her like she couldn't be bothered to actually *put* them on, but just mustered the energy to drape herself in whatever stained, wrinkled item was lying on her closet floor. Her tattered gray cardigan was too big, and the stretched-out cotton sleeves dangled past her wiry hands. Her kilt was askew, burned with cigarette holes and off by a button. Her dark hair was a tangled, spiraled mess, per usual. Her skin looked great, though, and I wondered if she was drinking more water and less artificially sweetened caffeinated beverages like she'd mentioned she was going to try to do last week. Was that really working? I kept meaning to start doing that. But didn't she just have that Diet Coke?

I felt another wave of ill come on, so I squatted and placed my head between my knees. Alex dismissed herself from the seniors to come over and rub my back as I dry-heaved.

"Are you sure you're okay?" She knelt down next to me, still rubbing me like a Yorkshire terrier. I stared at her threadbare, untied, green Converse that were not in uniform. "Maybe you should go home? To the nurse? Something?" she said.

"And say what? Sorry, I can't learn today, I'm busy doing my part in the fight against teen pregnancy?"

"Seems like as legitimate an excuse as any. Next time just use the damn condom correctly."

She didn't understand. I was Catholic, for Christ's sake. If

Alex got preggers, Nancy Holbrook would probably give her a hug, hold her hand through the procedure, make her matzo ball soup, and tell her she was proud of her for making such a hard decision. Honestly, she'd be so happy Alex finally had a boyfriend she'd probably let him sleep over, make him pancakes in the morning, and restock her medicine cabinet with condoms and edible underwear. I once suggested to my mom that going on the Pill might regulate my period and clear up my skin, and she cried for a week and sent me to confession.

Alex fed me more Diet Coke and helped me upright, just in time to catch a glimpse of Veronica rolling out of a Lincoln Town Car. Like she was Princess fucking Diana or something. If some heavyweight in a black suit with an earpiece had rolled out behind her, I swear to god she'd have gotten projectile vomit right on her smug, spray-tanned little bird face. She flipped her freshly coiffed and recently highlighted hair and slid on some new sunglasses that, from this distance, appeared to be Gucci, and thus new. I always know when anyone gets anything new, because I have a full mental inventory of all my friends' and family's worldly and closetly possessions—and Gucci sunglasses were not in my Veronica registry as of June.

She frantically began flinging her Tiffany and Cartier–clad wrists from side to side when she saw us.

"She's, like, out of control," Alex mumbled as she snatched the Diet Coke from my hand. Veronica was already skipping her sticky little legs over to us. Alex and I braced ourselves for a deluge of positive energy and some obliviously whorish story.

"Ladies!" she squealed, then took notice of my green face and crippled stance. "What's wrong?"

"Mollie's having a rough morning," Alex said, squeezing my shoulder. "We had to go with Plan B...."

"Again?"

Veronica kept talking, but I was in no place to listen to sounds higher pitched than dog whistles and Chipmunk Christmas albums.

I tuned her out to survey the school yard. Most noteworthy summer transformation awards went to Julie Goldstein, who'd gotten a much-needed nose job, and Margot Swan, who'd lost a solid twenty pounds. They looked good, I guess, but Julie still had that post-op cat-face, stiff-upper-lip thing happening. The swelling would go down, though, and she would undoubtedly be cuter than she was before. Good for her.

Christ. Had anyone else gotten fat over the summer? The whole boyfriend thing had really wreaked havoc on my ass. I'd spent my entire summer "splitting" nachos and sausage calzones and at the McDonald's drive-through at three AM. Sam eats like a sumo wrestler training at Walmart, and what was I gonna do? Be the lame barf jars girlfriend that picks at a garden salad with dressing on the side while idly watching him house carb-infused meat concoctions with melted cheese? Doubtful. At least I was puking today—that couldn't hurt things.

"So, Friday night?" Veronica said, pulling me back into the conversation I'd been ignoring. She looked at me, her vacant green eyes seeking approval.

"For her First Week of School party," Alex interjected.

"Oh yeah," I said, already stressed out by the prospect of another one of Veronica's momentous parties. I changed the subject. "Hey, V, did Alex tell you that she's trying out for *American Idol*?"

"What?" Veronica squawked.

"It's just a band," Alex said. "It's not a big deal."

She rolled her eyes. Was she annoyed that I wasn't taking this seriously? Was *she* actually taking this seriously? Since when was Alex serious about anything?

"Wait, are you actually trying out for *Idol*?! Or an actual band? Is it a new 'Band Idol' format? I'm confused."

Veronica was confused. Shocking.

"It's just a band," Alex barked. "A silly, practice-in-a-garage, just-for-fun high school band."

"With non-Crawford boys? Oh my god, are you going to be in the Battle of the Bands on Halloween?! You'll be like a celebrity! Remember those smokin' hot guys from that reggae band last year? Do you think you'll meet them? Invite them to the party on Friday!"

"Oh my god." Alex rolled her eyes so hard I thought she might actually tip over. "I'm not even *in* the band yet, calm the fuck down."

"Why didn't you ask if we wanted to do it with you?" V asked. "We could all be in a band; it could have been, like, our new thing? I love singing!" I actually wanted to hear Alex's answer, but V interrupted herself. "Oh, can you ask Sam if he can get us a keg?"

The question was directed at me.

"I guess," I said.

Asking Sam for favors always required a trade. *I picked you up from school, you buy me dinner. I let you watch* Real Housewives, *you blow me.* I puked one more time behind a red Jeep Wrangler before we all made our way into homeroom.

VERONICA COLLINS

n homeroom, I watched an even balder, though just as fat and sweaty as I remembered, Mr. Boardman shuffle through some papers on his desk and survey the talent in his homeroom. He caught my eye, gave me a wink and a wave, and said, "Welcome back, Ms. Collins. How was your summer?"

I sat up on my foot and leaned over my elbows on the cold linoleum desk.

"Great!" I said with a smile. "Did a lot of traveling…and tanning." I undid a button and pulled my white oxford shirt down over my shoulder to show him my tan line.

"Very nice," he said. "I'm sure everyone would love to hear about your adventures."

I leaned farther over the desk and pushed my elbows together. "Well, you know, I'm always happy to share them."

Alex scoffed under her breath.

I laughed it off. "What?" I asked her as I plopped back down on my foot, the hard new leather cold under my skirt.

She rolled her eyes, but I could tell she was smiling.

"What?!" I said. "Just giving him a little spank-bank material."

"I really don't think you want to be a part of the twisted depths of a man's spank bank. Especially balding, sweaty old men with lisps who take jobs at all-girls schools."

"Please, I just made his morning! And he's not *that* old...."

I felt him still watching, so I turned and twisted on top of my foot again, but this time, I turned out my hip to give him a nice little up-the-skirt shot.

I'VE ALWAYS DISCONNECTED FROM Mollie and Alex after I've been away for a while. I always break back into their little bond after a few weeks, or faster if Mollie happens to be annoyed that Alex is too clingy that week or if Alex happens to decide that Mollie is too bossy that day. But, without fail, as soon as I go on vacation or miss a party or go home sick, they re-fuse and I'm back at zero: alone on the swing set, pining for an invitation to take a turn on the two-person seesaw, like it's fifth grade all over again. It's really annoying. You'd think they'd just have accepted that we were a threesome by now, that they'd have gotten over the idea that I had to reinitiate myself and prove my worth every few months. But I knew the party would bring us back together—one drunken night of fun was all they needed to remember why they decided they liked me in the first place.

While I was in Europe over the summer, I'd decided that I was going to get a real boyfriend and try to do better in school this year, maybe attempt to get into a respectable college. I was tired of Mollie bragging about her *relationship* and thinking that because she and Sam went out to dinner together sometimes that she was somehow a better person than I was. Plus, even I was getting bored with the whole party-girl thing, and I should go out on top, right? My Last Week of School party last year ended with five police cars, a pool full of blood, an illicit video, and a pregnant sophomore—where do you even go from there? I debated even having my First Week of School party, but my First Week of School party is a tradition, so *not* having it would be downright bad luck, right? That, and the big empty house was starting to get to me. I'd been home for only two days, and already my dad had left for Asia and my mom hadn't left the gym or her new trainer, Roger. I was sort of looking forward to filling my house with warm bodies for a night, pumping some life back into that ancient history museum.

We resumed discussion of the party on our way to tennis practice that afternoon.

"Let's keep it just juniors and seniors," Alex proposed as she rummaged through leaves and papers and god knows what else to find cigarettes under the passenger seat of her car.

I agreed. "Though your brother can come with a few sophomores if he wants," I said.

"I'll mention it, but it's always weird when I see him out. Let him stay home and play video games. Get his own damn life, like I had to."

We used to torture Josh Holbrook when we were little. Nothing permanently damaging, just things like telling him that his freckles were a highly contagious rash or that every time he sneezed the snot that came out was part of his brain. He was also undyingly, annoyingly, and obviously obsessed with Mollie.

Freshman year, we found her picture in a drawer next to his bed. Mollie pretended she was grossed out by it, but continued to prance around the Holbrooks' house in short shorts and skimpy tank tops anyway. Typical, hypocritical Mollie.

"Aw! Come on. Isn't that what big sisters are for? Inviting you to parties? Getting you hammered?" Mollie said.

"You just want him there so he can fawn over you all night," I said, regretting the amount of sass in my tone.

Mollie spun around in the front seat, whipping her ponytail against her cheek. "Oh, stop it," she said. "He's like my second little brother."

I snorted.

"Are second little brothers like second cousins? Ya know, the ones you're allowed to bone?"

"*End* of conversation!" Alex screamed as she slammed on her brake. "Neither the boning of second cousins nor my little brother is allowed, okay? Everyone? Veronica? Do I need to make you repeat after me?"

"No boning your little brother or second cousins. Got it."

"Wait," Mollie said. "Can she not bone *your* second cousin or *any* second cousins?"

Gasping and giggling, we poured out of Alex's car and onto the Crawford campus, where the tennis courts were. We composed ourselves, stretched, and breathed in the open wild of the boys' school.

Our tennis team practiced at the courts at the boys' school because we didn't have tennis courts on our campus. We barely had a gym, but something closer to a barn with a basketball hoop because, well, I guess athletics are not exactly a financial priority in an all-female education. The Harwin athletics department pretty much consists of a bunch of lesbians in kilts and knee socks snapping the branches off some old maple trees, handing them to us, and telling us to play some field hockey. No one admitted it, but the fact that we practiced at Crawford was the reason that we were all on the tennis team. Or at least it was the reason I was.

I slid my new sunglasses on and puffed out my chest. I hadn't seen any of the boys all summer, so I needed to make a good impression. I needed a *damn, Veronica got tan and hot over the summer* buzz to drown out the *oh my god, Veronica blew Austin Markel in a Whole Foods parking lot* chatter from last spring.

Mollie took down her ponytail and straightened her skirt. Lex slammed the driver's-side door closed with her foot, crossed her arms, threw on a scowl, and lit another cigarette, right there on their campus, which I thought was a bold move. I looked around at the brick buildings and boys with floppy hair in navy jackets and striped ties and tried to look like I didn't notice them noticing us.

We made our way down the long trail to the tennis courts, balls and rackets in hand.

"Yo!" a male voice screamed from across the soccer field. It was Drew Carson. He waved his lanky arm in the air and ran from his pack of stretching ultimate Frisbee teammates over to the fence of the court, where Alex met him. I couldn't hear what they were talking about, but Alex's rough edges softened as she smiled and swayed between her long arms, which were clasped onto the green fence like a monkey's at a zoo. Drew was awkwardly tall, alarmingly skinny, and always had dark circles under his eyes, not in an *up doing blow all night* kinda way, but in, like, an *I have trouble sleeping because I'm so engrossed in this book and think so long and hard about the universe* kinda way.

Drew and Alex acted like they were dating, but Alex swore he was just her "guy best friend." And Drew seemed like the type of guy who was capable of actually being best friends with a girl, so I bought it, even though I'd never really had a male friend and didn't totally get how that worked. I didn't know him that well. He was "Alex's friend," but he'd always been really nice to me and paid attention to me in a way that didn't make me think he was just trying to get me into the backseat of his Pathfinder. Most Crawford boys were capable of only two kinds of interactions with girls: ignoring them and hooking up with them, and, well, I'd never been one for being ignored.

I ran up to Drew and Alex and joined their conversation. They stopped talking about whatever they were talking about when I got there.

"Carson, you coming to my party on Friday?" I asked, stretching my arms over my head.

"I didn't know I was invited," he replied.

Coach Potts blew a whistle.

"Call you later," Alex said.

I leaned through the fence to give him a little *of course you're invited!* kiss on the cheek. Alex gave him a fist bump through the green plastic-coated wire tangles. The coach blew the whistle again.

ALEXANDRA HOLBROOK

We didn't have tennis practice on Wednesdays, so, that first Wednesday back, I found Drew's white Pathfinder parked in my driveway when I got home from school.

"Hey, stalker," I screamed into his passenger-side window, "what're you doing here?"

He gestured for me to get in. "Smoke and drive?"

His car smelled of wet leaves, pot, and Polo Sport. "I have to be at that band tryout thing at seven."

"I'll drop you off. Can I watch?"

"No way."

He palmed the back of the headrest and swiveled his long, sun-browned neck as he expertly backed out of my driveway. I knew he wasn't intentionally putting his arm around me, but I liked to pretend that he was. I liked to think that if someone had seen us right then at that moment, they might have thought we were a couple.

"I'm probably about to make a huge ass of myself," I said.

"Please, they should have to try out to play with you."

Eyes on the road, one sturdy hand on the wheel, he reached into his pocket and handed me a CD. "I burned it for you."

On the shiny silver disc, Drew had written *Holbrook-Worthy Jams* in his five-year-old chicken-scratch handwriting. Seeing your name written by a boy feels almost as good as hearing one say it.

We drove through the leafy streets to the back roads that Drew liked to drive, but I always got lost on. It was still warm but was starting to get dark earlier and smell colder. We wound through the green and stone neighborhoods, listening to some new wave–trip-hop group that Drew had just discovered, tapping our feet and breathing the wind through the cracked windows. We drove up into the developments in the hills.

"Do you ever wonder if your happy childhood will keep you from becoming a great musician?"

I rolled my eyes and took a Camel from the center console. "What?"

He asked if I wanted to park and smoke the joint he'd been keeping in his glove compartment. I did.

We strolled out to a creek—one of those too perfect man-made ones on someone's private property, whose alarmingly loud trickling water sound was probably bought from the landscaper for an extra ten thousand dollars. We sat on a rock and stretched our legs out in the sun. Drew was still wearing his jacket and tie, but he'd untucked his Black Watch plaid shirt and traded the navy blazer for his signature yellow North Face vest.

"I wrote this short story yesterday," he said. "It was total garbage—sentimental, self-indulgent, dripping with forced emotion and cliché—and I got to thinking..." He took the joint to his lips and inhaled in a short staccato. "The best music, books, and movies are about struggle, pain, overcoming the odds. We want to be artists, but what is our pain? What's our struggle? This morning, I struggled to find a parking spot for my luxury SUV, because I was late arriving to my thirty-thousand-dollar-a-year private school, because I was smoking weed that I paid for with my dad's money. I'm not an artist, I'm a douche bag."

"Being a douche bag doesn't prevent you from being an artist, just the same as having money doesn't prevent you from experiencing pain," I said, touching my thumb and forefinger to his as he passed me the joint. I braced myself for another one of these conversations. These conversations that Drew and I always seemed to find ourselves in, about the self and the id and identity and confidence, which then always made me self-conscious and worried that one day Drew would see that I wasn't nearly as bohemian or revolutionary or as confident in the vision of my inner artistic self as I wanted him to believe that I was.

"I know it doesn't prevent me from creating art," he said. "I just worry that it prevents me from creating good art."

I passed him back the joint and I thought about it. He did have something of a point: when I sang, I didn't want to sing like sixteen-year-old Alex Holbrook, Jewish girl from Greencliff, Pennsylvania—she wasn't interesting. I wanted to sound like—and, in the privacy of my own living room, imagined myself sounding like—a three-hundred-pound black woman, possibly one who was alive during the Harlem Renaissance or the Black Panther movement, one who had seen and felt real struggle and had had to really fight for things that I knew nothing about, like love and survival. I sat at my piano, closed my eyes, and belted out notes of suffering and heartache, and imagined my voice filled with experience and soul. Two things I worried I did not possess, and maybe never would. But I didn't want to admit that to Drew. He loved starting these esoteric, self-loathing bourgeois conversations so he could sound smart and tortured. Only one of which he actually was.

"That's absurd," I said. "Plenty of wealthy people are successful and provocative artists, especially writers. Jane Austen? Edith Wharton? They wrote about the angst of life in high society."

"Someone this century?"

"Bret Easton Ellis."

"But he's a douche bag."

"Doesn't mean he's not successful. If anything, he owes his success to his douchebaggery."

He laughed at my use of the word *douchebaggery*. "Fine. Touché. I guess I have no excuse to suck as much as I do, then. Damn it, Holbrook! Foiled again."

He squeezed my knee until I flailed.

"You're a writer; you've got it easy. It's music that us suburban Jewish girls have no handle on."

"Ah, yes, Judaism. That must be what Drake meant when he talked about 'starting from the bottom.'"

We both laughed and stared into the creek.

I gazed at the back of Drew's neck and watched the short,

soft hairs perk and pulsate on the smooth, freckled skin as he laughed. I changed the subject.

"So, will you be attending the soiree of the century at Veronica's this weekend?"

The wind shook the trees, moving the shadows hovering over us. Drew scratched his fuzzy head and leaned back on his elbows. "Definitely. I think I convinced your brother to come, too."

"Why would you do that?"

"Because he's a cool kid and I like hanging out with him."

"You're just jealous that I have a brother and you're stuck with a house full of women. You can't take mine!"

"You just don't want fresh-faced little Josh around your cougar friends."

"Is it possible to be a cougar at sixteen?"

"If anyone can do it, Veronica can."

I laughed.

"She was looking pretty good the other day," he said.

I closed my eyes and took the punch. "Well, that's what she does, I guess."

"Did you think she was flirting with me? I think she might have been flirting with me a little."

Of course she was flirting with him; she flirted with everyone. After all these years of him making fun of "slutty ol' Veronica," all it took was one hair flip and a suggestive stretch, and he was a panting dog like the rest of them? Boys are the worst.

"Of course she was flirting with you. She flirts with

everyone. That's how she, like, relates to males. I think she's actually incapable of actual conversation."

"You're probably right." He flicked the roach into the rolling water. But I could tell his wheels were turning.

Suddenly, I was stoned and acutely aware that my mind was not working as quickly as it should be, and I needed to diffuse this Drew/Veronica thing immediately. Carefully, and immediately.

"So, do you, like, like her or something?" I asked.

He couldn't.

But maybe he did. Drew and I were just friends after all. Eventually, he was going to like someone. I'd always known that it was a matter of time before he had a girlfriend and I'd have to stop pretending that what we had was all I needed. Which it sort of was. As long as he didn't have a girlfriend. But Veronica? Really? Veronica was so *obvious*. Such an unoriginal choice. So everything Drew always claimed he was against. I imagined he'd go for someone deep, with good taste in music, an irreverent sense of style. Someone tall. Someone who liked the same things he did, liked to sit by creeks and smoke joints and have long insightful talks about art and life. Someone who made him laugh. Someone...more like me.

"Honestly, I never really thought about it. I mean, obviously she's smokin' hot. She's funny."

Funny? Veronica was not funny. Veronica was oblivious, and that was occasionally entertaining. Veronica wasn't witty or clever. Veronica loved Katy Perry for god's sake. Like, not ironically. She had all of Katy Perry's albums. *All of them.* Went to her concert. *Both nights.* How could Drew like someone who liked Katy Perry? All pillars of truth I'd held until that point began to slowly crumble around me.

"I could put a word in. If you really need to get laid that badly…"

"Would that be weird?"

He'd probably been thinking about fucking Veronica since the moment she shoved her push-up bra in his face on the tennis court. I was going to be sick. Fucking Veronica. Goddamn, fucking Veronica.

"It makes sense. I mean, you're two of my best friends. You could probably get her wasted and make a move at the party."

If I smacked my head against the rock we were sitting on, maybe I'd die. Or get a concussion. If I died, or even just ended up in the hospital, would he be too distraught to pursue this?

"Let's just see what happens. Don't say anything, okay?" He wrapped his long arm around my shoulder. "You're such a good wingman, Holbrook."

THE BAND'S GARAGE LOOKED like a real music studio. On the orange shag carpet lay an old gray amp, loose wires, and unstrung instruments. No sign of cars, old bicycles, toolboxes, or anything typically garagelike. Two redheaded boys—one in a Ramones T-shirt, the other in some shade of faded tie-dye—stood with a guitar and bass around their necks, respectively. I guessed these were the Farber boys. I felt deep pangs of regret and the urge to run home.

"Hello?" I probably should have changed out of my uniform; I must have looked like an asshole. Then again, they knew I went to Harwin; changing might have made me seem like I was trying to look cool for them.

The guy in the Ramones shirt smiled and came right over to me. The one in tie-dye and a Hispanic-looking one behind the drums just stared me up and down, which I suppose they were entitled to do. As I would have done if some private school bitch that I didn't know waltzed into my band practice like she had a right to be there.

"You must be Alex." Ramones extended a clammy palm and shook my hand.

"I am." I stalled. "Hi…"

"I'm Ned Farber; I play guitar. This is my brother Pete; he plays bass"—he shook my hand, too—"and this is Fernando, our drummer." I waved like an idiot to Fernando, who didn't rise from behind his drums. "Thanks for coming, and please don't think we're huge losers and that our mom recruits all our bandmates. We had a last-minute keyboardist-fell-off-a-building-and-broke-his-arm type of emergency."

I laughed. "Really? A building? How rock-and-roll…"

"What can I say, live free, rock hard."

I laughed again, hoping—assuming—he was joking. "Well," I said, putting some distance behind the awkward joke, "please don't think I'm a huge loser and that I join the bands of all my piano teachers' children."

They laughed. Genuinely. I started to relax. They seemed nice. Kind of dorky even. Not scary at all.

"My mom said that you were *very cool*, but that you didn't like music made by white people."

I couldn't believe she'd repeated that. I was joking. Sort of...

"I told her not to worry, because we have Fernando. He's Salvadoran. Is that enough ethnic flavor for you?"

"Token Latin drummer at your service," Fernando said with an easy smile. From behind the drum set, he extended his hand to me, and for some reason I blushed.

"What kind of music do you guys play?" I asked.

"We're sort of a funk–soul–jam band fusion. We do covers, but we write most of our own songs. We'll cover anything from Arcade Fire to Michael Jackson to the Stones, but we sound like us, not like them, ya know?" Ned said, showing me over to the keyboard. I didn't really, but I hoped I would soon.

I ran my hands over the plastic keys and wished I'd practiced more.

"Right up my alley," I said. "I have a pretty eclectic taste myself. Just no whiny white people music."

Ned and Fernando laughed; Pete seemed to be somewhere else.

"We try to avoid being whiny white people whenever possible," Ned said. "You wanna play something?"

"Anything?"

"Probably not Mozart," Pete chimed in. "He's pretty whiny and white."

Finally, a real laugh instead of a nervous one; my cheeks started to relax.

I vacillated between new-school and old-school. I didn't want to play anything too obscure, but I wanted to prove my musical street cred. Stick with a classic. The Cure or maybe Stevie Wonder. Bob Marley? I wondered what they liked, what they'd think was lame—if they were ironic or snobby or if they were the kind of musicians who loved all music or the kind who hated everything. I decided that everyone likes Stevie Wonder. Whether you're into rock, pop, oldies, gangster rap, or new wave Afro-punk—everyone likes Stevie Wonder.

When I'm nervous, I hum the melody to "My Cherie Amour," so I went with that. My dad always sang it to me, and I taught myself how to play it the day after he moved out. I always taught myself to play something new when I wanted to not think about something. He'd be so excited that I was in a band. Though he'd probably just tell me how much cooler his band was, how much better music was in the sixties, and how much harder he worked than I ever would.

Fernando hit the snare, and before I knew it, all the boys had joined in; I relaxed into the music, so much so that I didn't even realize that I'd started to sing. Ned was clearly the talent. Once he strummed his Fender the whole room melted around us, and my little ditty became full-blown, chest-melting music. I watched him play and transform. He was all over my slightly nuanced melody, and the song grew in a way that no song of mine ever had before, because I'd always played alone. Fernando fell right in with the beat, and Pete, too. And the next thing I knew, the familiar song became something completely different and completely beautiful, and I was completely in the middle of it. Holding it up, but being swallowed by it at the same time. They followed my changes through my key jump at the end, and I knew that these guys knew what they were doing. Hopefully I had fooled them into thinking that I did, too.

The song ended, and I realized I was smiling.

"Well," Ned said. He looked at Pete, then at Fernando, slapped his guitar, and nodded. "I'm comfortable saying, you're in!"

They liked me. I was good enough. I was in. It was too late to run.

MOLLIE FINN

Sam had his own little apartment in his basement. The walls were blue plaid and dusty, covered with sports paraphernalia. It was like our little windowless den of debauchery. His parents never went down there. Ever. We smoked, drank, fucked, everything down there; no one bothered us. Ever. It was terrifyingly liberating.

"I just think it's weird that Alex would join a band and not have mentioned it, or even that she was thinking about it, before." I groaned.

Sam's stomach rumbled as I lay with my head in his lap. I hoped that this position would lead him to stroke my hair or rub my arm or perform some sort of gesture of affection like he once would have in this situation. Instead, he took this opportunity to spread his arms over the couch like vulture wings and use my hip as a place to occasionally rest his beer.

"Yes! All right!" Sam jolted forward toward the TV, knocking my head into his knee.

"Babe," I barked without even turning around or moving from his lap, "are you even listening to me? Should I just stop bothering to talk to you?"

"No, babe. I'm listening. This is a great fucking game, though. Did you just see that steal?"

"Yeah, awesome."

"Fuckin' awesome!"

And he rested his beer back on my hip.

"So, you don't think that's shady of Alex?"

"It's a fucking gay-ass band of public school losers, babe. Who cares?"

"It's not the band; it's that she didn't tell us. She didn't even tell *me*. I just think that's weird. Why wouldn't she have mentioned it before?" I snuggled up closer to Sam's crotch and petted his thigh on top of his dusty khakis, hoping the movement would bring a comforting hand down to me. One stroke of my arm, cheek, anything.

"Maybe she's realizing that it's not necessary to consult you every time she takes a dump. Seriously, who fucking cares? Alex is getting a life. Good for her. Yes! Run, you motherfucker!" And he sprang forward, dripping some beer on my nose. I wiped it off and pretended to fall asleep.

A few minutes later, Sam leaned over me again, squishing my head as he set his sweating beer on the coffee table. He put his rough hand on the curve of my waist and squeezed my still-unsettled stomach.

"Ouch," I said. "Be gentle. I'm not a fucking football." I laced my fingers through his and guided his hand down my torso to show him how I'd prefer he just rub me lightly. I felt him stretch back and unbutton his pants behind my head.

"Gentle, huh?" he said, reaching into his pants with one hand and squeezing my ribs again with the other.

I flipped around on his lap to find his open pants and erect dick, which he'd so kindly already stuck over the elastic of his M&Ms boxers. The ones that had holes in them and were three sizes too small, but that he liked to wear so he could grab his crotch and say, *Melts in your mouth, not in your hand.*

"Oh yeah?" I said coyly as I began to stroke it.

"And go slow this time, babe—don't fucking rush it. You always rush it."

I rolled my eyes, but propped myself up and prepared for the task at hand. I decided this would be a good time to ask for the favor. "Babe, will you get a keg for Veronica's party on Friday?"

He nodded.

SAM DIDN'T SAY MUCH in the car on the way to the party, which made me nervous. I was wearing the pink miniskirt he loves, and he didn't even mention it.

"Thanks for picking up the keg," I said, staring out the dirty window, watching stone house after brick house after maple tree roll by. "I thought Veronica got a fake ID; I don't know why she can't get her own fucking keg."

"She probably just wants to owe me so she can thank me by blowing me later."

"You're so hilarious!" I punched him in the arm. Hard.

His hair was getting long, was starting to look like it did

when we first started dating, all floppy and sun-bleached. I thought it was so cute then.

"Oh, come on, Veronica sucking a dick is like anyone else giving a high five or a handshake. And I hear she gives a great handshake."

"Well, practice makes perfect.... Where did you hear that? Austin?"

"Austin, Parker, Davis, Phil Miller, Tim Miller. I think there's a note on the urinal in the science lab." Sam squeezed my knee and cracked himself up, as usual—no one laughed harder at Sam's jokes than Sam. "Maybe she could give you a little tutorial, show you some new tricks? You could use some new tricks, babe."

"Fuck you. If you want Veronica's expert tricks of the trade, don't let me stop you. I'd put in the order for the Valtrex now, though."

"It's really too bad she's such a slut," he said. "She's so hot. Usually only ugly girls need to whore it out like that."

"God, you're an asshole."

"It's why you love me."

I waited in the car while Sam dealt with the heavy lifting, and we drove the rest of the way to Veronica's in relative silence, listening to the radio—some angry, thrashing, noisy nonsense that I pretended to like. I wondered if Sam really thought Veronica was that hot. If everyone really thought she was that hot. I didn't think she was *that* hot. She was skinny and had big boobs, fine, but her face wasn't *that* great. Her eyes bugged out, and her hair was weird. Thin, frizzy. She wasn't *that* fucking hot.

VERONICA COLLINS

always get nervous before parties, even if someone else is throwing it, which seemed to never happen anymore. I was wearing my yellow Paris dress, the sparkly backless one, because it had brought me good luck with the Greek guy over the summer. First party of the year, no harm in being superstitious, right?

Alex and I sat on my patio and ripped tequila shots before people arrived. I figured I'd take this time to tell her about Austin and how I was trying to make him my boyfriend. I wasn't going to tell her about him coming over the night before, because I didn't want to make a big deal about it, because I was trying to be mature this year—girlfriends don't go around telling their friends every little detail about every little time they have sex with their boyfriends, because who cares, right? But I decided maybe I should, because I wanted to be sure that Austin wouldn't mention his visit to Sam, who'd mention it to Mollie, who'd then call me out for being shady, which I guess I had been, but whatever. Sometimes being shady is just way simpler and can save everyone a lot of melodramatic conversation and Mollie the opportunity to start with all the *Veronica's a slut* jokes. Why were we legally obligated to report all our actions to each other, anyway? I'd tell Alex that he came over and we hooked up.

I skipped the part about how I'd spent the entire afternoon cooking for him. I'd become a pretty avid watcher of Food Network in all my newfound time home alone, so I'd gotten into experimenting in the kitchen. I'd made myself coq au vin and beef bourguignonne, and learned how to julienne and render— whatever took time. I'd never been able to sit through movies or a full hour of homework or a book or anything, but I'd found that cooking was enough activity to keep me engaged. And then afterward, there was an actual reward! Eating! Eating legitimately way more delicious food than the Lean Cuisines and take-out Chinese that had been what I'd come to call dinner since middle school. I'd been begging Mollie and Alex to come over so I could cook for them, but obviously that never happened. They had mothers who cooked for them. Mothers who were big on things like dinner and curfews. Eventually, I got so lonely (and, okay, good enough that I wanted to show off to *somebody*) that I called Austin, Sam's friend who I'd hooked up with a few times last spring. I asked him if *he* wanted Veronica haute cuisine and to maybe watch a movie or something. He said he did.

Of course, he showed up at like ten and told me he'd already eaten. Of course, I told him that it was no big deal and that there were leftovers in the fridge if he wanted me to heat anything up or anything. Of course, he said he just wanted to watch the movie.

We were twenty minutes into some zombie nonsense before his tongue was down my throat and the condom was on. I know that *come over and watch a movie* is international code for come over and hook up, but I thought maybe since we'd already hooked up a few times (and everyone knew about it thanks to the Whole Foods parking lot debacle) and he wasn't so humiliated by it that he was still occasionally calling me that maybe he'd be interested in hanging out for a little or at least trying my freakin' Thai curry halibut. Operation: Date Austin was not off to a good start.

"You've gotta stop putting out for these lax assholes," Alex said. And then she said, "Heeeey…" and she dragged the *eeeh* out in a suspicious way. "Why don't you hook up with Drew?"

Drew? Her Drew? Guys like Drew weren't interested in girls like me. And I wasn't interested in guys like Drew—or was I? I wasn't getting anywhere with Austin Markel popular, athletic types. Did I like Drew? Maybe I did. Or, at least, maybe I should.

"Why? Did he say something?" I asked.

"Just that you looked good when he saw you at tennis the other day. No pressure, just something to think about." She poured us two more shots. "I think you guys could be fun together."

Fun together. So Drew probably just wanted to get laid. But he didn't seem like the type to just want to get laid. Had he ever even gotten laid? He'd known me for years; if he'd wanted to hook up with me, he'd have hooked up with me already, right? He was the kind of guy who likes girls for being funny and interesting. But he was also a guy, can never forget that fact when thinking about guys. No matter how many sappy movies they watch or long books they read, they are all, in fact, still guys. And guys like tits and blow jobs more than they like funny and interesting, which I'm not when you compare me to girls like Alex, so I had to rely on the boobs and BJs thing. And, thank god, I seemed to have been able to make a name for myself in both departments.

"Consider me thinking about it," I said, and we clinked our shot glasses. She took a swig out of the bottle after she threw back the shot. Alex drank like a rock star, yet always seemed to be the most sober of all of us at the end of the night. I swear, I've gone shot for shot with her, yet at the end of the night, she's smoking weed and making up songs on the piano, and I'm barfing in a bush wearing one shoe and no bra. She ran her fingers through her long hair, from root to tip, and blew smoke rings to the sky, which was starting to turn an electric shade of pink. Almost party time.

Drew showed up first with his stoner friends, then the seniors, then the soccer guys. I played my usual hostess game, made the rounds, greeted everyone, thanked them for coming, and pointed them toward the booze and the bathroom. I chatted, flirted, and kept an eye out for Austin, who'd promised he'd try to stop by.

"You throw the best parties," Drew said as he plopped down by me on one of the pool chairs.

"We all have our skills." I crossed and uncrossed my legs and dished out a smile.

"Why don't we hang out more?" he asked.

It occurred to me that he and Alex might be up to something, but I figured I'd just sip my Solo cup of vodka and smile along until I figured it out. What could she be up to? It's not like she was Mollie or something.

"Keg is here, bitches!" someone screamed from somewhere by the patio.

Mollie, Sam, and a few of his cronies rolled out of the bushes like a chain gang: Sam carrying the keg over his head like Conan the Barbarian, Austin nowhere in sight. I excused myself from Drew and skipped across the lawn and over to Sam to direct him to the trash can that I'd already filled with a garbage bag and ice.

"Happy now, whore?" Mollie scowled, playing with her phone as usual. "You have no fucking idea what I went through to get this."

"Don't worry about it, Collins," Sam said, patting my bare back with his wet hand.

"I'll give you cash," I said.

He looked me up and down and replied, "I'd prefer a beej."

Mollie rolled her eyes. I giggled and called him disgusting or something like that. It was unfortunate that Sam was so fiercely good-looking. Like, actually handsome, chiseled in a way that boys were just not these days. He looked like a young Robert Redford, if Robert Redford had had a gym membership and drank protein shakes in the seventies. He was always in some form of Crawford Athletics gear, as if the fact that his neck was the same size as his waist wasn't a clear enough indicator that he was a jock. It was a shame he was such a creep, and it was an even bigger shame that that only made him hotter.

In middle school, we all used to watch him make out with Stephanie Black and her blond ponytail at dances, and dare one another to cut in. We were obsessed. I even cut his picture out of the Crawford yearbook and put it on my wall. Like he was Leonardo DiCaprio or something—god, I was such a loser. I wondered if Mollie remembered that and had told Sam; that would be embarrassing. It's not like she didn't used to call him and hang up or pretend she was a telemarketer just like the rest of us.

The night charged on, bodies filled the pool, and Solo cups and beer cans littered my freshly manicured lawn. Boys did cannonballs, and I laughed and clapped and pretended it didn't pain me to see Petunia, my blow-up pool dragon, defiled like that.

After a few hours and a few more cups of vodka and shots of tequila than I could count, I started to feel a little spinny. I asked Drew, who had been following me around all night, to hold down the fort while I stole a minute upstairs.

"You want company?" he asked.

"No, no, you stay," I said. I needed, like, ten minutes to fix my makeup and maybe puke. "I need to pee," I told him.

I turned to go inside, and Drew took my hand—I wasn't sure a boy had ever held my hand before (not since nursery school anyway)—and pulled me in toward him. His hands were soft, almost like a girl's. He didn't tug or grab or pull me too hard or anything, just looked straight into my foggy eyes.

I found myself uncomfortable, nervous, twitchy. I knew what to do with my breasts when they were stared at, but my face was an entirely different story. I knew I was sweaty and that my breath probably smelled like booze and cigarettes. Then, just as I was about to burst or possibly throw up on him, he kissed me. Not with tongue or force, just a soft peck on my lips, seemingly for no reason.

"See you in a minute," he said after that.

I got sidetracked on my way upstairs, something with the lacrosse guys and Mollie being drunk and freaking out. I saw Alex and told her about the Drew kiss. She seemed excited about it, but honestly, this was around the point in the night where things got hazy.

MOLLIE FINN

Veronica's party was already crawling with the usual cast of heathens and barnyard animals when we got there. Alex was holding court with the stoners on the patio, per usual. Veronica was flitting around in the most aggressively hooker-tastic neon yellow dress I'd ever seen, batting her tits and eyelashes at anyone who'd listen. Drunk kids sat on marble countertops and played quarters on glass coffee tables. If it were my house, I'd have been having chest palpitations, but Veronica didn't seem to care—about anything, ever. She was having the best time of anyone, as always.

I left Sam with his posse to get myself a drink and play nice with the senior girls who I knew hated me but kissed my ass because I was dating Sam. I knew I'd get drunk quickly, because I hadn't eaten dinner. I never ate dinner on Fridays—Sam always got pizza with the team, so I told my parents I was eating with Sam and took the opportunity to skip a meal.

I sat outside with Alex and the ganja mafia for a while and pretended to know about the songs and movies they were talking about. After an hour went by without a peep from Sam (which was always a matter of concern), I got up to find him.

And lo and behold, where do I find him? In the foyer, at the center of a fiery mob flocking Veronica.

"I swear they're real!" she screamed, drunkenly fondling herself. She squeezed her overflowing tits together and then up toward her chin, then together, then up again. She raised one in her hand, then the other—like some sort of retarded titty line dance.

"Dude," said some nameless, pockmarked sophomore who I recognized from Sam's team photos, "real ones don't stay up like that. Just admit it!"

Veronica took the kid's hammy paw and placed it on her left breast. "Feel it!" she slurred. "Why would I lie?"

The guys all chuckled and snorted, pawing and prodding, taking turns groping her and snapping iPhone pictures. She squealed like a pig in pretend protest. Next thing I knew, Sam's hand shot out of the semicircle and grabbed a boob.

"Not bad, Collins," he said.

From three feet away, I flung myself like a rabid squirrel into the feeding frenzy. Veronica just stood there, pigeon-toed and tongue out like a brain-dead basset hound, Sam squeezing her boob like a rubber fucking ducky.

"What the hell?" I pushed Sam out of the herd. I yanked his arm away and pounded his biceps with my meager fist. "Get your fucking hands off my friend's boobs!"

"We're just kidding around, babe. Chill."

"Yeah, chilllllll out," V said through a string of drool, rolling on her heels, clasping my arm for balance. Her yellow loincloth had begun to droop and was stained with beer and excess self-tanner. "We're juss joking. Y'anna feel 'em, too? This guy said he'nt b'lieve me they were real. Tell 'em, Mollie, tell 'em. You'd know if I was lying."

And then I think I called her something to the effect of cum-guzzling crack whore, and there was a chorus of *ooooooh*s from the lacrosse team, but I didn't give a shit anymore. I ripped her off me and ran out the door.

"Babe!" Sam screamed, and followed me outside, as I'd hoped he'd do. "We're just fucking around."

Tears—drunk beer-flavored tears—started to fall. I knew I was being ridiculous, but I didn't care, I couldn't control it, and all I wanted was for Sam to feel bad that I felt bad and try to make me feel better.

"It's fucking embarrassing, Sam!" I sobbed. "Why do you always need to do shit like this? Why do you have to ruin everything?"

I saw his eyes drift over my right shoulder.

"Can I fucking help you?" he said.

I turned around. Josh Holbrook stood behind me looking all pale and concerned, and Alex-like.

"Mollie, are you okay?" He reached out for me tentatively, but I smacked his hand away, not wanting to provoke Sam.

"I'm fine." Sam's attention was wavering—I needed to make a power move. "Can you take me home?" I pleaded with Sam, falling into Josh.

I started to get woozy, see three of him, three of Sam, three of every car in the driveway, every bush on the lawn. I needed to get out of there. I was losing it, and I wanted Sam to notice. And care.

"Are you serious?" Sam asked.

"I'm really drunk." I steadied myself and looked him dead in the eye.

"Hell no, we're not going home yet. It's early."

My shoulders collapsed, and I started to sob again.

"It's okay," Josh said. "I'll take you."

Sam made a mock jerk-off splooge gesture and turned back inside.

"Are you sure you're okay? I don't know why you let him treat you like that," Josh said as we headed to his car.

"I really don't want to fucking hear about it," I said. I didn't. Because I knew.

ALEXANDRA HOLBROOK

It was a typical Veronica party scene, and I was having as good a time as I typically did. Ish. People came and went, swarmed and diffused around the pool and patio table, flowed in and out of the sliding glass doors, laughing and leaning ever so slightly more with each entry and exit. New kids, old kids, young kids, cackling, snorting, having the same conversations they had last week with the same people in new T-shirts. The beat was broken by an occasional splash or squeal; nervous girls and loud boys ebbed and flowed with every thump of the bass.

I kept talking, kept drinking, and kept an eye on Drew and Veronica, who kept crawling in and out of my line of sight. He was wearing my favorite T-shirt, the blue Bucks County YMCA one, the blueberry-cream one that turns his eyes the color of an indoor swimming pool, the one he'd worn the night I fell off my bike at the shore and sprained my ankle, and he carried me piggyback the whole mile home—it smelled soft, like suntan lotion and Downy fabric softener.

I kept my usual post on the patio for most of the night while Drew's friends all talked at me about music, but it's amazing how possible it is to appear fully engaged in a conversation while entirely absorbing every nauseatingly vapid remark from another one four feet away.

Oh, Drew, who makes your shirt? I love it....

You throw the best parties, Veronica....

Fucking club me in the face with a rusty crowbar—it was like she learned how to flirt from eighties porn.

I checked my phone to see if the boys from the band were coming. I wanted them to come as much as I didn't. My intention in joining this band was to make a new world for myself, separate from the fascist regime of the threesome. On the one hand, maybe having those boys at this party would defeat the entire purpose of the venture, but on the other hand, I kind of wanted everyone to wonder who my new, cool, interesting friends were.

I went inside to pee, only to be immediately poached by a half-keeled-over, half-dead-eyed Veronica. She yanked me into the black granite powder room with too many mirrors and a weird echo.

"Drew and I made out!" she said.

A faint, fading *nooooooo*...resounded from somewhere in the distant mine shafts of my mind. How had I let this happen? I feigned a smile as the blood drained from my face.

"That's awesome!" I said.

Like a fist in my throat, choking me from the inside.

Her usually wide sea-foam eyes were wet and pink. Her usually slick dark hair, fuzzy and tangled.

She hugged me, her body coated in a moist film. "I don't know what you said, but he's, like, so adorbs. I love you!"

And she stumbled out of the bathroom and was absorbed back into the party.

I stood by the patio door just breathing for a minute, processing what I'd heard, wishing I could unhear it, wondering if I could pretend that I hadn't. I stood for a moment while the party buzzed around me. Maybe two. Veronica was hammered—she'd probably mouth-raped Drew in a corner somewhere, and they'd both be embarrassed and awkward about it tomorrow. Maybe they'd gotten it out of their systems; maybe she'd have fucked a lacrosse player by the end of the night; it'd be fine. I kept breathing.

When I got back outside, Fernando and the Farber twins were standing by my spot on the patio, each holding a thirty rack of Natty Light. To my surprise, I was relieved to see them.

"This house is ridiculous!" said Ned, dropping the case on the terrace. Pete echoed the sentiment. I was starting to see how this Farber twin dynamic worked.

"We need to hang out with private school chicks more often," Fernando said.

He was wearing a white linen shirt and ripped jeans, lighter wash than a Crawford boy's, whose look was more khakis or corduroys, boat shoes, and belts with whales on them. He wasn't wearing his beanie, and I hadn't realized how long his hair was. His dark curls fell around his face—Mollie and Veronica would definitely think he was cute. I wondered if maybe I shouldn't have brought them here, if Veronica was going to ruin this for me, too.

I sat with them for the rest of the night. Smoked, drank,

talked about music, the band, about how flattered I was that they let me in. I tried not to think about Drew's tongue down Veronica's throat or god knows what else down god knows where else. It was nice talking to the guys. It had been a long time since I'd met anyone new, had an opportunity to be seen as anything but what I, over the course of my sixteen years in Greencliff, had accidentally given people the impression that I was—to not be the *chill* one, the least cute one who smokes weed and talks music and holds her liquor. It was nice to just be me, alone, whoever that was, not within the context of the other two. I introduced them to Marc Seidman and the rest of Drew's crew—naturally, the shared interest in pot and music united them instantly.

Fernando poked my side. "We're just psyched to have a hot, talented chick in the band, Alex."

I liked the way he inflected the *exxxxx* in my name. No one had ever called me *hot* before, at least not to my face, but I assumed not behind my back, either. Drew was nowhere in sight; I'd hoped maybe he'd heard it.

"Totally," said Ned, leaning over his furry forearms. "Just gotta get you to agree to sing at the show."

Pete nodded, puffed away at a blunt, and stared at the stars.

"I told you, I don't sing in public," I said. "It was a big step for me to even do it in practice!"

Eventually, Drew emerged from behind the glass doors looking lost. He walked out and stood over us.

"Where have you been all night?" I asked. I smiled and tossed my hair, acting drunker and dumber than I actually felt.

"Inside," he said.

"Drew, this is Ned, Pete, and Fernando. The guys from my new band. What are we called again? Adios Pantalones?"

"No!" Fernando said. "No, that was our old name. We're a new band now that you're here. Now we're the Cunning Runts, remember?" We all broke down in hysterics.

"We're between names at the moment," I said with a hint of a giggle—hoping Drew would see that he wasn't the only boy who'd ever made me laugh.

He shook their hands in that sincere way that guys do, still hovering over us, uncomfortably realizing he had nowhere to sit.

"The Cunning Runts," he said. "Clever."

I tried to gauge his reaction. Was he jealous? Happy for me? Was he looking for Veronica? And where was Veronica if not with him? I hadn't seen her in hours.

Drew put his hand on my shoulder, sending a chill up my arm.

"It's almost eleven thirty."

"Fuck," I said, looking at my watch. "Why am I the only person who still has a curfew?"

"Do you need a ride home? I can drive you," Fernando offered.

"It's cool. I'm going her way anyway," Drew said without pause. "Was great to meet you guys. I can't wait to hear you play."

I stood up and looked at Fernando, then over to the twins, then back to Fernando, who sat back with his wide grin and wily brown eyes. I couldn't tell if the grin was directed at me or if it was just a general oblivious, drunken grin.

"Definitely, dude," Fernando said to Drew. "Your girl's gonna make us rock stars."

"I bet," he replied.

We said our good-byes, and I thanked the boys for coming. Told them I'd see them the next day at practice.

We drove along Blackrock Road in silence, the dark tree-lined streets and curves of the road swaying me into a half-drunk half sleep. The glowing green car clock read 11:48.

"Fuck, I'm totally going to be late," I moaned.

"Chill out. You'll be home in ten minutes."

I shut my eyes and rolled my head back on the headrest.

"The guys in the band seem cool," Drew said, eyes fixed on the road.

"They are. I'm psyched they came."

"You like Fernando, don't you?"

What? No! The question was supposed to be phrased the other way. Fernando liked *me*. Fuck, this whole thing was going to backfire, wasn't it?

"Oh, stop it," I said, rolling my eyes. "I do not. He's just flirty."

"Whatever, Miss Oh-ha-ha-Cunning-Runts-we're-so-funny-with-all-our-inside-band-jokes-all-night."

"Whatever, Mr. Oh-Veronica-you-throw-the-best-parties-let-me-follow-you-around-and-carry-your-beer-all-night—like you should talk."

"Whatever. You should call your mom; we're probably going to be a little late."

VERONICA COLLINS

By the time I finally made it upstairs, I had to lie on my bed for a minute. The glow-in-the-dark stick-on stars on my ceiling blurred and spun in and out of focus, and I opened and closed my eyes to make them stop. They didn't. I sat up again, went to the bathroom, and kneeled over the toilet hoping I might puke, but I didn't do that, either. I just knelt there on the cold tiles with my head on my wrists, listening to the distant bass that was so loud the house shook. I decided maybe I shouldn't puke anyway, in case I went back downstairs and Drew wanted to make out more. I re-eyelinered, resituated my boobs, slapped my cheeks, and walked out of my bathroom as refreshed as I could be, prepared to reemerge, only to find one Mr. Sam Fuchs nosing around my room.

"Need the bathroom?" I asked, hoping he hadn't found anything embarrassing, like a cutout picture of himself from an eighth-grade yearbook.

"Yeah, can I use yours?" I could smell the whiskey on him from three feet away, and it turned my stomach. He stumbled closer to me and ran the back of his hand down my goose-bumped arm. "You're lookin' good tonight, Collins. Really good."

I smiled and looked up at his three beautiful blue eyes.

"You know, I've always had a thing for you," he said.

He kissed my cheek and I didn't stop him, then my neck, then shoulder. The room and stars on my ceiling still spun. I meant to slap him and run and tell Mollie what a creep her boyfriend was, but the words weren't coming out, my legs weren't moving, just crumbling underneath me.

"What about Mollie?" I managed to stutter, still thinking about pushing him away.

"You know you won't tell her. You know you want me, too." And he kissed me on the mouth. A wet, sour whiskey kiss, strong and long, forceful and passionate. I completely collapsed into it. Into him.

"This is wrong," I gasped.

Sam shushed me and locked the bedroom door. And I knew at that point that I was going to let this happen. The alcohol sloshed around in my brain and body. Images swirled, and words and thoughts and conclusions drained before they congealed. I had a quick flash of my kiss with Drew, which instantly faded into a montage of images of Mollie reaming me out in various scenarios—screaming at me in school, writing a mass e-mail or something announcing to the world what a slut I was, maybe even physically assaulting me. Maybe I'd tell her, maybe this would be exactly what she needed to hear to know what a jerk Sam really was. But I knew Mollie, and I knew that telling her that Sam came on to me would start a fight between the two of us rather than a fight between her and Sam. It wouldn't be worth it.

Fuck her and her self-righteous *monogamous* relationship. Fuck her for always calling me a slut. Look who she was dating. Look what he was doing.

We made out on my bed, and I ran my unfocused hands down his broad back. He'd said he'd always had a thing for me. I used to wonder what I had done that made him choose Mollie over me. That night freshman year at that party, I could've sworn I'd felt a heat between us, but then the next thing I knew he was dating Mollie. I pictured him telling her off. Me standing on his arm, him telling her that she was a miserable, anorexic bitch with an attitude problem who took him for granted and that he was going to be with a happy, fun-loving girl like me now. She'd go ape-shit.

He felt good on top of me, strong, powerful. He ripped my dress over my head and flipped me over. He was pretty rough, but I was so drunk I didn't even notice when he'd finished.

MOLLIE FINN

The day after Veronica's party, I woke up on the couch in my basement at five AM with no recollection of how I'd gotten there. Eyes stinging and head pounding. I barely even remembered the goddamn party.

We met at Eddie's Diner to recap the evening like we usually did. Whether it was noon on a Sunday or four AM on a Tuesday, there were always people at Eddie's, and the menu was always the same. Typical diner, with white linoleum counters and red vinyl booths, covered in a light film, and reeking of fried trash—the crust on the ketchup squeeze bottles had likely been congealing since the early seventies. Alex picked me up and on the way she assured me that no one, including her, had witnessed the scene I'd made and that Veronica had been drunker than I was, which was a relief, but not altogether soothing.

We sat at our usual booth in the corner. I refrained from offering any information first, as at that point who said what to whom when and in what humor was slightly questionable. I remembered saying some shit to V in regard to the Sam thing, but I didn't remember exactly what I said, nor did I remember if I'd said these things in a jovial manner or if we'd actually had some sort of altercation that I'd need to apologize for. V arrived late, and seemingly not totally pissed at me, so clearly she'd accepted my drunken venom as a joke, which was a relief. Alex complained about her hangover. Everything appeared to be business as usual.

"So what happened to you?" Veronica asked. "When did you leave?"

"Josh said you passed out in the car when he drove you home. He had to carry you inside," Alex said.

So that's how I'd ended up on the couch....

"I'm such a fucking mess," I said.

"Please!" Veronica exclaimed, still staring intently at the massive menu. "Don't even talk to me. I'm pretty sure everyone in the greater Philadelphia area now has pictures of my naked breasts."

"I'm pretty sure there's nothing that was photographed last night that the greater Philadelphia area and most of Europe hasn't seen before." Alex snickered.

"P.S."—Veronica coughed—"I'm sorry if I had a hand in your fight with Sam." She looked down at her lap. "I was really drunk."

"Yeah, we all were," I added, deciding that I needed to stop talking about this fucking party or I was going to become madder than I felt well enough to deal with.

"You and Sam will work it out," Alex said. "You always do."

"Yeah, I'm not that worried. Sam's an asshole. Veronica's a slut. Same old shit."

"Ha. Ha. Screw you, guys," Veronica said, still looking at her lap and rolling her eyes.

I sometimes wondered how she was able to brush off the jabs we all made at her. I guess it was because we never accused her of anything that wasn't true: we never called her anything she didn't seem to go out of her way to be called.

In sixth grade, some eighth graders on the field hockey team told me that my voice was so low, I sounded like a man, and they started calling me Manly Finn—I pretended I didn't care, that I thought it was funny.

One day, one of the girls told me to call the coach and pretend to be her dad to get her out of practice. She had me repeat things after her. Everyone cackled away, and I giggled along like I wasn't totally embarrassed that my natural, god-given, eleven-year-old voice happened to sound like Kermit the Frog after smoking six packs of Newports.

And then one day out of the blue, mid-"Manly, say…" bash session, Veronica, right to the eighth graders, no fear, no remorse, no sense of the backlash she'd receive, said, "I think her voice is sexy and you guys are just jealous." Just like that. Right to their faces. They were so awestruck that from then on they left me alone and started calling her Ballsy Collins, and no one ever called me Manly again.

The waitress brought our food, which distracted us for a few minutes. She glared at us through teal eyeliner and told us to enjoy. Veronica asked for a side of bacon. Alex asked for more soda. I wondered exactly how much this poor woman hated her life.

"Can we talk about Alex and the cute Spaniard in the band?" V asked, alarmingly spritely for being as hungover as she claimed she should be. She'd showered and was in some sparkly, off-the-shoulder monstrosity. She'd even put fucking earrings on. Fucking Veronica, god forbid she leave the house without fucking earrings.

"No, we can't," snapped Alex over her omelet.

"Oh my god, I can't believe I forgot to ask." I'd barely even asked Alex about anything band-related since she'd joined. I kept forgetting to take it seriously in the hopes that she'd realize she'd been joking all along.

"It's not a big deal."

"So, did you hook up with Fernando?" V asked.

"No!"

I loved Alex's fake shock and awe, like the fact that she could have made out with someone was such a preposterous notion. Even though it kind of was, but that was no one's fault but hers.

"You say no like you weren't cooing and giggling together all night," said Veronica.

"We're just friends. Some of us don't have to make out with every able-bodied guy in the tristate area."

V rolled her eyes. "Well, you guys looked cute together."

"Yeah, right." Alex's eyes stayed focused on her limp eggs. She jabbed the corner of her buttered toast into the side of her thin mouth and said, "Let's talk about how Veronica made out with Drew."

I gasped.

"Are you serious?" I directed my question to Alex, not Veronica.

"I am," she replied, with wide-enough eyes to let me know that despite whatever words she was about to spew, she was not happy.

Veronica, however, was smiling again, happy to have all the attention shining back on her. "He's, like, the sweetest guy. We talked a lot at the party. It wasn't really a *make-out*, just kind of a peck as I was going upstairs to get something. It was sweet."

I looked at Alex, confused. She clicked her tongue and nodded.

"So are you guys going to be, like, a thing?" I asked.

Alex stared painstakingly at the eggs and twirled her dark, unwashed hair.

"I don't know!" Veronica replied. "He said he'd call me, that we should do something this week. So I don't know. Just something new and fun and exciting, I guess!"

Was this yet another matter of importance in Alex's life that she hadn't discussed with me? If she hadn't, it was possibly because she knew my position on the Alex-and-Drew-ongoing-saga-of-self-indulgent-ridiculousness. It was obvious how she felt, obvious that Veronica was way out of his league—she just needed to nut up and tell him she wanted to date, because in the end, they weren't dating, so when he wanted to go make out with Veronica, she had no right to care, because she could have told him how she felt and given herself that right, but she didn't. Unlike me, who actually has the actual right to be actually pissed off when my actual boyfriend feels up my fucking gutter slut of a friend.

"Lex, did he say anything to you when he drove you home?" V asked.

"No, we didn't talk about it. I didn't ask and didn't want to make it seem like you ran right over to me and told me about it after it happened. I'll let you guys be adults and handle your own relationship."

"You're the best," Veronica replied, and returned to chomping contentedly on her bacon.

Alex reverted to her signature mess-making napkin tearing, and we all focused on our food. I had asked for no cheese in my omelet, but of course no one at Eddie's speaks English and I was lucky I even got an egg-based dish at all. I tried to pick out the vegetables and just eat those, because Sam never treated me this way when I was thinner.

"So did you and Sam make up?" Alex asked after a soothing period of silence.

"I haven't called him back yet." Which reminded me to look at my phone and see if he'd called. He hadn't.

Veronica coughed. "Oh god, I hope I'm not coming down with something," she said.

I snorted and said, "Guess it'd be a tall order to track down who you caught it from."

We all laughed. Everyone loves a slutty Veronica joke.

ALEX WAS UNUSUALLY QUIET on our ride home. She was fixated on the windshield, sucking back Marlboro Lights and flicking them into oncoming traffic. She wasn't even fussing with the radio. And though those hazel eyes that turned yellow when she was hungover or crying or really tired appeared focused, I knew there was a shitstorm brewing behind them. Her anxiety was palpable, and I wanted to be in on her plan, as I was sure she must have one. As I would if my Drew was banging Veronica. And my own anxiety about what exactly had gone down the night before was becoming unbearable. Sam still hadn't called.

"So." I had to break her focused silence. I was about to have a heart attack. "Tell me how you really feel about Drew and Veronica."

She paused, took a long breath, and shrugged.

"It's pretty annoying." She sighed.

"Why don't you just tell her that you're not okay with it? She's such a fucking whore, it's getting pathetic. You know that Drew's just going to use her up and throw her out like the tampon she is."

"Because"—she shrugged again—"I am. It's fine. I have no claim to Drew."

"I don't know about that," I said as I plucked a cigarette from her center console. "You and Drew have a thing. Whatever that thing is, it's still your thing, and Veronica should check her ho card at the door for one goddamn minute. She's supposed to be your friend."

"Maybe I should just tell everyone that she's got herpes, like you did freshman year so Sam wouldn't date her."

"Oh my god, I told *one* person she *may* have had a questionable cold sore...."

"On her vagina…" Alex laughed. It felt really good to make Alex laugh. Sometimes I felt like she didn't think I was as funny as she used to.

"Anyway," she said between chuckles and Marlboro puffs, "I really don't care. It's just annoying that Veronica has to molest every guy in town. Can't she just hang out with guys? Is she capable of having, like, a male friend? It's not that I'm jealous. It's more like…"

"That you're totally jealous! Because how can Drew be your pretend boyfriend if he's Veronica's real one?"

She tensed up in the driver's seat and turned up the radio. Some rapper's voice I didn't recognize that sounded tinny and far away through her tape deck from the nineties. I turned it back down.

"What about this band guy?" I asked, trying to change the subject, trying to make her realize that she was a hot commodity and could use that to her advantage.

"Fernando?"

"Oh my god, his name is really Fernando?" I regretted it as soon as I said it. I'd forgotten I was trying to be supportive.

She rolled her eyes. "He's cute. He's flirtatious, but I'm pretty sure it's just a cultural thing. Latin American guys are just like that."

"Oh, really? And how many Latin American guys do you know in Greencliff? Have you been engaging in romantic trysts with José the gardener that I don't know about?"

She laughed again. "You're such a bitch."

"It's why you love me."

We pulled into my driveway, and Alex shifted her car into park. I sat there, glaring at the ivy slowly swallowing my big white house, dreading having to deal with Sam. Deal with my parents. Deal.

"Wanna hang out and watch something terrible on TV?"

"I can't," she replied, shaking her head, green and yellow still bubbling in her eyes, which were still fixed on something past the windshield. "I have band practice."

I laughed. "Christ."

"I'll call you after," she said as I got out of the car.

"Yes, please do. And go for it with this Fernando! What do you have to lose?"

"My pride."

"Overrated."

She pulled away, and as I walked toward my front door, I decided that I couldn't handle seeing or talking to my parents, so I walked around the back to get in through the basement. I swung open the wooden gate, then walked across the patio and down the brick steps to the pool.

Josh must have carried me all this way last night.

He probably had to open the gate with one hand, haul me down the steps, slide the glass doors open, and lay me on the couch. I wondered how he carried me and how heavy I must have been. Over his shoulder? Or over both arms, like a fireman? God, and I hadn't even called him yet to say thank you. He could have just left me in a pile on the front lawn. That's probably what Sam would have done, if he'd cared enough to bring me home at all.

I wondered why Josh didn't call Alex and tell her to deal with me, but I'm sure he didn't hate the idea of having a moment alone with me while I was vulnerable and unconscious. After a wave of flattery, I had a sudden wave of creeped out, thinking about what could have potentially happened between a catatonic me and a kid who kept pictures of me in his drawer. I was fully dressed when I woke up on the couch. There was no way. It was Josh Holbrook—only creepos like Sam and the twisted bitches who date them have these kinds of thoughts.

As I walked toward the basement, I saw Sam standing there, wearing a baseball cap and sunglasses and his clothes from the night before.

"What are you doing here?" My heart throbbed and my headache returned. I hadn't even settled on how I was going to handle a phone call; I was by no means prepared for the in-person ambush.

"I wanted to make sure you got home."

I stood about a foot from him. I wouldn't go any closer until I figured out who was really at fault for the debacle of the night before.

"Come here," he said. "Give me a hug, you crazy drunken psycho."

I approached him and let him hug me but left my arms limp. He smelled of stale beer and cigarettes and outside and something else. I was still confused. Still angry. And now sad for a reason I couldn't quite put my finger on. Thoughts, memories, and feelings were all crossing wires. I just wanted to lie down and go to sleep. With Sam.

"What the fuck happened?" I said as I pulled out of his grip. "Josh Holbrook drove me home? You just let some kid take me home while you stayed at the party?"

"Babe, you were screaming like a crazy person! I didn't know what to do with you. Josh offered to take you home. You seemed okay with going with him. Are you telling me you're mad at me for this? I called to see that you were okay. You didn't pick up. I figured you were passed out, so I stayed at the party and had a few more drinks with the guys. You are not allowed to be mad at me when you're the one who went psycho."

He looked at me with bloodshot eyes, smiled, and threw his big arms around me again, kissing my head, which spun and ached as it rested on his beating chest.

"Why do you have to be such an asshole?" As the words came out, I felt myself soften in his arms.

"Cutie, we were all joking around, and you were just drunk and freaked out. It was nothing." He kissed my forehead. "Okay?"

"Okay," I said, not sure if I meant it, but not sure how to justify my sustained anger, either. "I'm sorry I lost it," I said. "I should really eat dinner on Fridays."

He kissed me softly. "All good. We're fine. Normally, you're cute when you're drunk." His hands sailed toward my ass, and I figured out where this visit was headed.

"Did you see my parents when you got here?"

"No." He coughed. "They were pulling out as I pulled up. I figured you were at brunch with the girls and I'd just wait for you down here."

"Look at you." I always got a little flutter when I felt like Sam paid attention to things, knew me in an intimate way or thought about me in a moment that I wasn't directly in front of him.

"Who knows you, babe?"

Wrapped in each other's arms, we stood, kissed, and nuzzled at my basement doorstep. I'd forgotten why I was supposed to be mad. He slid open the glass doors, took my hand, and led me to the black leather couch, and we just stood there by the sofa, glaring into each other's bloodshot eyes.

"What?" he asked.

"Nothing," I replied.

He kissed me again, unzipped my sweatshirt, and pushed me down on the couch. He poked and squeezed harder and with more violence than usual, like he missed me and needed me, like he wanted to devour me. He smelled gamy, was sticky, and, for a minute, I thought he might still be drunk. His kisses were wet and hard, but I surrendered and breathed in the comfort of his contact.

I was dry, not ready, but he stuck it in anyway. It hurt, but I needed it, wanted it. He held my wrists behind my head and grunted hot and wet in my ear. My chin pounded against his thick shoulder. He could never tell the difference between moans of pleasure and moans of pain.

When it was over, we both just lay there on my couch, naked, panting, feeling like ourselves again.

Part 2

THE FALL

VERONICA COLLINS

When Alex wore her glasses, it meant that she was hung-over or sick. But I hadn't heard news that she had reason to be either, so I was pretty surprised to see her wearing them that day in homeroom. She sat cross-legged at the desk under the map of the world—her cheek resting on her knuckles, skewing her already-crooked tortoiseshell glasses even more.

"Glasses today?" I asked.

"Yeah, couldn't deal this morning," she said. I wasn't exactly sure what that meant.

It had been about a month since my party, and I hadn't heard from Drew. Normally, this wouldn't alarm or surprise me, but being that there were so many wild cards in this particular poker game, I worried about who maybe knew what, why, and what they were doing about it. I didn't panic, though. I pretended that the whole Sam thing never happened. If I never told anyone, it may as well have never happened, right? The small pits of guilt and satisfaction in my stomach would eventually go away, and if it ever came out, I'd deny it to the death. It was his word against mine, but I had faith that it would never come to that—when a week had passed and Mollie still hadn't shown up on my doorstep with an automatic weapon, I assumed all was clear skies, bunnies, and rainbows.

So to solidify my new path to wholesomeness and respectability, I'd decided I was going to get proactive about the Drew situation. Not to mention that Alex had been so MIA with this whole band thing, I figured dating Drew would be a good excuse for us to hang out more.

"So, have you talked to Drew?" I asked, trying to snap her out of her daze.

"I talk to Drew every day."

"Well, has he ever mentioned anything about my party and our make-out sesh or anything?"

"He just wondered where you disappeared to after he mustered up more nutsack than he's had in his life to kiss you."

I sucked my cheeks. "I puked," I said.

"I figured." She bit the chipping purple polish off her thumbnail and spit it toward the front of the classroom.

"I was thinking he might call me or something."

"I think he was thinking the same. You're the one who ditched him to be groped by the lacrosse team, remember?"

Did she know something? Was that a dig? If I don't acknowledge it, it never happened.

"So you think I should call him? Is it too late?"

"Yeah, call him," she said, eyes closed behind her smudged, crooked glasses, words jumbled by the fist still at her cheek. "Why not?"

"And say what?"

"I don't know! Whatever you want! He likes you, not me, remember?"

Girls settled in behind desks, and Mr. Boardman called attendance. He reminded me of poultry, the way his clammy pink skin sweat, reddened, and pimpled under the neon lights. He seemed like the kind of guy whose dark apartment was covered in afghans and cat hair and reeked of chicken fat. I said *here* when my name was called, then stared out the window and scripted our phone convo.

WEDNESDAY SEEMED LIKE A good day to call Drew. Midweek, not too pushy, yet also not an afterthought. I waited until nine o'clock. Actually, I waited until 9:04 so it didn't look like I was just waiting until nine o'clock.

"Hello?"

I hadn't really expected him to pick up. I had to stop repeating the voice mail I'd been practicing and switch to actual casual conversation. I'd never really *talked* to a boy on the phone before, about anything other than when they were coming over anyway. I'd exchanged logistical information over the phone with my voice, but I'd never actually, like, sat and chatted for no reason with a boy. I didn't totally see the point—wasn't gossip what girls were for?

"Hey!" I dialed back my enthusiasm. If this was going to be a whole, actual conversation, I needed to pace myself. "It's Veronica."

"Hey...what's going on?"

I realized I had nothing to say.

"Nothing really." Seriously, I had nothing. "Just chillin'."

"Yeah, me too. Was about to watch a movie, actually."

In the past, I would have taken this to mean *come over and hook up.*

"Oh, yeah?" I stalled. "What movie?"

"*True Romance.*"

"Seriously?"

I wasn't sure if he was coming on to me or not. Was he watching a romantic comedy? Was this the way non-jocks got non-sluts? With movies called things like *Terms of Endearment* and *True Romance*? It was cute that he didn't immediately jump to the conclusion that I was a *Fast and the Furious* type of girl. Even though I kind of was.

"It's only the greatest movie of all time."

"I've never seen it. Is it, like, famous?"

He laughed. I probably should have lied and said that I'd seen it so that he'd think I was cultured and smart like Alex. I shouldn't have let on right away that I hadn't seen most movies most people had. I wasn't sure why. I wasn't sure where I'd been when everyone else was watching *The Wizard of Oz* and *Home Alone* and *The Breakfast Club*, but somehow I got to be sixteen and just had to pretend I knew what people were talking about when they said things like, "You can't handle the truth!"

"Famous." I could hear him scratching his scalp through the receiver. "I don't know what makes a movie famous. It's just... it's really good."

Another awkward pause.

"I like good movies."

"Good," he said through a muffled laugh. "It's good to like good things. Better than liking bad things."

At this point, the old Veronica would have said something like, *but sometimes it's good to be bad*, but I refrained. That was old jock-screwing, tit-flashing drunkie Veronica. New Veronica, who dated smart, sensitive, literate, good-movie-liking, good-SAT-scoring guys like Drew, didn't revert to sexual banter for lack of witty, insightful things to say, right? So I went with the truth.

"Well, honestly," I said, "I don't know much about movies, let alone good movies."

"Well, it would be my pleasure to introduce you to some good movies. And we'll start with *True Romance*."

"Sounds like a plan," I said, fighting a smile.

He paused again, then said, "I'm going to go watch it. But do you want to hang out this weekend? Start your cinematic education with a Tarantino tutorial?"

He was actually asking me out on a Wednesday for the weekend? He genuinely wasn't going to ask me to come over right then to "watch" *True Romance*. This really was something different it seemed.

"I'd like that. Call me."

"I will," he said. Then he inhaled deeply. I could hear the faint buzz of his TV hissing through the phone. "Take it easy, Veronica," he said. Then he hung up.

My room, my house, was silent. I swiveled in my creaky green desk chair and looked at all the dolls and stuffed animals placed on the wicker bookshelf, where they'd been collecting dust, untouched, for, like, ten years. Pictures of me, Alex, and Mollie were tacked all over my lavender walls. Us dolled up in too much makeup and braces blaring at middle-school dances and jumping around on the beach in not-well-filled-out bikinis at my old shore house. Me, Mollie, and Sam with cigarettes in our hands some night outside of Rizzuto's house. Me and Alex and Liz Masterson at my fourteenth birthday party. I'd always liked her; I strained to remember why we didn't talk to her anymore. I looked up at the fading stick-on stars on my ceiling and thought of how they were there every night, but I thought to notice them only once in a while.

ALEXANDRA HOLBROOK

Six weeks after the make-out that shook the nation, nothing else earth-shattering had really happened on the Drew and Veronica front. They'd each reported that they'd talked on the phone a few times and I saw them wave to each other through the fence at tennis practice, but they hadn't hung out one-on-one (thanks to a series of successful interferences run by yours truly) and hadn't made out again since the party. Thank god. I relished the possibility that this whole thing was really possibly going to blow over after all.

I found myself looking forward to band practice. Waking up excited on days that I knew we were going to play in the afternoon, skipping tennis so that we could start earlier and play for longer. And I really liked the guys. And I thought, it seemed, they really liked me, which for some reason made me feel more genuinely satisfied than anyone else ever liking me in the past had. Because they were different from anyone else who'd ever liked me in the past. They came from a different world, knew different things, had a different set of standards and values and ideas of what was cool and what was funny than anyone I'd grown up around. I had to shift my parameters around them, and at the same time, because it was understood that we were inherently different, could just be myself and be different from them, and they accepted, respected, and enjoyed me for whatever brand of different I was. They made me feel like maybe I was going to be okay out there, outside of the incestuous circle of Crawford and Harwin and girls with blond ponytails and boys with roman numerals after their names. And they loved music like I did. And they knew how to talk about it and roll around in it, analyze it, and create it in ways I'd never even considered to be an option.

"So, guys," Ned said as he tuned his guitar. "We got our first gig. We got accepted to Halloween Battle of the Bands."

I looked at Fernando and Pete, ready for them to laugh and say, "Dude, we're not ready!" But instead, Fernando said, "Awesome, man."

Pete just nodded.

Everyone went to Battle of the Bands. Everyone. All my friends would be there. I hadn't really thought about what playing in front of them was going to be like. I was so happy here in my little music bubble with Ned and Pete and Fernando. I wanted to live here, among people who understood, who were supportive, who weren't just looking for an excuse to mock me or for confirmation that I was a talentless wannabe.

"We're not ready," I said. I started to sweat.

"Sure we are," said Ned, completely unfazed. "But we should probably decide on a set list now. What do you think? Do you guys wanna do 'If You Knew'?"

He was so matter-of-fact. So unshaken. Wasn't there anyone he was trying to impress? Anyone he was worried about exposing himself to?

"I don't really know that one yet," I said, my heart still fluttering, head caving in.

"I'll teach it to you," Fernando said. And he came over to my keyboard and stood next to me. He placed his hands on the keyboard and hit A–A–C–G. Then he did it again and said, "A, A, C, G," as he played. I'd never really stood this close to him before. Never realized how much taller than me he was. He smelled like Irish Spring.

I repeated after him, "A, A, C, G."

He put his hands on my hips and shuffled me over. He nudged me with his elbow and said, "You try."

I did.

He said, "You got it. It's a really simple four-chord progression. You do way fancier stuff than this in your sleep, dude. The words are easy, too."

"Words? Oh, I don't need to bother with that," I said. "Right?"

"We're a band. We all learn the words," Ned said.

I nodded, bit the inside of my cheek, and looked down at the keys, chords, and patterns running together, the song already playing in my head, my hands already twitching, itching to play it out and connect the dots.

Fernando nudged me with his elbow again and cocked his head, shaking out his brown curls. "You'll be fine," he said.

Then he winked and put his hand on the small of my back before he turned to his drums.

THE ANNUAL BATTLE OF the Bands had become a Halloween tradition. It was held in a dingy old club on Franklin Avenue that was owned by the father of a Crawford boy in Sam's class (Billy Todman; his band was playing right after ours—his band also won every year). Mr. Todman didn't shut down the club for the event, but he made us wear UNDER 21 wristbands, which people like Mollie and Sam found "degrading." *Why pay ten dollars to go somewhere we can't drink when we have places to go where it's encouraged?* Four other bands from schools around town were playing. I threw up every morning the entire week before. If I were Mollie, I would have run around telling everyone I was pregnant.

But everyone said they'd come this year and root for me. Even Mollie promised she'd ditch the annual Dress as Your Favorite Slutty Animal lacrosse party and come, even if it meant ditching Sam. I'd believe it when I saw it. We'd been sounding pretty good in practice, and the boys were determined to make me sing at the show. Screwing around in practice was one thing, but I was not prepared to take lead vocals onstage. In front of people. In front of my friends.

We dressed as a mariachi band. I begged to wear a vest and sombrero like everybody else, but the boys insisted I go in a more Catalan/flamenco direction. I hate myself in dresses. I feel like a drag queen in them, but it was Halloween and the Cunning Runts' balls-out, full commitment to the cause seemed like it was going to be hilarious when we came up with the idea, so I said okay.

We stewed in a back office, hearts pounding, legs twitching, foreheads sweating, my hair slicked back in a bun, a rose behind my ear, a fake mole penciled on my cheek, and a dark premonition that my dress would split onstage.

"Alex, this is what we practice for!" Ned said. "Please stop looking like you're about to puke."

I couldn't even muster a polite laugh. My heart beat in my eyes.

I sat on a swivel chair in the stale old office that smelled like a taxi. Fernando knelt in front of me. He reached out both hands and held my shoulders. "Alex," he said, peering deeply into my bloodless face, "you are beautiful and talented and going to rock shit out there, man."

He rubbed his warm hands up and down my goose-bumped arms.

Our flirtation had continued, sort of. At least that's what I thought it was, but I wasn't sure, because I had zero experience in this area. I'd thought maybe boys had liked me in the past, but it never ended up materializing into anything. Things always took a turn, and they ended up with someone else and just being my "best friend," so I'd learned to be careful not to delude myself and accidentally think I was pretty or talented or special in any way, because I couldn't risk being humiliated and disappointed when it turned out that wasn't true. And even if he was flirting with me, I wasn't going to do anything about it. Even though I'd never had an actual relationship, I'd seen enough to know that this was the fun part: the imagining, the flirting, the possibilities. It was all downhill into boredom and jealousy and paranoia after that. Right now, he thought I was cool and interesting and fun. If he really got to know me, he'd see that I was actually not that cute and not that interesting and just a dumb insecure girl like everyone else. Or he'd become another Drew and learn to love me, but not like that. It wasn't worth it. It was better like this. Plus, sometimes boys just like to flirt, it doesn't mean they actually, physically, want to do and/or plan on doing anything about it. I resigned myself to stay focused on the music, assuming it was nothing.

"Please don't make me sing," I said, almost in tears. "I'm fine on the piano in the back. Please, just don't make me sing. Ned should sing."

"Is that really what you want?" Fernando asked. I felt guilty for thinking how right he looked in a sombrero.

"Fuck that," said Ned.

"What band has a chick and doesn't put her in the front?" said Pete.

"You're Gwen Stefani," Ned said. "You're Stevie Nicks, Grace Slick, Lauryn Hill, the chick from Garbage."

"Can't I be D'arcy Wretzky?" I pleaded. "Let it be. Please."

Fernando looked at me, and the tears welled again. He put his hand on my trembling face, turned, and said, "Dude, look at her. Give her a fucking break, man."

I looked at Ned and Pete, tears still mounting, heart still racing. I now not only feared I was going to be mocked and ridiculed by my friends and the audience, but also that I was about to gravely disappoint my bandmates, the only people who might even possibly still sort of respect me.

"Really, Holbrook?" Ned asked. "You're really that scared?"

"I'm not scared!" I shouted, tears now fully falling down my cheeks. "I'm just not good enough."

The twins threw their sombreros on the ground and rolled their eyes.

"Please don't cry," Fernando said, wiping a rogue tear from my cheek. "It's cool. Ned will lead tonight."

I was so embarrassed. I couldn't believe I cried in front of them; god, I was pathetic. No wonder no one ever wanted to date me.

Ned hugged me and said, "I'm sorry. I didn't mean to make you cry. Please don't cry. I'll sing tonight; you just do backup, okay? Just please, please do not cry."

I sniffled, nodded, and let him hug my limp body, totally humiliated that I had actually just let this happen. I never cried, let alone in front of boys. I was mortified but also entirely relieved that the pressure of singing, alone, in front of everyone, was off.

I reapplied my makeup and surrendered to the steady ratio of the rise of my heart rate to the building volume level of the crowd outside. Fernando twirled his drumsticks in his fingers, and the twins tuned their guitars. I needed a prop to fiddle with.

I checked my phone.

From Drew: **Good luck tonight. I'll be in the front row screaming your name. Can I get some backstage passes?**

From Veronica: **Gluck!!! Can't w8 2 b ur #1 groupie!!!!!!!**

From Mollie: **I may be late, but don't worry. I will be**

there, and I will be screaming for my favorite thrash metal pianist!

From Mom: **Sorry I can't be there tonight, break a leg! Love you. So proud. XOXO.**

I wasn't sure whether knowing I had all this love and support made me feel better or worse. Maybe I shouldn't have invited everyone to my first show. Maybe I should have given myself a trial run before I made a complete ass of myself in a motherfucking Chiquita Banana costume.

I thought I could faintly hear Veronica's high-pitched giggle from the office; it was then and only then that the inhuman timbre of her voice had ever soothed me.

"You can do it!" Fernando shook my shoulders.

"We can do it!" I replied, grabbing his wrists.

I listened to the muffled sound of Mr. Todman trying to quiet everyone down outside. I heard Drew's hoot and signature whistle.

"Please welcome," Mr. Todman said before clearing his throat, "the Cunning Runts!"

The crowd, the large crowd, filled with faces I'd never seen, screamed and clapped and glowed under the hot lights. The faces I did know melted into a mush of wide-eyed, face-painted animals, witches, sexy policewomen, sexy nurses, and sexy Village People. Veronica, Drew, Mollie, Sam, and four of Sam's friends who I knew, but who never talked to me, all stood right in front. Screaming, clapping, pointing, waving. I waved back as I made my way across the stage to the keyboard, hoping no one could see up my ridiculous dress.

Mollie was a murdered, blood-covered cheerleader and Sam and the rest of his friends were all vampire football players. Finally, she got to put on that cheerleading uniform: one of her dreams come true. I couldn't tell what Veronica was. A sexy teacher maybe? Britney Spears? Drew was Jay Gatsby; there was no way Veronica knew that there was any significance to that beyond a Leonardo DiCaprio movie. I wondered if she'd pretended to.

Ned took the mic. "We're the Cunning Runts," he said. Whooping, hollering, whistling. My friends went crazy. I could hear all their voices, Drew's whistle, even Sam's barking. I almost cried again.

"Please welcome our new keyboardist and lead vocalist, Alexandra Holbrook." And he picked up my keyboard and moved it from stage left to center stage.

Holy fuck.

"Wish her luck, everyone! It's her first show!"

Everyone screamed and clapped.

Ned adjusted the mic. I couldn't just *not* sing. Could I? He'd probably step in if I just didn't sing. . . .

"You'll be fine," he whispered in my ear. "You're the singer. You'll see."

I looked at Fernando, who smiled and winked at me. I looked at Ned, who was strapping on his guitar and nodding, looking confident that he hadn't just pushed me into an impromptu crowd surf.

Ned played a few notes, and I swallowed, not sure if sound would come out when I opened my mouth. White lights shone bright in my eyes and hot on my face. I was sure I was sweating. The crowd dimmed. They just stood there, staring at us, waiting for us to do something stupid. Waiting to laugh.

It was almost time for the lyrics. My fingers hit the keys, and I tried to remember the words. I knew the notes, but could I sing the actual words? Drew looked directly at me, smiled, and gave me a thumbs-up—the cheesiness of the gesture made me smile.

Then he turned to talk to Veronica, and I wondered what he said to her. If they were talking about me, if they had inside jokes or stories or things that I wasn't a part of, if I was still most of what they had in common. Mollie stood there with her arms crossed, biting her thumbnail, looking nervous. Like she was nervous for me. Like she knew how devastated I would be if I screwed up, and that there was a good chance that I might.

Drew put his arms around Veronica and kissed her. Just like that, right there in the crowd, right there in front of me, in front of everyone! Right before I was supposed to start playing. He stood there behind her, kissing her, holding her, looking at me. Giving me a fucking thumbs-up.

Fuck it.

I closed my eyes, leaned into the mic, opened my mouth, and sound actually came out. Everyone cheered. Drew whistled. I couldn't even hear myself. I just sang, like I was in the shower or my car. I closed my eyes, banged the keys, and belted out the words. People danced. We—our sound, our instruments, Ned's and Fernando's words—actually got people to move.

I stopped thinking and feeling, just sang and played and

smiled and took in the lights, the crowd, my friends, Fernando's dark hair shaking behind his flailing arms, the twins' onstage sureness that never came out in real life. The music hugged me, made me feel safe inside it, and protected us from anything the crowd could possibly do to us. It was all right. I sang some songs; Ned sang others. We sang together. I didn't miss one note on the keyboard, and I hadn't even lost the rose in my hair when it was all over.

We took our bows and bounced back to the sweltering office behind the stage. Sweating, laughing, panting, I felt like myself again.

"I can't believe you did that to me!" I screamed, and punched Ned in the shoulder.

"Aren't you glad I did?"

"Yes!" I said, unable to control my volume, my jumping, my adrenaline.

Fernando put his hands on my hips, steadying me, planting my feet firmly on the ground. "You were awesome. I knew you could do it!"

I smiled back at him, overwhelmed, unsure of how to feel, what to say, how not to scream or throw up. "I couldn't have done it without you," I said.

We hugged, moist polyester costume to moist polyester costume, heat radiating from our bodies. And just like that, right there in that stinky office, he took my sweaty face in his hands and kissed me.

MOLLIE FINN

It was my best friend onstage, but I felt like I was looking at a total stranger. All that makeup, the dress, closing her eyes and getting all emo into the mic like she was fucking Rihanna or something. I had no idea who this person was. Who this person thought she was.

And how could that bitch not have told me that she was the lead singer? I thought she just played the piano. She was a singer now? I had no idea why she was being so weird about this band stuff, and it was stressing me out.

The music wasn't bad. It wasn't mind-blowingly amazing, but it's not like they were off-key or anything. There's just something so cheesy about watching a bunch of teenagers taking themselves seriously playing Rolling Stones songs. They played mostly songs I didn't know, but I don't know if it's because they actually wrote them themselves or if I'm just a moron, because *oh my god, I only listen to music that's on the radio*—perish the fucking thought.

"Dude," Sam said over the applause as the lights went up. "Alex is a rock star."

He smiled and clapped. So did his friends.

"They were pretty good. I love their name. The mariachi thing is hilarious," said Austin. "Are they going to dress like that all the time, or just tonight, because it's Halloween?"

"That'd be fucking awesome if they did it all the time. If it was, like, their thing," said Sam, cracking up, again, at his own dumb joke. How different life would be if Sam were actually half as funny as he thought he was...

"Your friend the singer is kind of hot," said Austin. "Why don't you bring her around more often?"

"You've met her, like, seven times. You're probably confused by the fake mole and the twelve pounds of eyeliner."

"How freakin' good was she?" squealed Veronica. She and Drew were holding hands. So what, they were, like, dating now? Did Alex know about this? And more than that, if she did, how could she have not bitched to me more about it? More shit she doesn't tell me anymore. I'd be livid, injuring people, screaming to anyone who'd listen about what a backstabbing whore my friend was. They were officially making out in public and openly acknowledging their togetherness? It was totally fucked up and not right.

"Did you guys know she was gonna sing?" I asked.

"No!" V screamed again over the rowdy crowd. "I had no idea she was so good! Did you?" The question was to Drew.

"Not like that," he replied, still holding her fucking hand.

It was hot as balls in that dump of a suburban divorcée cougar pen. I wondered where they came up with this place. Was this the kind of place that "bands" played at all the time? Were all the tattooed, pink-haired, latex-wearing misfits in the crowd the type of people who often did things like *check out bands* in their free time? I wondered if that was what Alex was going to start doing now that she was such a hipster rocker-chick.

"I'm gonna try to get backstage," said Drew.

"I'll come with you," I said.

"I'm, like, overheating," said Veronica, fanning her glittering cleavage. She was wearing a loincloth and pasties—I could see how that must have been really oppressive for her. "Can we get some air and smoke a cig first?"

"I'll come with you," said Sam.

What was she trying to pull? Since when did Sam go anywhere with her?

"You're seriously too hot to come congratulate your best friend after her first show?"

She looked over toward Sam, who was already making his way toward the door.

"I'm, like, seriously about to pass out," she said, pouting.

"Seriously? You're wearing, like, no clothes. What the hell are you dressed as anyway?" I asked, like I thought she'd say *Oh my god, you're right, I'm not that hot. I'm naked! Silly me, I'll come with you.*

"I'm a Catholic school girl, get it?" And she twirled the cross at her neck around her finger.

"Because ya know"—the blood in my neck started to seethe—"that's what *I*, an actual Catholic girl who goes to school, look like every day."

"Well, what are you? A cheerleader? Because that's what cheerleaders actually look like every day?"

I looked down at my soiled outfit.

"I'm a zombie cheerleader, whore. I was gonna come dressed as you, but I couldn't fit seven dicks in my mouth."

Drew and Sam snickered, and Veronica said *ha, ha*, stuck out her tongue, fanned herself again, and said she'd be backstage with us in five minutes.

I didn't want her and Sam out there alone, but I figured Austin would follow and that she'd throw herself on him before she'd heave herself at Sam.

"Drew, let's go be good friends."

I followed Drew as he weaved through the crowd. I never realized how tall he was. It was easy to follow his little pinhead through the mass. I couldn't remember the last time Drew and I had been somewhere alone together. In middle school, maybe. He, Alex, and I used to hang out all the time. Somewhere along the line, the two of them stopped inviting me to things. Or maybe Alex and I stopped inviting him. Or maybe I started hanging out with Sam and stopped inviting both of them. We'd made out once in, like, eighth grade, maybe seventh, but it was during Truth or Dare, so it didn't count.

When we got to the creepy office door, Alex and the band were all huddled up, smiling, hugging. It was crazy to me that Alex had become so close with these people who I didn't even know. Since I was five years old, I don't think I'd ever hugged anyone Alex didn't know.

When she saw me, she pushed away the band guys, came over, and hugged me. Her costume was soaked with sweat, and her makeup was beginning to cake and congeal—but I've never seen her look so happy.

"You came!" she said, her voice cracked, as if she was maybe holding back tears. She smelled like melting plastic, like the pens Veronica always burned in chem lab.

"Of course we came!" I replied. She broke from me and hugged Drew.

"You were unbelievable," he said, patting her slick shoulders.

"Really?" She still seemed out of breath. "Tell me the truth. I feel like I was totally off-key during that last one."

"You were so into it, though!" I said.

"I know," she said, wiping her brow. "I, like, forgot people were watching."

"For a minute there, I thought you were going to keel over and fall off the stage!"

She laughed.

"Did Veronica leave?" she asked both of us.

"She was overheating. She wanted to get some air before braving the sweltering backstage."

She nodded sarcastically.

The cute Latino guy left the other ones and came over to us. He put his arm around Alex.

"So," he said. "You guys like the show?"

"You guys were so good!" I replied.

"Alex did great for her first time, no?"

Drew straightened his hat and put his hands in his pockets. "She killed it. Who knew she could sing like that?"

"We did," said Fernando, then he kissed her on the cheek. Both Drew and I flinched.

I watched Alex talk to the guys in the band, and I felt like she belonged with them. Like they were now this little unit, and she and I were not. Alex and I had never not been on the same team before, never not come at something from the same side. I didn't like what was happening here. It was hot in the office. My heart sped up, and I was starting to sweat and lose my breath.

"Well," I said, interjecting myself into the band conversation, "maybe next time you guys can sing some songs that people actually know!"

They all snickered at one another, and they didn't really laugh at my joke. And with their lack of laughter, the wall grew thicker. The more I talked, the harder I tried, I knew the wall would just get thicker and thicker, and it would become more and more obvious how different I was from them and how much closer Alex clearly felt to them than me. I had to get out of there.

And where the hell were Sam and Veronica? Were they a team now, too? Who was left on my team? What was happening to me? My cheerleader outfit was starting to stick to my skin, and I was finding it harder and harder to swallow.

"Drew," I said. "Let's go find Sam and Veronica." He nodded and followed me outside.

ALEXANDRA HOLBROOK

The next Friday, we sat at our usual table in the lunchroom, and I watched Mollie destroy yet another innocent turkey sandwich. Mollie's ingenious, personal brand of eating disorder was to destroy her food rather than consume it. I watched her pick slices of turkey out of her sandwich, then gnaw on some and discard others. She ripped the crust off her bread and poked at the insides with her nubby, pink pod-fingers. When she was done with a meal, most of her food was still there, it just appeared to have been attacked by wild, yet oddly anorexic, bears.

"Do you guys want to go bowling tonight?" I asked.

"Who goes bowling?" Mollie scowled. "Bowling is for fat eight-year-olds."

"Drew suggested it. Mix it up a bit."

"Pass," said Mollie.

The loud cafeteria static clanged and clashed around the table in the back corner of the lunchroom. Harwin's cafeteria didn't look like your typical high school cafeteria, but rather like something out of a gothic novel. It was a rickety old room in the oldest part of the school. The once white walls had soured and peeled around stained-glass windows over creaky hard-wood floors, and Victorian arches framed creepy portraits of thin-lipped schoolmarms being choked by their collars. Wobbly wooden chairs circled paint-chipped round tables filled with squealing, complaining girls, in the process of explaining why frozen yogurt was *totally* a well-balanced lunch.

"V?" I asked. This was her test, time to officially see if she'd jump at the chance to hang with Drew after big public Halloween make-out number two or make up some excuse to go social climb, and blow lax players with Mollie.

"Did Drew actually say 'invite Veronica,' because we talked about hanging out this weekend, but he didn't mention bowling. I don't want to just, like, show up and have him think I'm, like, stalking him."

"Aren't you guys, like, dating now?" Mollie asked. "Wouldn't it be normal for you all to hang out?"

Veronica rolled her eyes and leaned toward me, caging Mollie out. "You're positive he said *invite Veronica*?"

"Yes."

That wasn't actually what he'd said. He said something closer to *so what should Veronica and I do this weekend?* He said that he wanted to take her on a date, but I told him that was premature and that we should all do something fun together—then I pulled bowling out of my ass, because it seemed asexual and low contact.

I glanced at Mollie and said, "Molls, last chance?" Just for fun. Knowing she'd never give up a night in the infamous Rizzuto basement (lovingly referred to by Sam and his Cro-

Magnon cohorts as the 'Zu, because they're *fucking animals, bro*) for something so parochial as bowling with boys in her own grade who weren't on sports teams (ultimate Frisbee didn't count).

The 'Zu was just Lindsay and Tom Rizzuto's basement, an institution and Greencliff legacy. All the "cool" kids from all the private schools partied at the Rizzutos' and had for years. Lindsay was a senior at Harwin when we were freshmen. She was a legendary whore, but was one of those "knows everybody" and "friends with all the guys" types. Tom Rizzuto was a year older than us at Crawford. He didn't seem to be anything particularly special or exciting, but people hung out with him because of his house and his sister's cachet. Both Mollie and Veronica were weirdly obsessed with it. I had gone a few times and didn't see what the big deal was. It was just a bunch of douchey guys and drunk girls vying for their attention. The only topic of conversation allowed there seemed to be either how drunk you currently are or how drunk you were when you were there last week.

I wanted to see if, just for a passing moment, I could make Mollie confront her own agenda and admit that going to the 'Zu was more important to her than hanging out with us, her "best friends."

"Still definitely pass," she said. "I told Sam I'd do the 'Zu thing tonight."

V CAME OVER TO get ready for our big bowling night. She tried on a million of my T-shirts, claiming she wanted to go for my *chill, retro-chic* look, before inevitably, and predictably, going with the lowest-cut leftover baby tee from sixth grade she could find. I hated when she tried on my clothes. When she stood there, in front of the mirror, wiggling around in various items saying, *Oh my god, Lex, do these fit you? This can't fit you! It's huge!* They're my clothes, whorebox. They fit me. Unlike her clothes, which were made for bulimic preschoolers.

I debated inviting the band boys, but I decided I needed to stay focused on running interference between Drew and Veronica, which was the whole point of my orchestrating this whole date insurrection in the first place. Despite my initial instinct to use Fernando to make Drew jealous, I decided that keeping a watchful eye on the progress of this bullshit relationship was more important. I couldn't let a Fernando-type distraction result in another stolen kiss or back-alley tryst. I also didn't need Drew's reaction to seeing me flirt with Fernando to be a full-throttle plunge at Veronica. I wondered what I'd started here and if I had the stomach to see it through.

Drew texted me: **Hope you're stretching and hydrating. You're about to get schooled in the art of bowling.**

I replied: **Game on.**

I fought every impulse I had to check Veronica's phone and see if he sent her the same thing. Or, worse, if he sent her something else—something cute and mushy or, oh god, sexual. I wondered how he talked to her, if they joked around or if they were earnest and romantic. An eerie panic rolled over me, and I left Veronica to rummage through my closet while I went downstairs for food.

My mom sat cross-legged at the kitchen table, her new super-hip cat's-eye glasses perched at the tip of her nose. She was thumbing through the Arts section, as she usually did at this particular time in that particular spot. My brother stood at the counter twirling spaghetti in a Tupperware. My mom looked up at me over her glasses and proceeded to rattle off everything we had in the fridge, as if I hadn't just opened it and wasn't staring directly into its contents.

"There's leftover spaghetti—and I bought that expensive cheese you like."

I grabbed the fork and spaghetti out of Josh's hands.

"I was done anyway," he said.

I smiled up at him with my mouth full. The dynamic between us hadn't quite adjusted to his growth spurt. I chose to ignore his new size and structure and continued to treat him like the snotty runt I always had. Even though sometimes I felt like I was standing next to a stranger, or worse, my contemporary.

"Where are you going tonight?" my mom asked, not looking up from her paper. "See if your brother wants to go."

Her gray roots were growing in. She never had roots or holes in her sweaters or wore clogs when my dad was around, but she did now, all the time, and seemed to be pleased as punch with her newfound languor. She'd started smoking again, too, even though she wouldn't admit it. She'd caught me with cigarettes a few times, and she was always completely unconvincing when attempting to scold me about the danger they presented to my health and general image. I could see the sides of her mouth turn up when she called it *a disgusting habit*. I wondered when we'd both be able to come out of our bathrooms, untowel the doors, put away the air freshener, and be able to sit at the kitchen table and smoke together like two civilized adults.

"I can make my own plans, thanks, Mom," he said, grabbing the Tupperware back.

"We're going bowling," I said as I gathered an armful of assorted snack crackers and baked goods to bring upstairs.

She burst into a loud guffaw, slid her glasses off her nose, and let them hang off her fingers.

"Bowling?" Sometimes she was way too amused by things that just weren't that amusing. She dabbed her watering eyes with her knuckle. "Like when you were little? That's a riot."

Feeling patronized and belittled, I rolled my eyes and left the kitchen. Josh followed me up the stairs.

"Is Mollie going tonight?" he asked.

"No, she's too busy social climbing with Sam," I replied, not bothering to look back at him.

"Fuck that guy," he said.

"Did she ever thank you for Veronica's party?" I stood at the top of the staircase, he three steps below me, which allowed me to be taller than him again.

"No, but it's okay." He looked down at the tan specks in the navy carpet. "She doesn't really need to. What was I gonna do, leave her there with that guy?"

I gave him a little pat on the shoulder. "You're too good for her, Josh."

"That's a nice thing to say about your best friend."

Veronica busted out of my room in a T-shirt and no pants.

"How do we feel about this top?" she said, pulling and twisting the T-shirt around her hips. "Oh my god, Josh! Whoops. Sorry!" she said, sheepishly covering her lady parts with cupped hands. Not running back into my room, or retrieving a pair of pants or anything of that nature—just standing there, half naked, in my hallway, in front of my fifteen-year-old brother, twisting and posing. He turned bright red and looked at the floor.

"It's fine," he said. "Don't mind me."

"Whoops!" she said again, before spotting the buffet in my arms. "Oh, yay! I'm starving."

D rew and his gang were already bowling and drinking 40s out of paper bags when we got there. People liked to hang out at the bowling alley, because it was one of the few places kids could still drink without much hassle.

He hugged Alex first.

Then he said, "Hey, you," to me. He poked my stomach and kissed me on the cheek. "You look pretty."

The boys were already on their way to drunk and Alex seamlessly rolled herself right into their game. I wondered what the guys knew about us, about me, if they'd heard things about me and if they knew that Drew and I had kissed. Twice. In public. If guys told each other stuff like that. The second kiss meant that we were dating, right? Or at least that he wanted to date or that we were on our way to dating. It meant that he wanted to kiss me on a relatively regular basis and wasn't embarrassed to do it in front of other people, right? None of the jocks had ever kissed me in public, not soberly anyway. It felt like a big step to me.

"So," Drew said, plopping down as I tied my rental shoes, "you gonna be on my team?"

"If you'll have me," I replied, hoping he'd get a nice flash of cleave while I took my time stroking and bowing my laces.

"You any good?"

"I've been told I know how to handle balls."

He laughed, but I kicked myself and swore I'd lay off lines like that.

"Drew!" Alex shouted from the red line thingy. "It's your turn, buttface."

He popped up, grabbed the ball from her hand, and said, "What the hell is this girly light ball shit? I thought you were an athlete."

"You think you can handle the heavy one, Rocky? Please. My biceps are bigger than yours."

He grabbed her arm. "Woman, I could bowl you."

"She *is* like a bowling ball," shouted Marc Seidman from the sidelines. "Ya put three fingers in her and throw her in the gutter."

The group roared with laughter.

Alex swiveled her neck around and stood at the ball dispensary with her hand on her hip, black Led Zeppelin T-shirt dripping off her square shoulders like she was a closet hanger.

"Well, you're so fat that when you wear a yellow T-shirt, kids line up for school," she said.

The group roared again. High fives were exchanged. I giggled along, wishing I could be that quick and clever. And that I was getting as much of Drew's or anyone's attention as she was.

I took a medium-heavy ball and walked toward the line, looked back at the boys, winked, and told them I'd show them how it was done. I bent over, slowly, hoping Drew was watching and that my new jeans were doing what I'd bought them to do.

WHEN THE LANES CLOSED at ten, Alex decided that she was too drunk to drive home. Drew stood between us, hands in his pockets, eyes darting to Sam and then me, to Sam and then back to me.

"I can drive you guys home. I'm fine."

"V, are you sleeping over?" she asked.

I hadn't planned on it, but I said sure, figuring that I'd rather us both get out of Drew's car at the same time than give them time alone to talk about me—I knew there was no way to justify him taking Alex home first, though that would have been ideal. Goddamn Alex for living on his street and making it impossible for him to come up with a slick way to take her home first! Seriously, goddamn. If Alex was a good friend, she would have thought about this in advance and we would have come up with a plan, right? Why hadn't she thought about this and come up with a plan?

We said good-bye and walked out to the parking lot. Alex hopped in the front seat without even calling shotgun. The two of them bobbed their heads to some song I didn't recognize but Alex seemed to know the words to. Drew occasionally glanced back at me, over that puffy yellow vest, to ask, *are you okay back there?*

I said I was, but I found myself becoming increasingly discouraged. I was always in the backseat, straining to hear, feeling like I missed the day when everyone else learned the words to the song. Whether it was Alex and Mollie or Alex and Drew,

I was always somehow in the backseat, always a beat behind. I was still trying to figure out how I'd orchestrate a kiss good night around the logistics of this car ride. The logistics of this whole night, really. Drew and I had barely talked at all—I felt more like I'd taken a supervised field trip to Drew/Alex-land only to now head back to slut/jock-land with tales of bowling and banter from abroad.

We pulled into Alex's driveway and sat in his car in front of her house while we all smoked a joint. Even I took a few hits; clearly all that was left in my night was cleaning out Alex's fridge and passing out, so for that, I could handle getting high.

"Thanks for driving, buddy," Alex said, and she leaned across the console and kissed him on the cheek.

"No problem, ladies," he said. Then he looked back over his shoulder at me, grinning his cute, crooked grin. I smiled back, leaned forward, and gave him a long, soft kiss on the cheek, half openmouthed, hoping maybe I could get something started. I caught his eye for a minute and held it there, about an inch away from his face, hoping he would have the balls to kiss me in front of Alex. He stayed there for about four seconds before he pulled back. Alex let out a deep sigh, said, "See you tomorrow!" and jumped out of the car.

I raised my eyebrows and looked at him one more time, try-ing to imply that he had one more chance.

"Maybe we'll hang out this weekend?" he said.

"Yeah, call me."

And I scooted out the passenger side and slammed the door. Alex fiddled with her keys before letting us in.

"You hungry?" Alex asked.

"Always," I replied.

Alex's house was warm and smelled like laundry and spicy food. Mail, mugs, and reading glasses were always strewn over the kitchen table, like people actually lived there. Sweaters hung on the backs of chairs; sneakers and slippers were thrown by doorways and under coffee tables. Her mom sold antiques, so there were all sorts of interesting, old-looking things everywhere. Weird things like red wagons, tapestries, and copper pigs. Things my mom would call crap. My house was like a museum. The rooms were all too well lit and too big, and nobody had been in most of them in years.

"Tonight was fun," she said, basking in the glow of her refrigerator light.

"Totally."

My phone beeped, and I reached into my purse to see who was calling. Maybe it was Austin, leaving the 'Zu and looking for a booty call. Or maybe even Sam...

It was a text from Drew: **I wish I'd gotten to kiss you again tonight.**

A smile spread across my face. *Phew*, I thought, though if he wanted to kiss me, why hadn't he when I gave him the chance?

I texted back: **Me 2 :(**

He immediately replied: **I will kiss you again soon. I promise. Good night, Veronica.**

"What are you smiling about?" asked Alex, pulling some leftover spaghetti out of the microwave.

"Nothing," I said. "Booty text."

MOLLIE FINN

Alex had been pretty closemouthed about the Drew/
Veronica thing. V and I had bio lab together, so I took the
opportunity to get her side of it—to see if maybe she had some
idea of what a self-involved cunt she could be.

"So," I said over Bunsen burners, "what's going on with you
and Drew?"

She looked at me, her cow eyes peering out from under the
plastic lab goggles. "I don't know," she said, still focused on the
beaker. "We talk on the phone sometimes and had fun bowling
the other night. It's all been pretty PG. We've only kissed, like,
twice."

She hovered over our lab station. The sleeves of her white
coat were rolled up, exposing her tan, bony wrists stacked with
Tiffany charm bracelets and a Cartier watch. Veronica and her
fucking charm bracelets. It always cracked me up that someone
so lewd could be so obsessed with something so precious. But
she's worn them, and has just continued to stack them farther
up her bony little arm, since I've known her. She used to let me
borrow them, back when we used to go to all the 'Zu parties
together and I'd stay at her house to avoid curfew.

"Do you like him?" I asked.

"What's not to like?" she said.

"Do you think Alex is weird about it?"

"I thought she might be, but she's been cool. She was the one who told me he liked me in the first place, right?"

She was?

"Well," I said, taking the forceps from her limp fingers and rearranging our test tubes, "if you actually want to date Drew, my advice is to take it slow."

She rolled her eyes. "Trust me, we are," she said.

It was ironic, me giving Veronica sex advice. I used to look at her as my sex guru. When I first decided to sleep with Sam, I asked her about everything—condoms, positions, underwear, pacing. I figured people keep wanting to have sex with her, so she must be pretty good at it.

That was actually how we even really became friends. She was always Alex's annoying friend who I tolerated because her parents were never home, and, well, you don't have a girl who looks like that running around and not keep her on your side. But when Sam and I started sleeping together, I'd run right to her, not to Alex, with everything. I'd asked if it was normal that it was over so quickly, that it hurt sometimes, that he really liked doing it from behind, that we stopped making out before-hand after a while. I couldn't talk to Alex about that stuff; she'd just get awkward and think I was bragging or that Sam was a weirdo and hate him even more than she already did. But Veronica could make a joke and funny story out of anything—it was one of her greatest and most annoying qualities. Whatever strange, embarrassing, scary debacle happened during sex, nothing was a big deal, everything was normal, and happened to everyone all the time. I used to sleep at her house every Friday night after 'Zu parties. She even used to let Sam come over, and we would have sex in one of her guest rooms. Until everything came out about her parents, and my mom found out that there were never any adults in that house and stopped allowing me to stay over there.

"Remember what a big deal it was when I first slept with Sam?" I asked her as I scribbled down the lab notes. "We'd been together, officially, for, like, months. Unlike the rest of the dipshits you hook up with, Drew is potentially interested in being your actual boyfriend."

God, what would Veronica be like with an actual boyfriend? Would she be able to accept adoration and attention from only one guy for an extended period of time? Would she be able to handle it when the adoration and attention stopped and she'd have to come up with legitimate things to talk about? Or would her head spontaneously combust if the entire world wasn't gawking at her at all moments? I admit, I was somewhat curious to watch her crash and burn.

"We've literally just made out," she said. She perched on her stool, admiring her nails, having apparently given up entirely on even pretending she'd help with the lab.

"I'm just saying, had I flashed my cleavage and put out for Sam right away, I'm not sure we'd be what we are today. If you want a real relationship, you need to work for it. Play the game. Boyfriends don't just pop out from your Bunsen burner the second you decide you're in the mood for one, and boys don't date girls who put out on the first date. Fact."

"Thanks, Dr. Phil," she said. "I'll keep that in mind."

"Fine then, whore. I'm just trying to help." And I pushed my notes over to her so she could copy them.

"I guess you would know more about relationships than me," she said in a tone I didn't appreciate.

"I never really pictured you with a guy like Drew," I said.

"Trust me, me neither," she said as she shrugged and begrudgingly copied my answers.

"So why Drew, then? Why now?" I couldn't figure out her game here, if she was really into Drew or if she was doing this to mess with Alex, to prove a point. I looked at the clock and nudged her to get a move on the lab copying.

"Because he likes me, and keeps calling me and wanting to hang out, and that's more than I've gotten from the 'Zu guys. I figure I should mix it up and hang around someone who actually likes me for a change." She became distracted from the answer copying and began poking the tip of her pen in the fire from the Bunsen burner.

"What the fuck!" I yelled, snatching the hot, bubbling blue plastic from her grip.

"Sorry!" she yelled back. "I like the way it smells when it burns."

ALEXANDRA HOLBROOK

I sat on my bed staring at my calculus textbook, unable to think about anything but Drew and Veronica. I thought about what they were doing; if they were talking, kissing, more than kissing; what they were saying; how they were saying it; if they were different around each other than they were around me; if they talked about me; what they thought of me; if they made fun of me, lauded me, pitied me.

It was all downhill after Halloween. They weren't calling themselves boyfriend and girlfriend or anything (yet), but they went out to meals together, went to the movies. He started driving her home from things—her and not me, like I didn't still live down the street and it didn't still make logistical sense that we consider the environment and carpool. He hung out at her house on school nights instead of mine, and when he stopped telling me about what happened there, I knew it was really over. For the first month, I oversaw and edited every text, choreographed every hangout, but by Thanksgiving, preambles like *Veronica told me* and *Drew and I saw* were followed by information that was news.

Drew and I still talked, but not like we used to. We still

went on our smoke 'n' drives (sometimes) and watched our movies (less), but something was different. Something that left earlier and came later. Something that drove us to say *hey, stranger* when we saw each other, even if it had been only a few days since our last encounter. They'd try to not be awkward around me and invite me to meals and movies, and to play mini golf—and I went to show them how secure I was with myself and how supportive I was of this whole miserable fucking thing. Seeing her all over him, watching him try to be funny for her—it was excruciating, but I grinned and bore it—after all, I had no one to blame but myself. I let this happen. Fuck, I practically made this happen.

I stared at that calc book: the *x* and the *a* and the square root sign and the silly blue graphs in the top left corner of the glossy paper that, as far as I could tell, had nothing to do with either the *x* or the *a*. I saw their faces close to each other's, heard them whispering, felt them smiling; her all gussied up at the prom in some boob-baring, exorbitantly expensive techno-colored number holding his flowers and slow dancing to sad Beyoncé songs with her face in his neck. I slammed the book shut.

I went downstairs. I opened the refrigerator, but I wasn't hungry. I turned into the living room and saw the piano.

I sat on the hard bench, felt the cold wood through my jeans and the slick ivory under my fingers. I ran my nails over the keys like it was my pet. I always felt like I had to greet it, say hello, exchange pleasantries, before I played. That came from my dad. When I was little, we'd sit on that bench and he'd tell the piano what he was going to teach me that day, and he'd ask if it thought I could handle it. I'd laugh to humor him, as I was never the type of child that believed the piano would answer or that Santa fell down chimneys or that wishing on stars or on pennies or at 11:11 made any sort of difference in getting me any closer to anything I wanted.

I flipped around through some of the sheet music we had, but I didn't feel like playing any of that. *Stevie Wonder: Greatest Hits*, *The Sound of Music*, Beethoven. I started to mess around.

I played a C chord, just because, then E minor—that sounded eerie and soothing and sad and exactly how I was feeling, so I kept going. I let my fingers run around with the major and minor chords until sound filled the room and I wasn't thinking about it anymore. I got dramatic and started pounding the keys and really just letting it out; it got angry, then sad and soft, then angry again. I pretended there were little mini Drews and Veronicas under the keys and I was beating them, shoving my notes and punches and everything I wished I had the balls to say down their smug little throats. I kept going. I didn't even know what I was playing. It just felt good to be making something, changing the sounds in my head—to hear music instead of noise. Fuck the noise in my head, I thought, their faces in mine. Fuck it all. I could push them out, fill my head, change the noise....

Fill it with sound. Fill my head with sound, fill the room with sound, fill it with anything but the noise—drown out the noise, turn off the words, black out the pictures...I got up and found a pen.

Part 3

THE HOLIDAYS

ALEXANDRA HOLBROOK

As a quasi-nonpracticing Jew, I found winter break to be a pretty lonely time. Drew and Veronica had spiraled into coupledom, Mollie's family was all in town, and the guys in the band celebrated Christmas like normal people, so there wasn't much for me to do but lie on my bed, listen to Radiohead, and think about how cold and lonely the world could be. I'd been doing this for a few days when Josh knocked on my door and asked if I wanted to get high in the garage; I said okay.

"So, what's wrong, big sister?" he asked as he packed his little bowl that I'd bought for him on South Street the week after he got caught with weed in his sock drawer. "You've become a complete cliché of teen angst, and I need you to cheer up and be a bitch again, because I'm bored without someone to spar with."

I laughed and took the first hit when he offered it to me. "I'm sorry, little brother," I said as I coughed, then patted him on the shoulder. "The holidays are just shitty and depressing. All my friends have boyfriends."

"You're the lead singer in an awesome band," he said, forcing a smile. "That's so much cooler than having a boyfriend!"

"Gee, you're right.... Lucky me." I perched on a box full of our dad's old albums and patted the box next to me. He obliged and plopped down.

"I mean, think about it...." He took a long inhale. "Would you really want to date Sam? The greatest jerk-off in Crawford history? Or Drew, who is, like, practically related to us?"

I looked at my lap. "No."

"Cheer up, Al." He handed me back the bowl. "I know it seems like having a boyfriend is a big deal, but what you have is actually going to make you way happier in life. You're just in high school. You'll be talented for way longer than they'll have shitty boyfriends."

I looked at Josh and laughed. "When did you get so wise, little one? Aren't I the older sister?"

He patted me on the back and laughed, too. "I've always considered myself wise beyond my years." He exhaled and blew smoke rings, like I'd taught him to do.

"Nice rings," I said.

"See, there are still some things to learn from you."

"Do you think Dad's really gonna come visit after Christmas?" I asked.

"Nope," he said, still holding smoke in his throat, and handing me back the bowl.

The garage door started to rumble. We looked at each other in panic, waved the smoke around, and stumbled over each other as we ran back inside.

*   *   *

FERNANDO AND I HAD kissed four times since our kiss on Halloween: three times after practice and one time we went to a movie and made out in his car when he dropped me off.

I was acutely self-aware when I was around him, always looking at myself through his eyes—trying to figure out how he saw me; what he was thinking about what I was wearing; how I was standing; how I was singing, playing, acting, coughing, laughing; and what he thought that all meant. He knew so little about me, saw such a small part of my life. I was curious as to the conclusions he drew about the little glimpses I chose to give him. It was exhausting. I was trying to enjoy it, but I couldn't. I just kept waiting to fuck it up, for him to get bored or annoyed or grossed out, or to find out that he lost a bet or something. I knew it was only a matter of time before it all went away and things went back to the way they were. Me, Alex, the bud, boyless—that was the way of the universe—me having a quasi-boyfriend/boy I sometimes made out with had to be throwing off the whole balance of the cosmos. Somewhere in the world, the sun had to be rising at night and puppies were dying and red meant go and green meant stop. Something had been thrown off, and surely there were going to be repercussions.

Every time we kissed, there was a solid chance that it would never happen again and order would be restored. I kept waiting for him to initiate some sort of *what are we* conversation, or to acknowledge with actual spoken words that we were something more than buddies and bandmates, and that I could start to assume we'd kiss every time we saw each other, but he didn't. We never actually spoke of our rendezvous, just the band, the weather, music, what we did that weekend. It was like starting from zero every time. Every time we kissed I was surprised, like it was the first time, like it happened by accident. How many times did we have to kiss before it was expected that we would?

I wondered if this was how it always was with these things or if this was just how it was with me, if I was doing something wrong and screwing this up, perpetuating my own self-fulfilling prophecy. Like, when did Mollie and Sam start actually dating and telling people they were boyfriend and girlfriend? I couldn't remember. She met him at some party at the 'Zu that I wasn't invited to, told me she actually spoke to the famous Sam Fuchs, but that he was an asshole and Veronica threw herself at him. Next thing I knew, he asked her to homecoming, they went to homecoming, and then they were boyfriend and girlfriend. That was probably normal. This was probably not normal. The fact that we didn't kiss or touch or flirt or act like we were anything more than friends in front of Ned and Pete (except for that first time at Battle of the Bands, which I'm pretty sure they didn't even see) probably meant that he was embarrassed by our "relationship" and didn't want them to know about it. Didn't want anyone to. I guessed I was fine with that. Better to have a secret make-out buddy than no make-out buddy at all. Plus, it was something for me to talk about (and slightly/grossly exaggerate) when Drew talked about Veronica.

The night of our last practice before the holidays, Fernando and I walked out to our cars together. That happened only sometimes. Sometimes he stayed at the Farbers' after practice to write with Ned. Sometimes when we walked out together, he kissed me; sometimes we just hugged good-bye and smiled at each other knowingly. I pretended both were totally cool and normal and neither action on his part resulted in either glee or disappointment on mine.

It was bitterly bitingly freezing cold, and my heart beat sharp and hard, wondering which way it would go that night. The naked trees stood petrified against the white ground and navy sky, and our slow clouds of breath seemed to be the only thing warm enough to move in the silent, frozen world.

I opened my car door, and the sound echoed against the cavernous night.

"Well, good practice tonight. See you tomorrow?" I stuttered through chattering teeth.

The sleeves of my puffy jacket crunched and shushed as he rubbed his mittened hands up and down them in the silence of the snow.

"Your songs are really good, Alex. I can't wait to sing them." His teeth knocked, too, and the words blended together on his thick tongue.

I smiled.

"Really?" I said. "They're not stupid?" My teeth chattered some more, feeling like foreign objects behind my numb lips. If this was pre-make-out nonsense talk, I wondered how long it was required to last before we could just cut to the chase, because it was fucking freezing.

When he leaned in to kiss me, I couldn't even feel his lips on mine. He pulled back and smiled. I smiled back.

"What're you doing for New Year's?" he asked.

Suddenly, an unexpected warmth.

"Not sure yet."

"Well, let's do something," he said. His mouth was now purple and he was still clasping my puffy jacket sleeves. I breathed hot and wet into my wool scarf.

"Okay," I said. I wasn't sure if this was my chance to ask if this meant that we were dating and if this meant that we could kiss in front of the other guys in the band and my friends and at midnight on New Year's—if I could tell people I had a boyfriend, if I could tell Drew I had a boyfriend, if Drew, Veronica, Sam, Mollie, Fernando, and I could start going on triple dates.

"Okay," he said. "Get home safely."

"Okay," I said, and I got into my car. Face still frozen in a smile, I called Mollie to ask her what she thought the New Year's thing meant.

VERONICA COLLINS

By Christmas vacation, Drew was, like, officially my boyfriend. Me, with an actual boyfriend—I had no idea how I'd pulled that off. All of a sudden it was December and we were holding hands in public, going to winter formals together, and making New Year's plans. Yay, Veronica! Merry Christmas to you.

My New Year's resolution was to stop sleeping with Sam. Yeah, it had happened only a few times, but I knew even once was too many. I don't even know why I kept doing it. I tried not to think about it, and honestly it had worked. I was amazingly talented at talking myself into things. And he was so hot. How could I have said no to a chance to bone-dance with Sam Fuchs? Thirteen-year-old Veronica never would have forgiven me. And Mollie was such a self-righteous bitch; it's not like she was even making it hard for me to not feel guilty.

The first time after that time at my party was when we were having a cigarette outside Alex's Halloween concert and neither of us had a lighter, so he somehow talked me into going to his car to get one. Getting a lighter from his car quickly escalated to doing it in the backseat. I don't even remember how he got me to agree. I don't even know why I wasn't totally weirded out when we both had to get into the backseat to look for the lighter in the first place. I know I said no at first. (I wasn't positive I had at my party, but I know I did the second time.) Maybe it was because of the football uniform. Maybe it was because of that night freshman year when Steph Black told me he was going to ask me to homecoming, but then he mysteriously asked Mollie instead. I heard later it was because Mollie had told Steph that I had chlamydia (which I totally freakin' didn't—it was just a yeast infection). Maybe it was what a bitch Mollie had been to me lately. Whatever it was, it was wrong, but it's not like I was getting any from Drew, which was starting to concern me a little.

When Drew and I first started hooking up, he tried and I told him I thought we should wait, because I was trying to be all *new boyfriendy wholesome* Veronica and that's what Mollie told me I was supposed to do. He, of course, being Drew, stopped immediately and said he was happy to take it slow. But it had been three months since then, and I was starting to worry that he wasn't even interested anymore. He knew me now so that probably ruined it—he didn't think I was hot anymore or something. He never tried again. They always try again. You always say, *No, I can't*, and they say, *Aw, baby, but I want you so badly*, and you say, *No, I shouldn't*, and they say, *Oh, come on*, and you give in and that's how it's done. *No* never means no. *No* means try a little harder, right?

For the first time in my life, I was in town for Christmas

vacation. My dad had basically relocated to the Far East, and my mom and I were supposed to go to St. Barts like we normally do, but then she invited Roger, the greaseball trainer with too many rings and too much chest hair who she met freakin' online. I told her I'd rather kill myself than go away with her and Roger, and she said fine, then don't come. So, I didn't. So fuck her.

So Drew invited me to his house for Christmas Eve. I'd never met a boy's family before. Not even, like, a guy friend's family. I'd maybe seen a mom or dad in passing at a Bar Mitzvah or Sweet Sixteen or something, but I had never actually sat down and had a meal and conversation with the parents of a member of the opposite sex. Marcia, his mother, was a hefty little nugget who ran around in kitten heels and a flour-covered Santa apron. She waddled on a constant loop between the dogs, the kids, and her husband, filling and refilling water bowls, cheese plates, and scotch glasses. She kept telling me how much she loved my outfit and how glad she was that I wouldn't have to spend Christmas alone.

Drew's dad was really tall, like him. I'd never seen him before that night, just heard how creepy he was from Alex. He didn't say much now that he was here, just sat in the corner, reading a paper and drinking scotch. His only movements were looking up from his paper, crossing and recrossing his legs, pushing his glasses to the bridge of his nose, and jerking his chin toward his wife when he was ready for a refill. Drew had two little sisters; one gave me a lot of stink eyes and I got a lot of *Do you know Alex? Can you play the song from* The Little

Mermaid *on the piano, because Alex can, and she always does that when she comes over* from the other.

I'm not really a little kid person, so I wandered into the kitchen and asked if I could help with anything. His mom told me not to worry, and to go play with the girls, but I sidled up to her and started chopping onions anyway.

"Oh my!" she said. "You're like a professional!"

I'd learned the right way to chop onions from all my time watching Food Network. My knife skills had really improved, and I was excited that she even noticed. I beamed a little from the compliment. She asked me if I'd check on the stuffing, which I did happily.

"I actually made a stuffing like this a few weeks ago," I said as I took a little taste and put it back in the oven.

"Really?" she said mid–potato mash. "You make stuffing?"

I laughed a little; I guess that probably sounded sort of weird. What kind of sixteen-year-old makes stuffing in her spare time? But it had been Thanksgiving, and all that food on TV looked so good, and I knew that I was never going to get to eat a Thanksgiving dinner unless I made it myself. "I watch a lot of Food Network," I said. "And eventually, you can only watch so much delicious food before needing to eat it!"

She let out a belly laugh. "Good for you!" she said.

"But you know what's really good in stuffing that you'd never think?"

She shook her head.

"Apples!"

"Apples?" she asked. "Red or green?"

"I used green. I think red would be a little too sweet, but it would also probably work to the same effect. If all you have is red, just maybe add a little lemon juice to cut the sweetness with some acidity."

She put the potato masher down and looked at me with wide eyes. "Sweetheart, that sounds delicious. I think we have some green apples in the crisper in the bottom drawer of the fridge. You lead the way?" And she handed me an apron.

I tied it around my waist, opened the fridge, and counted out four apples. I asked her if she had a paring knife, and cored them all in one fluid motion, the way Ina Garten does it. She stood behind me, watching and asking questions; I felt like I was hosting my own cooking show.

"What other tips do you have?"

"You really wanna know?" I asked as I slid the apple cores into her garbage disposal.

"Of course!" she said as she went back to mashing her potatoes.

I gestured over to her potatoes and said, "The key to potatoes? More butter."

She laughed again, and said, "With a figure like yours, you eat real butter?"

"Oh please!" I said. "I don't believe in imitations. I don't buy fake purses, and I won't use fake butter. In my experience, when you think you've added enough butter...double it."

She laughed wholeheartedly.

Drew popped his head in. "What're you girls doing in here?"

"Drew, you didn't tell me Veronica's a gourmet chef!" She

patted me on the shoulder and gave me a squeeze in that motherly comforting and prideful way that no mother had squeezed me before.

I looked over at Drew and shrugged, unable to fight the hard smile my face had been frozen in since the last time I'd remembered to think about my face.

"She's a natural," he said, and he came over and kissed me on the cheek. His mom giggled.

"Okay, so what's next?" she asked.

"I'm just going to add the chopped apples to the mix and put it back in the oven," I said.

"Is it bad that everything's already been cooking and we're adding them late?"

"Actually, it's totally better to add them now, because if they cook too long they'll caramelize and get soft, and the whole beauty of this apple thing is to give an otherwise ball of mushy stuffing a little texture and crunch, you know?"

Drew and his mom sat back, crossed their arms, and just watched me as I stirred the apples into the mixture and added some seasoning. Drew scratched his head and smiled at me in a way he never did, almost like his smile when he sat back and watched Alex when she was onstage. He was making me feel like I was doing something awesome, even though all I was doing was stirring apples. And it was a strange feeling, because his mom was also watching, so I couldn't bend over or flip my hair or do what I normally do when I know a boy is watching me, but he was watching me anyway, and smiling anyway.

"Okay!" I said as I wiped my hands on my apron. "Ten to fifteen more minutes, and we'll be ready to eat!"

"Veronica," Marcia said as she stood up and cleaned her glasses, "next year, you're coming over at noon and running the show!"

Drew smiled and winked at me, and I blushed a little.

Once we sat down, I'm pretty sure I handled my end of the conversation. His mom asked me where I wanted to go to college and what I planned to study. As if anyone actually *planned* to study in college. I told her I thought I better get my SATs back before I got my heart set on anything. She asked if I'd thought about going to culinary school; I couldn't tell if she was joking or not. She started bragging about Drew's writing and asked if I'd ever read anything he'd written. I told her I hadn't, then asked Drew if I could. He said, "Thanks a lot, Mom," and she smiled lovingly and went back to the potatoes.

All in all, the meal was a success and I felt like they liked me, even his dad, despite the fact that he never really talked to me. They all hugged me and said it was nice to *finally* meet me. I still couldn't believe that I'd gotten so lucky. I wasn't sure what I'd done to deserve this, but I had an overwhelming feeling of gratitude for it. Look at me with this great, smart guy, proud to stand by me with his great, loving, totally functional family. I wanted to call my mom and tell her how proud of me she should be for being someone's real, in public, in front of your parents, girlfriend. Though I doubted she'd believe it.

After dinner, Drew took me home and came inside to hang out for a little like he usually did.

"So, when am I going to get to read one of your stories?" I asked, turning on the TV. *Love Actually* was on again. My favorite.

"You really want to?" he said, extending his bony arm around me.

"Of course! Have you written anything about me?" I asked, then started to really wonder what he'd say if he did.

He laughed. "Not yet," he said, and kissed my head, "but I might."

We sat there for a while, watching the movie, my shoulder hooked underneath his. But I'd had enough of Hugh Grant's shenanigans, so I turned around to make out. He smiled and kissed me back, like he always did.

I climbed on top of him, took my shirt off, and kissed him again. This time harder, my hands clasping his skull, hoping my aggression would ignite his. I pushed him back so he was lying down and put his hands on my boobs. I leaned down and kissed him again and could feel that he was hard. So he did want me. So what was the problem?

"Do you want to?" I asked. For the first time in my life.

"Do you?" he replied.

I sat up, still straddling him. "Well, only if you do!"

He propped himself up on his elbows and put his hand on my thigh. "Of course I do."

I smiled, pushed him back down, and continued kissing him. He ran his hands up and down my back, but still made no attempt to take off my bra or anything. Was he that lazy? Was I going to have to do all the work?

"Veronica," he said mid-kiss. I ignored him, figuring he was going to say something cheesy and romantic or something that I'd have to try to not be totally turned off by. "Veronica," he said again, and pulled away. "You know that this is my first time, right?"

I sat up on him, still wearing my festive red Christmas bra. He was no longer hard.

I did know. I'd asked Alex months ago. I wasn't sure what to say. Was I supposed to care? Was this supposed to change anything? Was there, like, a special blessing or something he wanted me to say? I'd lost my virginity on a dare.

"Oh," I said. "Do you not want me to be your first?"

He sat up, too, his legs still extended straight on the couch; I was still sitting on them.

"No. I do!" He paused. "I just…I'm worried I'll be bad or disappoint you or something."

I smiled. He looked so scared sitting there, all wide-eyed and pale and shaking. I told him not to worry, that we all had first times and that I was honored to be his. That I'd hold his V card near and dear to my heart, treasure it always. He asked if I had condoms. I did, but I had never actually had a guy not bring his own. I got one from my upstairs bathroom and came back to find him still sitting upright with his legs extended in the exact position I'd left him. He asked if he could be on top. I said sure.

So we resituated on the couch and saddled up. We started kissing, and once I felt him get hard again, I grabbed the back of his sweater and pulled it over his head. He lost his balance and fell on me, leaving me with a mouth full of wool and an eye full of elbow. Once the sweater was off he said sorry. We kissed some more. Eventually, he slid my tights down to my knees and my skirt up and undid his pants. He wiggled them down to his ankles and lay back on top of me. I felt his heart beating on my still-bra-clad chest. His normally sweet, gentle kisses were now all over my face and neck, and his wet, meatball breath was right on my ear.

"You're doing great," I said. I even threw in a little moan to let him know that I was enjoying myself, which I was, in a way.

He didn't reply, just pumped away, and asked me if *I liked that*, which he must have heard in a porn or something. As soon as I could tell him that I did, it was done.

"Well," I said. "Merry Christmas."

"Merry Christmas," he said.

And then he fell asleep on my shoulder.

ALEXANDRA HOLBROOK

I decided I was going to have a party on New Year's Eve. I never had parties, because I had arguably the smallest house of anyone I knew, but I wanted to do it my way, with my friends, on my turf for a change. My mom was having a little dinner party, too, but said that I could have people in the basement if I wanted, as long as Josh could also invite friends. And that no one would drink and drive.

My basement wasn't big and nice and adjacent to a pool or tennis court or helipad like Mollie's or Veronica's or anything. It was an actual basement-type basement. We had old TVs and furniture and mousetraps, a ratty old brown corduroy couch, and a white art deco coffee table down there. It smelled like a combination of mildew and what I imagine the eighties smelled like.

It was a rare occasion that everyone was home for New Year's. Mollie's family usually went to Florida and V's family usually went somewhere posh and exotic, but this year, Mollie's mom made her stay home and study for the SATs and the Collinses, well, they didn't do a lot of things they used to, so we had a stacked team. Normally, when I was the only one around, I'd end up at one of Drew's friend's taking bong rips and watching the ball drop. I stole some liquor from my mom's cabinet and told everyone to bring as much alcohol as they could fit in backpacks, as they'd need to bypass my mom's party to get down to mine.

Drew came early to help me set up. Move boxes, that sort of thing. When all that was done, we sat on the smelly gray carpet and ate pizza, figuring we should carbo-load before the drinking marathon.

"So, how are things going with you and Fernando?" he asked, stacking my discarded pepperoni on his dripping slice.

"Good, I guess," I replied, not entirely sure how to answer. Not entirely sure if I was even playing this *make Drew jealous* game anymore or if I'd already lost.

"Are you guys, like, official?"

"We haven't had, like, an official talk or anything." I hadn't hooked up with anyone else, but that didn't mean that he hadn't. I couldn't help but worry that he had a whole other girlfriend at public school. Maybe multiple. That I was his post–band practice make-out, and that he maybe had a post-math-class make-out, a post-football-Sunday make-out, and maybe even a post-Friday-night-stoner-movie-with-Alex blow job. I hung out with too many boys to believe in the benefit of the doubt. And it was my fault anyway for never sacking up to ask him what our deal was. I wasn't even sure I wanted to be his girlfriend, but I was sure I wanted him to want to be my boyfriend.

"Well, is he coming tonight? Do you plan to kiss at midnight?"

"He is coming, and I guess."

"Then he's your boyfriend! Alex has a boyfriend. Who'd have thought we'd see the day...." He smiled and patted my shoulder.

"What about you? Are you sick of Veronica yet? I can't believe she came to your house for Christmas Eve. That's so in-lawy. I've never been invited for Christmas."

"You're Jewish!"

"So! That doesn't give me the right to celebrate the birth of Christ? One of my own?"

He laughed.

"I had no idea you felt such a kinship to our Lord and Savior. You can come next year, too. It was cute; Izzy kept asking her if she knew you."

That hurt my heart. Thinking about Veronica being there and infiltrating that family. My family. Good girl, Izzy. At least one of the Carsons has a sense of loyalty. I chuckled a little, picturing Marcia choking on her Santa apron, aghast at whatever inappropriate low-cut getup Veronica had decided to wear. I wondered what they talked about, if Veronica put on a show and pretended to be into school or tennis or anything that made Drew's interest in her look more complicated than that she was hot and easy. I wondered if Marcia liked her. I wondered if she wished it were me there—if afterward she said something like *She's sweet, but she's no Alex*. I wonder if Drew's dad was nicer to her than he ever was to me.

"Aww," I said, using every muscle in my throat to restrain myself from saying *Good girl, Izzy* out loud.

I took another piece of pizza, plucked off the pepperonis, and gave them to Drew. He handed me his crust.

"So," he said, dropping his slice back in the box. I put mine down, too, and sat up straight, responding to the urgency in his gesture. "I kind of have something to tell you."

My heart dropped, because I knew what he was going to tell me. It was bound to happen eventually. It was Veronica, for fuck's sake. I took the fact that it took this long to mean that he was holding out, that he had grander, more romantic notions about sex than most guys and that he wanted to wait until it was special. For someone special. For me. Did this mean he'd decided that she was special? Was she?

I didn't want to hear him say it. So I did.

"You fucked Veronica." I used the word *fuck* on purpose, hoping the word would cheapen it for him, too. That it would not only make it seem like less of a big deal, but actually make it less of a big deal. It sounded fake coming out of my mouth, like a joke we'd told a thousand times already.

"Did she tell you?"

Holy shit. I had been half kidding. Kidding myself, I guess. Part of me thought he'd laugh and say, *Yeah, right,* but he didn't. He'd done it. With her. I couldn't cry; I didn't even know why I wanted to. I was prepared for this. I'd been preparing for this since that moment in the creepy fun-house bathroom when Veronica told me they kissed. After all, Veronica doesn't just kiss people. Once you've kissed Veronica, you may as well consider your dick sucked.

"No, she didn't tell me."

Which I couldn't believe. Though I guess we didn't talk much anymore, especially about Drew. Did she think I'd be mad or weirded out or something? Why would she all of a sudden think I'd be mad about this, but not about the fact that they'd been making out and jerking each other off in my face for the last three months?

"You could just tell? Do I look different? More like a man?"

"You're such a homo."

"Actually, now that I've had sex with a woman, I am officially not a homo. I am an actual, practicing heterosexual."

He wasn't funny. I wasn't laughing.

"Yeah, you are!" I yelled. "High five!" I actually made him high-five me. I had a very sudden urge to drink heavily and punch myself in the face. "You've officially left me alone in the virgin club. How does it feel? How was it?"

He smiled and picked up his pizza again. "It was good," he said. "Different than I thought, I guess.... But it's not like I have anything to compare it to."

My mouth was frozen in a smile, but the rest of me was slowly dying, hardening, decaying from within.

I asked if he told her it was his first time. She already knew it was, because she'd asked me if he was a virgin when they first started dating.

"I did. She was really cool about it."

"You down here?" someone called from the top of the stairs. It was Mollie.

Thank god.

Mollie rolled in with a backpack full of tequila and some story about her vagina being sore. Drew and I both rolled our eyes and put her to work setting up beer pong on the pool table.

I helped myself to the tequila.

By the time Veronica arrived, I was drunk.

She showed up in some sparkling, slutty, typical whore-casing and draped herself on Drew. Drew's crew all arrived together and brought a lot of beer, as requested. Fernando came around ten; I was already half past blacked out.

"Hey, baby," he said when he bounced down the stairs into the party, "looks like you've already started!"

"Haaaaaaaappy New Year!" I screamed in his ear, then looked around to make sure Drew was watching and kissed him. With tongue.

"Tequila?" he asked.

"Tequila!" I handed him the bottle, from which he took a giant swig. "No twins?"

"No twins tonight," he said. "Just me and you."

Sam and his friend Austin, who I'd met a million times but who never remembered me, showed up shortly thereafter. Mollie immediately started yelling at him about something, but I could no longer hear.

I played a game with myself: every time either Drew or Veronica or the combination of Drew and Veronica was in my eye line, I took a shot. I seemed to be winning. Josh loitered around, not saying much. A few people he invited showed up, too, but I didn't particularly care who they were or bother to introduce myself.

"'Sup?" Sam said to me as I stood by the overturned camp trunk that was serving as our evening's bar, trying, unsuccessfully, to put some ice into my Solo cup.

"'Sup?" I replied. Curious as to why all of a sudden, after all these years, Sam deemed me worthy of speaking to directly.

"Sweet house," he said.

"Sweet fleece," I said back.

He chuckled and said, "So let's spice this fucking party up, Holbrook. Let's play some games or something."

I was intrigued. "What do you suggest we play?"

"How about Truth or Dare?" he said.

"If you can rally the troops, I'm diggity down like Chinatown."

"You're fuckin' hammered is what you are."

"Fuck yes, I am."

"Ya know, you were always my favorite," he replied smugly.

The entire party formed a circle, terrified and eager for whatever exciting disaster this game would surely and always did inevitably bring.

Mollie sat next to Sam, her face white as a polar bear's ass. Fernando sat next to me, his hand on my leg, which was a bold but welcome gesture. I wondered what his agenda was, what he wanted from me, why he came without Ned and Pete, and what he thought was going to happen. Did he think I'd put out tonight? That had to be the reason he was so all over me, he figured it was New Year's and I was drunk and this was his shot to get laid. Fuck it, maybe I would put out. Maybe I wanted to. Would having sex with him be the end of our fun make-outs, though? There was some sort of electric charge in the room. In myself. I felt capable of damage.

Josh took me aside. "I'm going upstairs to check on Mom's party so she won't come down."

"You wuss, she's probably hammered. Play the game," I said.

"I really don't think I want to see this. I've played this game before, and you're my sister. Shit's about to get weird."

I snorted and laughed a little.

"Pussy. But good call." And he bounced up the stairs with one of his little friends. Fine, good. I didn't want to see him make out with Mollie anyway. "Who's gonna start?" I asked.

"Why don't you start?" said Sam. "It's your party after all."

"Fine!" I screamed back at him, having lost the ability to control the volume of my voice.

I scanned the circle. Mollie bit her thumbnail and looked too scared to mess with. I couldn't deal with Drew or Veronica yet, and clearly, I wasn't going to subject Fernando to the first one. . . .

"Sam, you want to play so bad. It's your turn. Truth or dare, motherfucker?" I said, or more likely screamed.

"Dare." He smiled at me, his blue eyes glowing with mischief.

"Show us your cock."

"Hey!" screamed Mollie. "What the fuck? No!"

"Babe," he said. "It's a game. This is how the game is played. Truth or Dare is a get-out-of-relationship-free-card game."

"Wait, wait," I said. "I don't really want to see your dick. I was just kidding. Molls, I'll do something else."

She looked at me and looked at him. Then looked at me and looked at him again, and said, "No, fuck it. Do it. Show them. I don't fucking care. Show everyone your big fucking dick. You want a get-out-of-relationship-free-card game? Fine by me!"

So he stood up, undid his pants, and showed everyone his penis. Mollie always talked about how big his dick was: it didn't look that big to me. But then again, what did I know?

"Happy now?" he said.

"Okay, babe. Your turn." He looked over at Mollie and smiled.

"What?" she said.

"Truth or dare, woman?"

"Dare."

He looked around the circle, at me, Drew, the paralyzed and panicked sophomores, then over to Austin, who per usual had yet to speak to me or thank me for inviting him into my home and providing him with free alcohol and all this grade-A entertainment.

"I dare you to make out with Veronica for thirty seconds."

"No fucking way! Ew!" she said.

"Wait, I'm not done . . . and for bonus points, I dare you to do it with your shirts off. You can leave your bras on."

"Fuck you!" she screamed. "You can't do that because it involves Veronica and it's not her turn!"

"Collins," Sam said, "will you participate?"

She looked at Drew and then at me and then at everyone, confused, but clearly excited, as Veronica lived to be the object of perverse gawking. Drew gave her a shoulder shrug and said, "You don't have to if you don't want to."

She looked at Mollie, who gritted her teeth and exposed the whites of her eyeballs, like she was about to bark or pounce.

"I'll do it if Mollie will."

"Babe," Sam taunted. "Come oooooon…it's just a game. You told me you'd make out with Angelina Jolie. Veronica is totally just as hot as Angelina Jolie. It'll be so hot, please?"

The boys started chanting: "Do it! Do it! Do it!"

And Sam said, "Please, babe? For me? It'll be so hot…."

"Fine!" she said. "You fucking perverts."

They both got on their knees and crawled to the center of the circle.

"Shirts off!" Sam screamed.

"Thank god, I wore my fancy New Year's bra today!" Veronica said to the crowd behind her as she ripped her shirt over her head in one graceful movement. Mollie took her time and used both hands to unbutton her pink top.

"I hope you all enjoy this," she said. "V, I hope you brushed."

And they leaned in and went for it as Sam and all the other boys counted to thirty. I couldn't watch. It was like watching your parents make out or something. Except it was two girls, little lips, little tongues, both of them just standing on their knees, skinny arms straight at their sides, both of them clearly trying not to make any more contact with the other than necessary. I was oddly repulsed and jealous simultaneously.

At about twelve, Mollie broke from the lip-lock.

"Okay, enough!" she said.

A chorus of "awwwws" echoed in a wave around the circle.

"Sam," said Marc Seidman, "you're the fucking man."

And they fist-bumped each other.

"My turn," Mollie said, her eyes darting around the circle.

"Alex," she said. She blurred in and out of focus. "Truth or mothafuckin' dare, bitch?"

She was practically foaming at the mouth. Mollie knew way too many of my embarrassing truths, so I went with dare.

"I dare you to kiss Drew. With tongue. For ten seconds."

The words pierced my gut, letting out everything that was holding me up. I felt hollow, deflated, and shaky, at risk of being pushed or dropped and shattering. What did she think she was doing?

"You're not fucking serious!" I said.

"Oh, I am. Do it." She smiled and nodded, her wise eyes pleading with me to trust her, promising me she was doing this for my own good, that she had a plan.

The crowd chanted again: "Do it! Do it! Do it!"

I looked at Drew. He smiled, bowed his head toward his lap, and shook it. He looked up, still with a big smile, which I hoped meant that he wasn't completely disgusted by the suggestion.

"I don't know if I like this!" Veronica squealed, putting her shirt back on.

"You just kissed me topless!" Mollie screamed at her. "You don't get a veto. Drew. Alex. *Kiss! Now!*"

I looked at Fernando, who looked extremely uncomfortable.

"I'm so sorry!" I said. "I don't have to do this."

Fernando ran his fingers over his dark hair.

"It's a game. Whatever."

I looked back at Drew, who stood on his knees, grinning goofily, with his arms open.

"Come on," he said. "It won't be that bad. Just pretend I'm Fernando."

I hid my face in my hands, then crawled to him.

"On three," said Mollie. "One. Two. Three!"

And he went in. Kissing him was exactly like I thought it would be. Sweet. Safe. Warm. Almost like it was something I'd done a million times before. He tasted like he smelled, felt like he sounded. I tried to become undrunk, to enjoy it, savor it, make it count for the millions of times I'd wanted to kiss him before and would want to in the future, but wouldn't be able to. He put one hand on my cheek, one hand on my waist, and pulled me in closer before breaking.

MOLLIE FINN

My cold, black heart almost broke when Alex and Drew kissed. I wondered if she was aware of what a favor I'd done for her, if she'd thank me later, or if she'd be pissed.

Veronica stared at Alex, whose facial redness was probably a combined result of the liter of tequila she'd guzzled and the general flustered, weak-in-the-knees, singing-birds type sensations she'd likely experienced from having finally kissed the guy she'd been secretly in love with for the better part of a decade. God, I remember when kissing Sam felt like that....

I saw Alex mouth *I'm sorry* to Veronica, but V just shrugged. Muahaha. Stupid slut. Now she knew how it felt.

Alex crawled back over to Fernando and kissed him. I couldn't hear what they were saying, but she sat back down next to him, and he put his arm around her, all happy and snuggly-like. Poor guy. He had no idea what he'd gotten himself tangled up in.

"Anyone else?" Sam asked around the circle. The meek, terrified sophomores just stared into their shaking laps. They seemed to have figured out that this game wasn't really a game and they weren't really playing. "Alex, it's your turn again," he said.

"I already went. Give someone else a turn," she replied, her dark, drunk, tangled head buried in Fernando's neck.

"Fine," he said. "Carson, you go."

Drew rubbed his eyes and took a big chug of beer. "I dunno, man. I can't think of anything. I'm done."

"Fuck that." Sam looked around the circle. "Seidkick, you go."

Marc Seidman: Drew's second-in-command in the stoner troupe, thirty pounds overweight, fancied himself a wiseass, and was always saying grotesque and hilarious things. Not my least favorite to have around. I wished Sam had friends like that. Fat, funny ones. I always enjoyed that type. Jocks were good-looking and all, but not so much in the wit department.

"Okay, fine then. Carson," said Marc, scratching his stubbly chin, "truth or dare?"

"Let's mix it up a little. Truth," Drew said.

Marc leaned his chubby forearms over his soft lap and said, "Why are you fucking Veronica Collins when you're obsessed with Alex Holbrook?"

The room went silent, with the exception of a few snickers and suffocated giggles. I gasped and threw my hand over my mouth to keep from bursting out laughing. Slow clap for Marc Seidman.

"Fuck you, dude," Drew said.

"Right?" he asked, addressing the whole circle. "It was the obvious question!"

"You're an asshole."

I looked at Alex, who just sat there, hiding her drunk smile behind her long fingers. Marc Seidman and the rest of Drew's posse keeled over in laughter, heaving and pointing and smacking their legs. Veronica rolled her eyes and looked around lost, per usual.

"This is a joke, right?" she asked.

"Yes, he's kidding," Drew said to her, rubbing her bare, bony back. "Seidman, you wanna ask another question or is this dumbass game over?"

Sam and I elbowed each other, but touché Marc Seidman. The ultimate silent predator and clear victor of this retarded game. I had a sick desire to take him aside and join forces. Unite our camps in the name of perpetuating good (i.e., getting Alex and Drew together) and fighting evil (i.e., Veronica).

"Okay," interjected Alex, "this game is over. It's almost midnight."

We all got up and refilled our drinks, as the game brought on an unwelcome gust of sobriety. We turned on the TV to watch the countdown.

"Babe," I said, falling into Sam's arms. "Happy New Year! I'm so happy to be starting another year with you."

"Me too, babe." And we kissed. God, I'd kill myself if I didn't have a boyfriend on New Year's. What do those girls do? Sloppily make out with Marc Seidman–types, I guess, as it looked like some of Josh's sophomore friends were gearing up to do.

"Okay, everyone!" screamed Alex. "Get the confetti!"

Then it was five...four...three...two...one! Happy New Year!

Sam and I made out for a while, which was weird, because we never made out anymore. We kissed all the time, but lip-to-lip smacks. Kisses were an obligatory preamble to sex, unconscious extensions of hi and bye or occasionally a public declaration of our relationship when I felt we were in a situation in which our relationship needed to be declared. The making out—like full-on, tongues, hands, face touching, body groping hours of kissing—stopped months ago. Maybe even years. It used to be hard for us to even talk, because I couldn't look at his face without kissing it. Nowadays, it was harder for me to look at his face without punching it than it was to not kiss it. I wasn't sure if that was normal.

I looked around: Drew and Veronica were passionately groping each other and sucking face on the brown corduroy couch. Alex and Fernando were kissing, too, hugging, smiling, looking sloppy and drunk. The other boys were making out with the sophomore girls who Josh had invited. Though I hadn't seen Josh all night. Thank god, taking my shirt off and making out with Veronica in front of Alex's little brother really would have been an unnecessary addition to my shame list for the year. Christ, and thank god it was New Year's, and I got to start a fresh one.

AFTER MIDNIGHT, TIME SEEMED to move really fast. I played some beer pong, took some shots, and for once didn't feel like the drunkest person in the room. Alex had disappeared. Were she and Fernando sleeping together? There was no way that could be true and she wouldn't have told me.... I know she's all into not telling me things anymore, but there is no way she wouldn't have told me that. We planned the logistics of my virginity loss for weeks. How could she not have told me that she was at least thinking about it? She probably went upstairs to check on her mom's party or something. There was no way she'd have sex and I'd hear about it later. Had she even given Fernando a blow job? Had she given anyone one?

Veronica flitted around the stoners and Sam and Austin, and when they all went into the back room to smoke a joint, I had to pass, because weed makes me paranoid. As if I weren't already paranoid. But then I was left, sitting alone, on that crusty corduroy couch, hungry, wondering what kind of delicious food the Holbrooks were hiding upstairs, willing myself, begging myself, not to break the seal and eat something, because I was drunk enough that once I started, I knew I wouldn't stop.

But then Josh came over and sat with me. I hadn't really seen or talked to him since the incident at Veronica's party in September. God, had I really not been inside Alex's house since September?

"Hey there," he said with his goofy smile that looked like Alex's dad's. "Having fun?"

"Always," I said with a sarcastic smile. "Josh, I..."

"Don't worry about it," he said, shaking his head and patting my back. "Seriously, you're like my sister. I got your back."

I smiled and let my shoulders relax for the first time all night. I gave him a hug.

"Well, I'm not your sister, and you didn't have to do what you did that night, which I guess now is like embarrassingly long ago. You could have minded your own business, or left me on the lawn. You saved the day, so just shut up and let me say thank you."

He smiled, leaned back, and switched his baseball hat from backward to forward. "You're welcome."

"Any cute sophomore girls you have your eye on?" I could always feel it on my skin when I tried to be sweet. I saw myself from the outside, saw how stupid I looked and could hear my inner bitch laughing and rolling her eyes. Many people out there only saw this person, and probably believed she was real. My teachers, parents, older girls at school. I truly wondered if anyone was actually sweet. Who truly cared about whom Josh Holbrook had his eye on or recycling or that someone gets well soon or has a safe trip. Did everyone fake that, or was it just me?

"Nah," he said, giggling, "my eye's not on any of them."

"None of these girls are good enough for you anyway," I said.

"So, Sam is good enough for you?"

I giggled uncomfortably, staying actively in Sweet Mollie mode. "Sam is the hottest guy in school! He's out of my league....And that's what you deserve, too, Josh, a girl who's out of your league—date up, that's my advice."

Josh shook his head. "Mollie, that doesn't even make any

sense. Anyone who treats you the way Sam does is fucking bush-league."

"That's adorable, but that's just not how life works."

"That is actually exactly how life works. And despite what it looks like, I know your life's not working."

I knew it was wrong that what I got out of that sentence was that *it looks like* my life is working, and that the words washed over me like a compliment and a wave of relief.

"Yes, it is. I'm as happy as I've ever been." I swallowed hard, and my spine twitched as I said it. "I have everything a girl could want."

Josh smacked his palm to his forehead and spun toward me. He put his hands on my shoulders, grabbed them hard, and shook me, quite aggressively, making it seem like his melodramatic actions were an act of playfulness, but I knew that despite the sass in our tones we were having an actual serious conversation.

He spoke loudly and enunciated every syllable: "GIRLS SHOULD WANT DIFFERENT THINGS, MOLLIE."

Sam, V, and Austin all came out of the smoking room, reeking. They'd decided in there that they wanted to head over to the 'Zu after-hours party, and though I would have loved to have gone home, hooked up with Sam, and gone to bed, I didn't put up a fight. It was New Year's, fuck it. Party on. Drew had to be home in an hour, so he couldn't go. I looked for Alex to say good-bye, but she was nowhere to be found. I figured she was either puking or hooking up, and she wouldn't want me to interrupt either.

Sam claimed he was fine to drive, so Drew went home and Veronica came with us, which I couldn't believe. Drew was her boyfriend! It was New Year's! I knew that no one cared when she got home, but how could she ditch Drew? Maybe she was mad at him about the Alex thing. I'd never seen Veronica actually express anger or displeasure before. Or maybe she was still just a pathetic social climber at heart and secretly missed flirting with jocks at the 'Zu parties and was tired of lying around and watching movies she didn't understand, pretending she was in love. Still, who leaves their boyfriend on New Year's? Stupid sluts, that's who.

We got to the 'Zu and it was a typical scene. Dingy white walls, crunchy gray carpet, haggard old faces. It was about five hundred degrees and smelled like old beer, old vomit, and old money.

It was after two when we got there, so I ripped some shots because I needed to loosen up a little more to have the same conversations with the same blond-haired, blue-eyed half-wits that I did every weekend. It was kind of nice to have Veronica there with me again—like the old days, when we were *the hot freshmen* and all of this was still exciting, glamorous, and fun.

She handed me a bottle of Malibu and said, "Bottoms up!"

Sam motioned for me to come over to him, so I squirmed through the sweaty people across the basement to where he stood by the stairs. I clasped the Malibu for dear life.

"I can't stop thinking about you making out with Veronica," he said. "It was so hot."

"You're such a perv!" I flirtatiously grabbed his waist, cut and hard underneath his shirt.

"Seriously," he said. He ran his hand through my hair the way he used to, then kissed my neck and my ear. "It was, like, the ultimate fantasy. I can't believe you did that." His fingers rested in the top of my pants, and the rum buzzed through me. It had been so long since I'd felt so wanted by Sam. I wondered if I should make out with girls more often.

It used to be like this all the time. We used to flirt and play and have all sorts of raunchy fun. We'd leave these parties and go have sex in his car, or in an empty bedroom. We hadn't had sex in relative public in ages. I wondered if we were about to go do that. I hoped we were about to go do that.

"I can make a lot of your fantasies come true," I cooed in his ear. "Let's go fuck in one of the bedrooms upstairs."

"I have a better idea," he said with a devil in his eye.

"Oh, where should we go? It's too cold outside...."

"Let's see if Veronica will come with us."

"What do you mean?"

"Come on! You guys already kissed. It's, like, you're just letting me play, too, this time," he said with a smile and a pinch of my ass. I was drunk. I wasn't even sure I understood what he was asking.

"So you want us to hook up in front of you? Or, like, both of us, with you? At the same time?"

I couldn't figure out fast enough how bad this was, if this was bad, or what it meant in regard to how he felt about me or what he ultimately wanted from me. Maybe this wasn't that big of a deal. Was I supposed to say yes or no? What was the good girlfriend thing to do? Would he lose respect for me if I said yes, or would he think I was boring and a prude if I said no?

"Whatever, babe! Let's just see what happens once we get up there! Go with it. Thinking about you, like that, so hot. You'd be, like, my own personal porn star."

My heart raced. Maybe this was what Sam and I needed. Maybe this would make him see me as hot and wild and fun again, not just his jealous girlfriend who wasn't as cute as she used to be.

"Do you promise that this isn't just an excuse to hook up with Veronica without cheating?"

"Babe, I swear. Let's just ask her. I bet she'll do it."

I motioned to Veronica to come over, and the three of us went upstairs. I finished the bottle of Malibu on the way. We made our way to Lindsay's room, which I told myself had seen way kinkier and more disgusting things than what it was about to witness. I sat on the mint-green-and-eyelet-covered bed and bit my nails. Sam sat next to me.

"Do you guys have coke?" V's eyes lit up.

Sam laughed. "I wish. Mollie and I have a proposition for you."

She stood by the door, biting her lip and twirling her fingers. Sam walked over to her and stood proudly, there next to her, with his arm around her, and looked at me. "We were talking, and we would like to invite you to join us."

"Join you...where?" She looked at him and then at me, confused as ever. I completely regretted agreeing to this, wasn't sure I even had yet, but I knew it was too late. I scanned the room for more booze, wondered if Lindsay had a stash of anything in one of the wicker drawers. Xanax, Valium, Percocet, heroin, anything. Did I have time to raid the bathroom? Would I get a buzz if I snorted enough Advil?

"We want to have a fucking threesome with you, okay?" I blurted out.

I stared at the white dollhouse at the foot of the bed. I used to have a dollhouse. I loved that dollhouse, played with it every day, dragged my mom to every store in the tristate area collecting all the little clothes and the little furniture and knickknacks. I accidentally kicked it and broke it doing On Demand Tae Bo.

"Are you kidding?" she asked.

Sam grinned. "No, we're not. What do you think?"

Veronica held back a smile, which I thought was an odd reaction. I knew she'd die for a chance with Sam. I fucking knew it.

"Guys! I have a boyfriend! I can't!" she said, with her hand on her hip, her wiry form swaying in the door frame. But she could, and she was going to. I could tell.

"Oh, come on," said Sam. "Like you didn't just watch him make out with your best friend? Like you and Mollie didn't just kiss?"

Her face dropped a little. I stayed quiet.

"It's not cheating, because it's the three of us. It's more a rowdy group activity, not, like, actual sex, which is between two people. This is just fun, silly drunkenness between friends."

He ran the back of his hand down her arm; my skin crawled. I could have cried, but I swallowed it. I thought about the sacrifices people made for love, the desperate things people do to keep relationships together. There were swingers and fetishes and open marriages. People did weird shit to please their partners and keep things interesting all the time. If seeing me and Veronica together was what it was going to take to renew Sam's lust for me, well, then that's what I'd do. I guess. I convinced myself that this was badass. That this was the shit of models and rock stars. That I was about to be the coolest girlfriend ever. Sam would love me for this.

"Come on!" I said, knowing she'd need to see my enthusiasm for reassurance. "It'll be a hilarious story to tell later. Well, way later. Like, after college later. Before that, this is our secret. We tell no one."

V looked at Sam and looked at me, rolling her skinny ankles back and forth over her black platforms.

"Molls, you're sure this won't get weird? I've never done anything with another girl before...."

I walked over to her and Sam, stomach in knots but mind made up. I looked him square in the eyes and kissed him, again. Then I kissed her, again—her lips still thin and wet, and tasting like cigarettes and coconut rum.

Sam pushed our heads together, took our hands, and led us to the bed. We sat. Then he leaned down and kissed her—my stomach turned, again. I didn't know what to do now. I didn't want to watch. I needed an activity. I undid his pants in an attempt to wedge myself between them, and it worked. He stopped kissing her and sat between us. He lay down and put our hands on his chest. I just kept looking at him looking at her, wondering what he was thinking. Wondering if he wished I weren't there, if he thought she was hotter than me, a better kisser, if he was thinking about how her boobs were bigger or her thighs were thinner. If he liked her better.

I kissed her again, trying to refocus this ordeal on that instead of them. He sat up and kissed my neck, while I kissed her. Then hers. Then mine. Our shirts came off, again, and I wondered what she was thinking. If she noticed I'd gained weight. If she felt satisfaction in knowing that she was hotter than me, thinner than me. If she was elated to finally get her shot at hooking up with Sam. If she thought this counted as that, because it didn't. What was her motive in agreeing to do this in the first place? I wished I were drunker.

She kept looking at Sam and smiling. Never at me. Something felt so wrong. I almost got up and ran out, but then Sam looked at me and smiled—that same smile I got from the sidelines at lacrosse games, from when he opened a door and saw me standing on the other side, the one that was happy to see me, the one that was just for me—so I went in to kiss him more, so I could shut my eyes and pretend this wasn't happening, that it was just the two of us, that this was fun, and that I was enjoying it. Veronica went right down and put his dick in her mouth. Of course she did. Stupid slut.

ALEXANDRA HOLBROOK

After *Happy New Year!* all I saw was Drew and Veronica attached at the face. Like they were doing it out of spite, purposefully to illustrate to me and everyone else that they were together and Drew and I were not. I couldn't process our kiss or Marc Seidman's question—why he asked it, if he knew something I didn't, if he, like everyone else, liked to joke about how we were *obsessed with each other*, or if he, as Drew's other "best" friend, really knew something. Like how Mollie did, like how she had reasons and motivations behind her dare. Maybe he did, too?

But none of that really mattered. Here I was thinking about Drew and the kiss and the question and what it all meant and there he was thinking about Veronica and all the sex they were going to have. He laughed off the comment. Everyone did. So, so would I. Ha, ha. Drew and Alex, always hanging out. They're so *obsessed* with each other. Ha, ha. Suuuuuch a funny old joke.

I snuck Fernando up to my room, briefly stopping at my mom's party to wish her and all her friends a happy new year. She asked if I'd been drinking. I told her someone had brought one bottle of champagne and we'd toasted at midnight. She, who had clearly also been drinking, made me promise that no one who drank would drive. *Obviously, Mom! How irresponsible do I look?*

We made out on my bed for a while, and I couldn't believe that I actually had a boy to make out with on New Year's. This was so unlike me. I was never the girl with the boy. Drew was the only boy who'd ever been in my room.

"Sweet posters," Fernando said of my wall full of concert posters. "We should go see some of these bands sometime," he said between kisses.

"We should," I said. I took a fistful of his thick hair. I continued to maul him, because I didn't feel like talking.

We kissed for a while, and I went for his pants. Fuck it. Fuck it all, I thought.

"Hey, stop," he said.

"What's wrong?" I asked. "I want to."

"Alex," he said, the inflection of the *exxx* on my name and the fact that he said my name all the time, like after he said anything: *Cool, Alex. Great practice, Alex. That's an awesome T-shirt, Alex. You're such an awesome, hip chick, and I love secretly making out with you, but I am still not asking you to be my girl-friend, Alex* was starting to get annoying. "You're really drunk."

And I was officially humiliated. Officially, no one would ever have any desire to have sex with me. I'd be the last virgin in the world.

"It's not that I don't want to," he said, rubbing his eyes. I got off him and sat there, on my blue bed, legs straight before me, my shoulders hunched in shame. "You're just so drunk," he said. "You'll regret it."

"What makes you think this is my first time?" I snapped back. I was starting to get the spins. I wanted to lie down, but I focused on my feet instead.

"I didn't say that...." He paused. "It's just our first time, and I'd like you to remember it."

I was such an asshole. I stared at my A Tribe Called Quest poster. I tried to think of one of their songs. Get it in my head, and let it relax me. But it didn't work. Nothing would. What had just happened? Did I get rejected? Did I just offer my virginity to someone and he turned it down? Turned me down? This was not how it happened on TV. The girls were supposed to say no, not the boys. Of course, I'm a freak of nature. Of course, I'm that repulsive. I knew it. I'd always known it.

"Plus," he added, "I'd rather not sleep with you the same night you've made out with another guy."

"Oh, come on!" This night was just getting better and better. "It was Drew! It was a game!"

"Whatever," he said, shaking his head. "We should probably go back downstairs."

"Fine," I said.

I stood up, and the room spun, Fernando spun, and what had just happened spun in my head, as did my emotions around and around between pissed, embarrassed, relieved, and confused. Fernando and I got to the top of the stairs to find my mom standing at the bottom, barefoot, arms folded, black eyes glaring at us.

We slowly descended with our heads bowed. I sent Fernando to the basement and stood on the second step, towering over my mother, who I was taller than anyway.

"What the hell are you doing with a boy in your room?" she screamed. It appeared her friends had gone.

"I was just showing him my posters, Mom. Calm down." I stared at my bare feet.

"Do I look like I was born yesterday?" she asked.

"Mom, it's not a big deal."

She took my face in her hands, and I felt my stomach gurgle. "You are way too drunk, young lady. What the hell is going on down there?"

"Mom, chill. Nothing. Just my friends hanging out."

I hiccupped. I knew what was next. I swallowed hard.

"Well, we are going downstairs together and kicking everyone out. It's almost three AM. Party's over."

She grabbed my wrist, and the second I took one step, it was over. There it came. I swallowed the first wave, but another one was right behind it.

I threw up. On the first step. A little on her. Mostly on the step.

Part 4

THE WINTER

MOLLIE FINN

School started on the second, and we spent the lunch period listening to Alex bitch about being grounded and laughing at her, because, seriously, who pukes on their mom? Fucking classic. Veronica'd been eerily quiet, not once interjecting her own projectile vomit story or mother gripe or whore antic, which was very unlike her. I wondered if Alex noticed that she was being weird and would be suspicious that something was up.

The thought that Alex could potentially find out about what happened on New Year's made me want to rip my fucking throat out. I wondered if she'd be disgusted, jealous, feel left out even. As pathetic as it was, I knew that's how I would feel if I found out that Veronica and Alex had had a threesome and I wasn't invited. I almost felt like a traitor having done it with Veronica instead of Alex, not that she ever would have done it, but that's really not the point.

I went over to Alex's after school to spend some quality time with her before her mom got home and laid the smackdown on the grounding. One of my New Year's resolutions: to be a better friend. That, and to eat less. And to stop caring so much about what other people thought about me. We plopped down on her bed, and I thumbed through the pile of magazines on her nightstand. *People, SPIN, Rolling Stone, Vanity Fair, Cosmopolitan*—sweet, *Cosmo.*

"So you never really told me what happened with Fernando," I said as I flipped to the "50 Things That Will Drive Him Crazy in Bed" article.

She sat cross-legged on her fluffy blue comforter, yanking the sleeves of her green sweater past her palms.

"I kind of want to kill myself," she said.

"Oh god, that bad?" I sat up, leaving the magazine open to #10: LOVE HIS ASSHOLE.

"We were making out, and he basically told me he didn't want to have sex with me." She raised her eyebrows and stared at her tie-dyed socks.

"Like, ever? Is he saving himself for marriage or something?"

She laughed. "He said he didn't want to sleep with me the same night I made out with someone else."

I snorted a little bit in disbelief. Really? These fucking sensitive musician types. This is why I dated jocks. "That's a joke, right?"

"I guess I understand...." She trailed off, glaring at some poster on her wall—some rappers scowling, standing back-to-back with their arms crossed, exactly like how our moms used to make us pose together when we were little.

Alex's room was pretty, pastel, just the way it was when she was seven, but now hiding under all sorts of chintzy crap like band posters, dirty clothes, creepy pictures, and cryptic words cut out of magazines. I wished she'd just get it together and stop trying to cover everything up with all this angsty hipster crap, and just be the girl I knew with the best toys and funniest laugh in the baby-blue bedroom who stood back-to-back with me and smiled at the camera. When did we stop posing like that?

"That's retarded. There has to be more to the story. Maybe he has an STD or something and doesn't want to give it to you?"

"That's mean," she said.

I thought it was a valid statement. He did go to public school.

"I've met the kid twice. I don't know. I'm just saying: that's not normal. Guys don't turn down opportunities to have sex. Ever. Trust me, I know."

"Ugh." She groaned. "This is so stupid. I'm going to be a virgin forever."

"No, you won't," I said. Though, part of me wanted her to stay a virgin forever. Wanted her to stay pure and objective and nonthreatening, and to keep cheering from the bench, because once she was in the game, she'd officially no longer be on my side, but playing for herself. I needed to hold on to *someone* I could trust. Once she was out there, flirting—and, like, really flirting, not like Alex flirting, but flirting like she actually had an end game. Once she was really pulling from the same artillery Veronica and I've had at our disposals, it'd be over. Officially. It'd be every woman for herself.

"What happened at the 'Zu, after you guys left?"

A sharp chill ran down the back of my throat, but I swallowed it, as I'd gotten used to doing.

"Nothing," I said. "Same shit, new year."

"I can't believe Veronica ditched Drew on New Year's," she said.

"I know. What a social-climbing whore."

My eyes drifted back to the magazine. #35: GET CREATIVE. BE SOMEONE ELSE FOR A NIGHT.

SAM PICKED ME UP at Alex's after basketball. He pulled into her driveway and honked the horn. I gave Alex a hug and told her to hang in there, that a month would go by, and in no time, she'd be back out there on the streets, at the parties, angsting away, wishing she were still grounded so she had an excuse to wallow in her room, with her notebooks and magazines and CD collection, where I knew she was secretly the happiest. She laughed and said that I was right, that she was actually relieved to have an excuse to hide out. I understood that impulse; I found myself a little jealous.

When I got into Sam's car, he told me he wanted a burrito. The last thing I wanted was a fucking burrito. I asked him if we could get something healthier, maybe go to a real restaurant, but he said he'd been craving a burrito all day and that was what he wanted. I swallowed again. I was starving, so I wondered if I'd be able to just eat a few bites of a burrito and then throw it away. Probably not. I'd just get chips and salsa. Take a bite of his burrito. That's what I'd do. A burrito would ruin my whole week—it was sad, but it was true. I wasn't going to let Sam get me fat and hate me again.

"So how's Alex?" he asked, and then put his hand on my knee.

Things were better. As much as I cringed to think about why, I did feel closer to Sam. We'd shared this thing, had been through something together, had an inside joke of sorts. Even if Veronica had shared it, too. We'd have to do other things without her now so that this could just be one of our many things. Maybe I'd dress up as a sexy nurse or schoolgirl or tie him up—then we'd just be this couple that had weird, kinky, fun sex. The threesome would be just one more kinky thing we did together.

"She's okay," I said, putting my hand on his. "Annoyed that she's grounded, embarrassed because she asked Fernando to have sex with her and he said no."

"No way!" he exclaimed. "What a fag!"

"He said he didn't want their first time to be the same night she'd made out with someone else."

Sam took his hand off my knee, wiped his nose, and put it back.

"What a homo," he said. "Well, if Alex wants to be our next guest star, I'm more than happy to add her V card to my collection."

I laughed. And tried to mean it. I was also going to try to be less sensitive this year. Laugh things off, stop getting so mad about everything and being so miserable all the time.

"Seriously," he said. "I'd bang Alex. She's gotten pretty cute. I'm diggin' this whole band-chick thing she's got going now."

I brushed my hand through his hair, rubbed the back of his neck, and took a deep breath.

"No more guest stars," I said lovingly. "That was a one-time deal."

I looked sincerely into his face, hoping he could tell that I was serious. That this meant something to me, that I didn't want to fight about this or make gross jokes—that I was trying to have an honest moment with him and tell him how I felt.

"Aww, really?" he said.

"Really."

He didn't say anything, just looked out at the road. Both his hands were on the wheel now. He seemed disappointed. And I wondered if *just me* was ever going to be enough. What I had to do to make that so.

"But we can do other stuff...," I said.

His eyes perked up a little. "Yeah," he said. "Like what?"

"I could dress up for you," I said. "I'll be anything you want...."

He looked over at me with that familiar devilish spark and rubbed his crotch a little.

"How about some road head?" he said.

"Right now?"

He took my hand and put it in his lap.

"You're all sweaty and gross from practice!" I said, pulling back my hand.

"You said you'd be whatever I wanted, babe. Be a chick

who's into shit like that, who takes care of her man after a tough practice."

He yanked my ponytail and nibbled my ear a little, which he knew I liked. We were at a stoplight, so he leaned over and kissed me, had this *please* behind that devilish sparkle in those glass-blue eyes.

I unbuckled my seat belt, put my hands back in his lap, and took a deep breath. I gagged a little at first, but I tried to breathe through my mouth and be a chick who was into this sort of thing. The smell was ripe—sharp and pungent, like hot garbage, and my eyes watered. It was almost unbearable. I told myself to stop, that I didn't have to do this, that if he loved me, he wouldn't care if I did this or not. But I didn't stop. I sucked it up and kept going, kept thinking that maybe after something like this, he'd realize that no one else would do shit like this for him, and he'd hold on to me, appreciate me, love me.

VERONICA COLLINS

Alex's grounding was lifted on Valentine's Day, which, as it turned out, was a Friday. They decorated the cafeteria in red and pink with streamers, and all the girls were bustling around with carnations and little packets of those chalk-tasting candies that say weird stuff on them, like *Be Mine*, which always sounded a little too *I'm gonna lock you up in a basement* for my taste. The seniors ran an exchange where you could send a carnation with a note to Crawford and vice versa. They delivered them throughout the day. By lunch, none of us had gotten one yet.

"So, Lex," I said. "How will we celebrate your return to the social world?"

"Isn't it Valentine's Day?" Mollie snapped. "Don't you have something to do with your boyfriend?"

I gulped a little, because no, I didn't have anything to do with my boyfriend. He hadn't mentioned Valentine's Day at all. In fact, he hadn't mentioned much of anything at all lately. At first, I figured that it was the sex, and the fact that we weren't having it. I assumed that was the distance between us, the thing that wasn't connecting. The reason I didn't feel like how

I always thought being in a couple would feel. We had that great night with his family, and I thought we were really on our way, but there was still this sense I always got around him that I wasn't quite sure what he was thinking. I saw Mollie and Sam and other couples around school, and they just appeared in sync and like they were subconsciously connected or something. I'd been waiting to feel that with Drew, and I figured the sex would be the binding agent that we were missing. But not so. It didn't change anything, except put another thing that we never talked about up in the air. We kept hanging out, and even kept having sex, like everything was normal and fine, but I was pretty sure it wasn't. But he never said anything to make me think it was something specific (like an illicit act at an after-party on New Year's), so I kept rolling with it, hoping it would iron itself out.

After New Year's, he was *allegedly* very busy with the lit magazine and SAT stuff and had been *working on some new short stories*. But he was the romantic type, right? All writerly and thoughtful and sensitive, he read long books about epic love stories and cried when we watched *Legends of the Fall*. I hoped maybe he'd planned some big Valentine's Day surprise, but I knew better than to expect anything. He was still a guy after all.

"The Runts are playing the Greencliff High dance tonight," Alex said. "I figured neither of you would want to waste your Valentine's Day with your boyfriend hanging out with a bunch of public school kids."

"Shit," Mollie said. "Sam and I would totally come see you,

but I think he made some fucking fancy reservation some-where." She chewed her thumbnail and stared into her empty yogurt container.

I really wanted to know what the fallout of New Year's had been for them, if it had or hadn't affected their relationship. Sam had texted me once since New Year's. He'd said: **What are you doing right now?** I didn't respond. I didn't know how to anymore, so I just didn't. I erased it and pretended everything was normal. Pretended Drew was my boyfriend, Mollie was my friend, and Sam was her boyfriend. That was how it was after all. I needed to just live in the simplicity of that. Whatever allure hooking up with Sam had for me was squashed that night. The good way in which Sam and me hooking up had felt like a screw-you to Mollie didn't feel good that night. It just felt evil. Hooking up with Sam, in front of her, knowing that it wasn't the first time, knowing where to touch him and pull him, and her not knowing that I knew. It felt mean, and not in a satisfying way, but in an *I'm a bad person* way.

Why did I do it, then? I guess I thought it would be more suspect and out of character for me to say no than it would be for me to go along with it. I guess I somehow thought that maybe the threesome would bring Mollie and me closer together again. Give us, like, an inside joke and something to bond about, or something. I guess that was stupid. I guess there was no way that a threesome with me and Sam would some-how unite us against Sam, even though at the time, in my head, that's what I saw happening.

"I figured," Alex said, ripping her napkin into long shreds. "V, I assume you and Drew are doing something, too."

If Drew was planning a surprise, Alex would probably know about it, right? I took the fact that she was asking what we were doing to mean that we weren't doing anything. Or maybe she did, and she was playing along.

"Actually, we're not," I said. "He hasn't mentioned a thing. I don't even think he remembers that it's Valentine's Day."

"He's been really obsessed with his writing lately," she said.

I hated it when she did that, told me stuff about Drew that she assumed that she knew and I didn't. Like she secretly competed with me over who knew him better. She had, like, ten years on me, I get it, but at the end of the night, he was still going home with me and not her, so I wished she'd just let it go sometimes.

"Well, I'm sure he'll want to come support you, so we'll totally go," I said. "It'll be fun. A public school Valentine's Day safari adventure!"

Out of the corner of my eye, I saw Gabby Sherman waddling up to our table with an armful of carnations, flushed and panicked, like she always was. I thought about the time that she farted during the Thanksgiving assembly, and giggled to myself.

"Carnations for you guys!" she said.

She handed one to me and one to Alex. Then another one to Alex.

Mollie just sat there, staring her down, ready to accuse her of some great crime.

We thanked her. She said no problem and that *this wasn't all of them*. That there was *another batch coming later*, and then she scurried off.

My note said: *Happy Valentine's Day, beautiful. xoxo, Drew*

Alex scooted her chair back and giggled away to herself.

Mollie peered at her. "Who sent you two, Miss Popular?" she asked.

"One's from Marc Seidman," she said through chuckles.

"What's funny?" I asked.

"Marc Seidman. He wrote, 'Roses are red, violets are blue, I'm sorry you got grounded and for being an asshole to you and Drew.'"

"Is the other one from Drew?" Mollie asked, still with the squinty eyes and bitch face.

Alex looked at me, then back down at the card. She said, "Yeah, just congratulating me on my freedom. Happy Valentine's Day...yada yada." Then she said, "Nothing from Sam? What a bastard."

Mollie looked into the empty yogurt container and crossed her legs. "Please. Sam is hardly the cheesy carnation type."

"I thought you guys had big fancy plans tonight?" Alex asked.

"We do. Hence why he doesn't need to spend more money to send me a cheap stupid flower." She grabbed her bag and the yogurt and stood up. "Lex, save me a seat in English?"

Alex nodded, and Mollie stomped off.

It was just a stupid flower sale. She'd be fine. And not mad at me, because he didn't send her one. At least he didn't send me one. Or both of us. Better none of us than both of us...

"So, I'm serious," I said, rerouting my train of thought. "Drew and I will definitely come see you guys at the dance tonight."

"Super," she said.

We took our carnations and headed to class.

When I told Drew about seeing Alex's band at the Greencliff dance, he said he was psyched that I was down to go. He was afraid that I'd want to do something dumb and romantic for Valentine's Day, which was a stupid holiday created by Hallmark to extort money from bored, fat, consumption-obsessed Americans. I told him that it would be fun to be somewhere where no one knew us. But that maybe I'd cook him a fancy meal afterward. He said maybe, that he'd been on a roll with his writing and was anxious to get home and work. Because right, going home and banging away on a dusty laptop definitely sounds better than getting fed and laid by your super-hot girlfriend....

IF CRAWFORD AND HARWIN were different countries, Greencliff High was a different freakin' planet. Everything was oversize and cold and made out of linoleum and tile and aluminum—no mahogany, stone, or carpet. The kids looked pretty much the same, just a little rougher around the edges and slightly more racially ambiguous. And the guys looked older than the Crawford boys for some reason. There were a lot of cute ones actually, and I wondered why we hadn't tapped this public school resource sooner. Seemed to be heavy on the guy to girl ratio, too.

The dance was in their gym, which was dirty and smelly and neither woody and quaint like Harwin's nor massive and opulent like Crawford's.

The band was already setting up when we got there, looking all professional, tuning their instruments and whispering official, informed-looking things to one another. Alex looked cute in her little skirt and funky tights, very rock and roll. I found this whole thing to be so funny, that there was, like, this whole side of her, this whole thing that she did and liked and was good at that she never talked about or shared with us, the people who were supposed to be her best friends. In all the years I was friends with Alex, I'd never once heard her play or even talk about the piano. I knew she took lessons, but I always figured it was something her mom made her do, like how Mollie took tennis lessons and I used to take ballet and horseback riding and ice skating. I knew she was into music, like finding songs and bands and stuff that weren't on the radio, but that wasn't the same as having, like, an actual drive to play with strangers, like, in front of strangers.

They started playing, and everyone cheered. People in the crowd screamed for Ned and Pete and Fernando, so Drew and I wailed and whistled for Alex as loud as we could. They sounded so much better than they had at Halloween. Totally different, too, more funky and soulful, more Alexy honestly, like it was really her band now, as opposed to her just playing in the boys' band. Everyone in the crowd stood and listened, and then when the beat picked up danced. Everyone around us (not knowing that we were her friends) was buzzing about the

Cunning Runts, and her voice, and how hot she was, and how much better they were now than they used to be when some other guy was their singer.

Drew gazed at her up there, mesmerized, a smile plastered across his face. He had his arm around me, but he stared at her, and not in the way that guys stare at me. We swayed and bopped back and forth to the music, and I put my head on his shoulder. He kissed my hair and squeezed my ass. I wasn't sure in that scenario who the lucky one really was. I knew that I had what I wanted, maybe even what Alex wanted—him, a boyfriend, in body. I knew that he was my boyfriend, that he was down here with me, physically holding me, but he was completely entranced by her.

When their set was over, a DJ went on and they joined us in the crowd.

"Congratulations!" I said, and hugged them all. They were all kinda moist and sweaty; it was kinda gross.

"Thanks for coming," Fernando said.

Alex grinned from ear to ear, clearly pleased with her performance. I told her I couldn't believe how good she'd gotten, how everyone in the crowd was talking about how hot she was. She just laughed and asked if I liked the new songs. I was embarrassed to tell her that I didn't know which ones were new and which were old, so I just said that I did.

Drew couldn't stop hugging her and punching her in the arm and telling her how *fucking awesome* she did, that he wanted her to record her songs so that he could listen to her in the car.

"Happy Valentine's Day," the DJ said into a microphone. "This one's for the lovers."

A slow song came on, and, in unison, all the public school kids sucked themselves onto one another and started making out. Before I could say anything, Drew said, "Oh my god, Alex, it's the song! We have to dance to this song."

I didn't recognize the song.

She said, "Ew, I'm all sweaty, you don't want to dance with me."

And he said, "Shut up, I don't care," and held out his arm.

"Do you mind?" he asked me.

I shook my head and smiled and watched the two of them go off and hug and sway.

So, I was left standing there in the dusty gym in the midst of all these strangers, couples, on Valentine's Day, while my boyfriend went off to dance with his (my) best friend. Perfect.

Fernando tapped my shoulder. "Well," he said, "would you like to dance?"

A wave of relief. I told him I would, more than anything, and thanked him for saving me.

"No problem," he said. "You don't know anyone here. It's really cool that you guys came to support us."

It's always weird being alone with your friend's boyfriend. I never really know the rules here. Well, I mean, other than the *don't have sex with him* rule that I had already broken. But in an attempt to do it the right way, what can you say and not say? Where is it okay to touch and not touch? He seemed nervous, but damn, he was cute. I never really had a chance to look at him up close before, or maybe I just never really bothered. Dark hair, dark skin, bright brown puppy-dog eyes. He looked cute in his little vest, clearly he'd tried to look nice. How could Alex not be falling all over him?

"So they're pretty close, yeah?" he asked, gesturing to Drew and Alex.

"They're *best friends*." I looked over at the two of them talking up a storm, laughing away about god only knows what.

"It's annoying, right?"

I laughed. "Extremely!" But I looked at pretty Fernando, and he wasn't laughing. "I wouldn't worry, though," I said. "They've been tight for years. If they were going to hook up, they'd have hooked up by now."

"I guess so," he said, eyes still fixed on the gruesome twosome. "I just wish I knew where I stood with her."

I shrugged, realizing the strangeness in the fact that Fernando and I had the same problem.

ALEXANDRA HOLBROOK

After the dance, Fernando asked me if I wanted to *grab some pizza*. I'd seen him at practice, but we hadn't really *talked* since New Year's, seeing as how part of the stipulation of my grounding (which included seizure of my phone and computer) was that I had to come right home after band practice (after negotiating even being able to *attend* practice). Part of me hoped I'd drunk-hallucinated the whole ordeal. I wondered if there was a statute of limitations on "we should probably talk about this" and if it was past the point already. For all I knew, Fernando had a new girlfriend. For all I knew, I was never his girlfriend in the first place.

He opened the door for me when I got into his car. I smiled. He got in on his side and smiled back. Was I supposed to say something? Apologize? Was he? What was this? Was he taking me out on a Valentine's Day date, or were we bandmates *grabbing pizza* after a gig?

"I think we're really coming together," he said.

"Yeah," I said, assuming he was talking about the band.

He looked over at me and smiled yet again, and put his hand on my leg. I smiled, again, wondering when either one of us was actually going to say anything—if either one of us had ever actually said anything during the entire duration of our relationship or if it had really just been a series of smiles, and in my naïveté, I assumed that was all relationships really entailed.

We walked into the pizza place, which was almost empty. Blasts of spicy meat and bubbling cheese wafted around us like hot thunderclouds. I immediately started to salivate. Apparently, ten o'clock pizza isn't a popular Valentine's Day activity for young lovers, but it seemed as romantic as anything to me. I was self-conscious about my frizzy hair and shiny skin under the bright fluorescent lights. I fussed with my skirt and twirled my split ends.

"Two slices of plain," he said to the guy behind the counter, handing him a ten-dollar bill. So he was paying. And he ordered for me. Maybe this was a date.

We sat down. He cracked his knuckles, looked at me, and said, "I want to apologize for New Year's."

Massive. Overwhelming. Bowel-cleansing relief.

"No, I want to apologize!" I said.

"It's been frustrating not being able to talk to you."

"Trust me, it's been frustrating not being able to talk to anyone."

He folded his pizza in half and held the bread on both sides like a sandwich. "We don't need to make a big deal about it," he said, chomping away. "But sex isn't nothing to me."

Oh god, he'd said the word. I was going to have to look him in the eye and talk about sex. Not just *sex* in the abstract, but actual physical penetration between him and me. Gross.

My actual vagina may as well have been sitting on the Formica table between our pieces of pizza.

"Me neither," I said. I wanted to make eye contact to show him that I could, that I was cool. I was a sexy, mature woman who could talk about this stuff, but I couldn't, I wasn't. So I didn't.

"Okay, good," he said. And he reached his hand across the table, presumably to take mine. I smiled again and put my hand in his. My other hand sat awkwardly in my lap, as I eyed my pizza, wishing I could pick it up and take another bite.

"We don't have to talk about this," I said. "It's cool. I was so drunk."

"I know," he said. "But I wanted to make sure you knew that I still think you're cool, and I still want us to hang out and stuff."

My hand was still in his, and I didn't know how long I was supposed to leave it there. It was starting to sweat and it was greasy from the pizza. *Hang out and stuff.* What the fuck did that mean? Part of me wanted to ask what the fuck that meant, but most of me didn't want to have the *am I your girlfriend?* conversation, because I knew I would be uncomfortable with either answer. My dried sweat was starting to itch under the fluorescent lights. I wanted to wash my face.

"Good," I said, taking my hand from his and wiping it on my skirt. "Let's just pretend that night never happened, okay?"

"Well, I don't want to pretend it *never* happened," he said, winking at me. "I like that it happened."

He had finished eating; the crust of his pizza sat discarded on his plate. My favorite part. I was still hungry. I wanted to eat it.

He looked at his watch. "We should probably get you home soon," he said. "Can't have you getting grounded again."

I nodded and eyed the pizza crust, debating if I should just ask for it. A big, thick piece that still had some sauce on it. He rolled up the plate and threw it in the trash.

DREW CALLED AT ABOUT midnight, asking if I was awake. I told him I was. He asked if I was down for a sesh. I told him I was.

He pulled into my driveway and around to the side of the house by the garage. There were no windows there, so my mom couldn't see what we were doing, even though she probably knew. I told her that I'd be right back—that Drew was just dropping something off. She asked where he'd been, why she hadn't seen him around lately, asked me to tell him that she missed him and to invite him over for dinner. Like it was completely impossible that there was an actual complicated reason that Drew hadn't been around; like it was my fault he hadn't been around, like I had been too busy for my old friend Drew. Like I was the selfish one.

It was unseasonably warm for February in Philadelphia. A cool dampness sat in the air instead of the frigid bite that had loomed for the past few months. The snow was starting to melt and trickle down the sides of the streets. We sat for a while, with the windows down, letting the wet air in, while he rolled a joint.

"No Veronica sleepover tonight?" I asked.

"I have SAT tutoring in the morning," he mumbled mid-lick.

I kept my eyes straight. Tried not to catch myself staring into the soft nape of his neck again. I watched the dark street sit there purring in the wet moonlight. Every few minutes a car would shush by, and I'd get nervous, like we were about to get in trouble, even though I knew we weren't. My mom was inside and couldn't see us, and my neighbors couldn't possibly care what we were doing. How were we affecting them? We're just kids being kids after all.

"Do you and Veronica ever smoke together?" I asked.

"Not really." He leaned back in the seat, shook the joint between his thumb and forefinger, and twisted the top. "She says she doesn't really like it, and honestly, I don't really like it when she smokes. She gets really stupid. Says shit that makes no sense, eats a lot, then falls asleep."

I laughed as, having smoked with Veronica, I knew this to be true. We always had fun when we got high, but Drew never really saw that silly girl part of me, the part that was friends with Veronica for a reason.

He lit the joint, took a long inhale, and passed it to me. I did the same and exhaled out the window.

"It's good to have you back, Holbrook." He reached over, placed his hand over my shoulder, and gave my neck a little squeeze. "I missed you."

I turned to him and smiled. "I missed you, too." I looked back out the window. "I missed everything! I missed daylight. I missed the moon."

"Bet you missed Fernando."

The weed started to kick in. The streetlights glowed brighter, lining the trees and houses in an iridescent haze.

"Not as much as I missed you!" I said, and pinched his cheek. "Why aren't we listening to music?"

"Good god, I don't know! What do you want?"

"Something chill."

"Perfect," he said, and lit the joint again. "So Fernando's a good guy," he said as he inhaled, and the beat filled the car.

"Yeah, I know...." I trailed off. I wondered if every time we hung out now, we'd have to talk about Veronica and Fernando. I couldn't remember the last time we'd talked about anything else.

"So are you gonna make me ask?"

"Make you ask what?"

"If you guys have *done it* yet."

The weed, my head, the lights and music. All of a sudden, it all became too much.

"I've been grounded for a month!"

"So you haven't?"

I don't know why, but I said, "I didn't say that."

"You little minx! And you thought you could get away with not telling me...."

"You didn't tell me the second you slept with Veronica."

"Yes, I did!"

"I just haven't felt like talking about it."

What was I going to tell him, the truth? That I tried, but Fernando didn't want me? That I was totally unsexual, undesirable, and that, just like him, Fernando thought I was fun to hang out with and great to talk to about music, but didn't want me.

"So that's it," he said, inhaling again. "You're done."

"What does that mean?" The lights pulsated, and the bass on the car shook my seat.

"You gave it up. You gave it to Fernando. You've gone to the other side."

"Oh, don't be so dramatic. It's just sex. You had it with Veronica."

"Yes. Yes, I did." He looked at the glowing green numbers on the stereo.

MOLLIE FINN

In geometry, Veronica asked me if I'd told Alex about New Year's.

"Oh my god, no!" I said. "Why? Do you think she knows?"

"I don't know," she replied, doodling stars in my textbook. "Drew's just been so distant. I thought maybe you told Alex and Alex told him or something."

"Well, I didn't. And you better not, either!"

"So." She crossed and uncrossed her legs and twirled a thin piece of hair around her pinkie. "Have you and Sam talked about it much? I've been wondering...."

Why was she bringing this up now, in math class? We'd successfully managed to pretend it never happened, and I was really relishing in her newfound ability to follow fucking directions. The truth was that Sam and I didn't talk about it much, but when we did, he got smiley and flirty and raunchy, and as miserable as the fucking experience was and as creepy and dirty as I'd felt since, it had worked. Sam was back with me again, I could feel it—he wanted me again, paid attention to me again, was excited to see me, touch me, have sex with me again. So fuck her, thinking that she had some sort of place in our relationship now. Thinking that she was some-how involved.

I drew a bear and a pig in the margin of my notebook next to her star. Then some lightning bolts.

"Not really," I said, "and I thought we agreed that we weren't going to talk about it, either?"

"Even me and you can't talk about it?" she asked with genu-ine sadness in her eyes. "Because Drew's been weird. I can't tell if it's me, if he subconsciously can sense something...."

She was provoking me. Wanting me to ask about her rela-tionship, wanting us to be girlfriends who talked about this kind of stuff, who gave each other advice and supported each other and told the other that everything was going to be okay like we used to.

The first time I ever hung out with Veronica alone was one time in seventh or eighth grade, when Alex was out of town. She was this tall, glamorous creature who came from New York who'd decided that she liked Alex, which made me jealous of Alex, but also wonder what it was about her that was attractive to someone who came from somewhere where everyone was attractive. And why she'd chosen her to bond with and not me. I hated her, but I also wanted her to like me.

We raided her mom's closet and dressed each other up in fur coats and leather pants and all sorts of ridiculous things that my mother had probably never even heard of, let alone worn, and took pictures of each other. I put on some neon hot pants, and she said, "Your butt is amazing. I could fit it in the palm of my hand." Every inch my butt grew after that, I always thought about whether it could still fit in the palm of somebody's hand, and that if it couldn't, it was too big and I no longer had anything that Veronica didn't.

It was always like that with Veronica, always a competition, and I always felt like I was losing—until I got Sam. Finally, *I* earned something that she wanted, because I'd *worked* for it. For once, the world didn't fall effortlessly into her lap like it always fucking did. Boys just naturally flocked to her; her parents just threw money at her and let her do whatever she wanted. She ate whatever she wanted and stayed thin, did whatever and whoever she wanted and people still liked her, never studied and got good grades. I didn't understand it, and it wasn't fair. Alex and I were best friends for years, and then Veronica came along and they were instantly close. Sam met Veronica and immediately liked her. I killed myself for everything I had, and it all still felt like it was slowly slipping from my grasp—fuck her. I was going to make her work for my friendship; for once in her life, she would have to fucking earn something she wanted.

"I think you're just being paranoid," I said.

"Girls!" Mrs. Matthews screamed. "Can either of you tell me what kind of triangle this is?"

"Uhh...equilateral?" Veronica guessed. She was wrong.

Part 5

THE SPRING

VERONICA COLLINS

figured I'd have a St. Patrick's Day party, because, well, I was
bored out of my mind and was starting to get that disconnected vibe I got from time to time. I was starting to wonder
if I'd gone about this year all wrong. All I'd wanted was for
things to be good with Alex and Mollie again, for the three
of us to laugh and make inside jokes and dance around like we
used to. I thought dating Drew would bring me and Alex closer
together, give us something in common, be an excuse for us to
hang out all the time but, of course, stupid me, it did the opposite. We barely even talked anymore.

I guess I didn't know what I thought sleeping with Sam
would do for my relationship with Mollie, but I just wanted
to prove her wrong about him, prove to myself that I was right
about that night freshman year and that I could have had him
if I wanted him. If I could show her that she was wrong about
him, maybe she'd realize she was wrong about a lot of things.
Maybe she'd feel knocked down a peg or two, get over herself,
get over it all, and come back to me and Alex and be able to
just say *fuck it* with us, relax, be silly with us, and have some

fun again, stop trying so hard and caring so much, maybe start eating, like, actual meals again.

We needed an excuse for everyone to get together and have fun again. March had been totally rainy and miserable, so I figured I'd give us all something to do and look forward to and have a party.

I decided to mix it up and make it a day party, have everyone over at, like, noon and start boozing from there. Also, I was tired of trying to fill my Saturday afternoons alone. I always wondered what other people did all day when they were alone. When we were younger, Alex, Mollie, and I used to hang out, go to the movies or the mall, make mischief in one another's houses on Saturdays and Sundays, but that wasn't happening anymore. They were always busy now: band practice, homework, SATs, jogging, family stuff, Sam. And Drew never wanted to hang out in the daytime; he was always writing. Writing, writing, writing. About god only knows what— he still hadn't let me read anything.

One could spend only so many Saturdays at the mall alone. I tried to watch some of the movies that Drew told me were so good, but I always found myself zoning out or falling asleep. Same thing happened with homework. I got more involved in my cooking; I went out and bought myself really fancy knives, got a fancy French cookbook, and challenged myself to make every dish in it. When I finished the French one, I got a Chinese one. I'd eat as much as I could in two days, and then bring Tupperwares full of leftovers to Gabby Sherman and the do-gooders to take to the homeless shelter, because what a waste. I started cleaning, too. Furiously. Rosie asked me if my mother was upset with her, if we'd gotten another housekeeper to come in on her days off, because the house was always so spotless when she arrived. I just told her it was my new *domestic* phase. That I wanted *to be a good wife some day!* She laughed.

I called the party for noonish, and by two PM, some of the jocks had shown up, a few seniors, some randos from our grade, Josh Holbrook and some sophomores, but no Alex, no Mollie, and no Sam or Drew.

I called Drew a few times, but there was no answer. It was taking him longer than expected to get the green streamers and leprechaun cutouts I'd asked him to pick up.

I called Alex.

"Hey," I said. "What're you doing? Why aren't you here yet?"

"Oh shit, what time is it? I'm just reading," she said.

"You're doing homework on a Saturday? On St. Patrick's Day? Put on something tight and green and get your ass here."

She laughed. "No, I'm reading, like, an actual book. For fun. I know. I'm a loser."

I laughed. "Seriously! Stop being a nerd and come hang out!"

"I'll be there in a little," she said. "I'm actually really into this right now. I'm lazy. It's raining. I haven't showered."

"You suck."

She paused for a minute.

"I know. Maybe tomorrow let's just you and me hang out and get dinner or something? We haven't really had any bonding time in a while," she said.

I smiled, because I couldn't believe she'd even noticed.

"I'd really love that," I said.

"Okay, I'll see you soon."

I hung up the phone smiling. I couldn't remember the last time Alex and I hung out just the two of us. That night before my First Week of School party maybe? We used to hang all the time. When Mollie disappeared into Sam world, the two of us would get into all sorts of wacky trouble. She'd make me smoke pot, and we'd go to fancy dinners and charge them to my dad's credit card, sneak into Penn parties and make out with frat boys, or just sit around my pool and talk about life and sex. Well, I'd talk about sex. She'd talk about life. And life without sex. I wondered where we'd go for dinner. Sushi maybe, because they never carded. I wanted to get drunk with her and really bond. I felt like we had so much to talk about. I wanted to talk to her about Drew, see if maybe she could give me some advice. I was dying to ask her about Fernando, and tell her how happy I was for her and what a great guy he seemed like—maybe she was thinking about sleeping with him! Maybe I could give her advice, too, like I used to with Mollie. I wanted to figure out some way to ask her if she knew what was going on with Mollie and Sam and if she was as worried as I was that Mollie was really losing it and possibly about to snap.

I tried calling Drew again, still no answer. And there was a small pit in my stomach that didn't even care. That knew I'd probably have more fun without him, and was sort of relieved to be free and unburdened at a party again, and that maybe that meant something. I took a swig of green beer and went back to entertaining my guests.

ALEXANDRA HOLBROOK

It was raining, and I was reading *High Fidelity*, thinking about the top five songs I'd want played at my funeral. I couldn't decide between wanting something tragic and emotional like Radiohead or the National or something whimsical and ironically appropriate, something that might make people laugh and say *Oh, this is so Alex*, like "Crossroads." My mom was working in New York for the day, Josh had already gone to Veronica's party, and I was alone in my house. I loved being alone in my house. No questions, no noise, no feeling of being flocked and watched, just the freedom for me to do as I pleased at a pace of my liking. I knew I had to go to Veronica's party, but I couldn't have been less in the mood. All I wanted to do was sit in bed and keep reading what was quickly becoming my new favorite book. I told myself I'd go at four o'clock. By then people would be drunk enough for me to unabashedly mock them to their faces and I could sneak out an hour later but convince people I'd been there all day.

Hours passed, and I hardly noticed. New song lyrics started to seep into my thoughts, something about rain, something about being alone, but then I worried if Fernando would read into my lyrics, which led me to think about how I didn't really feel like thinking about him.

Then Drew called.

"Hello?" I said.

The line was quiet, but I heard him breathing.

"Drew? What's up?"

"Hey," he said. His voice was shaky, off.

"What's up?"

When he said he was at the hospital, my throat swelled, and I knew something was really wrong. I knew no one had sprained an ankle playing basketball or cut themselves slicing bagels. I don't know how I knew—I just knew.

"Are you okay? What's going on? Is Veronica okay?"

"My dad was in an accident."

My heart pounded in my face and fingers. I didn't know what to do, how to feel, where to go, what to say. Thunder cracked outside my window.

"Is he okay? Are you okay?"

"No." His normally soothing, sturdy, NPR tone rattled like my windowpanes. I hung up and ran to my car. I didn't look in the mirror, didn't turn off the lights, just went.

I shuffled through the wet emergency room. Through the maze of strange faces and white coats. The smell of disinfectant made me a little dizzy, but I darted through the wide white hallways until I found them. Drew sat on a plastic chair with his head down, elbows on his knees and white-knuckled hands clasped together. His mom sat next to him; she was crying and holding Isabelle, who was still in her blue-and-pink polka-dot pajamas. Christina, wearing denim overalls, sat next to Drew and stared expressionlessly at the wall.

One time, Drew's dad drove us to the shore. He made us listen to classical music the whole way. Drew whined and complained and told his dad that he should try to be a little cooler. His dad said, "I don't need to be cool. I'm your father." And I thought about how nice it must be for Drew to have a dad who cared more about being his dad than being cool.

My dad was always competitive with us about who was cooler—who listened to cooler music, had more disdain for authority and convention, did harder drugs. Sometimes it was exhausting. I was the only girl in the world who told her dad that she was checking out some local band when she was really at the library. My dad, with his band and his underground music and his ratty T-shirts and hand-rolled cigarettes, was so cool that he decided that he was too cool to even be a dad at all.

It seemed to take Drew forever to stand up. Once he did, his body melted again in my feeble arms. He was clammy and shivering. He didn't say anything, just rested his wet cheek on mine.

"What's going on?" I'd already started to cry.

He took my hand and walked me out into the hallway, around a corner from the waiting area where his family sat. He stood square in front of me, legs sturdy on his flat feet and head stiff and strong on his broad shoulders. Then his face slowly collapsed.

I threw myself around his shaking shoulders and felt him

entirely crumble into me. Tears streamed down his cheeks and mine, and I didn't know what I was supposed do, what I was supposed to say. So I didn't say anything for a while. We just stood there in the hospital, hugging and crying. I wanted to call my mom.

"What happened?" I finally asked, my elbows still locked around his neck.

"An accident," he said. "Hit a tree on Blackrock Road. He was drunk, they think. They don't know. I'm sure he was...."

There was pressure around my chest; my ribs closed in on my lungs. I pulled away from him and grasped his arms in my shaking hands. Intercoms and announcements buzzed around us, but it was all muted and in slow motion.

"Is he okay?" But I knew that he wasn't. There was a panic in Drew's eyes that said that he wasn't.

He shook his head and lunged toward me, buried his face in my hair.

He sniffled in my ear, and I looked around the corner at his mom and his sisters. They had all collapsed into one another's chests and shoulders. They all seemed so small, this whole thing so big, and all of them, so small.

"What can I do?"

"Can you take me and the girls home? My mom is going to stay here with my aunt to deal with stuff. We can't be here anymore. Please?"

I thought about my own father, where he was, if he was okay. I hadn't heard from him in months. I wondered how I'd feel if he died, how it would be different from how Drew was feeling. I wondered how Drew felt. I hated myself for not being able to really know. I wondered if this truth would inevitably make me a huge failure as a best friend.

But I didn't have time for that kind of thinking. Not today. I kept looking over my shoulder for Veronica. Wondered if she'd know what to do and if that was the reason he was with her and not me.

We drove back from the hospital in silence. No talking, no radio, just the patter of rain on windows and tires over wet gravel. The sky was bright white. The girls got out of the car; Drew sat.

"Can we go back to your house?" he asked.

"Are you sure you want to leave the girls?"

"Christy can watch Izzy. I can't be in that house right now. I don't want to talk to anyone but you."

When we got inside, I asked if he was hungry. He shook his head and went straight upstairs to my room. He kicked his wet sneakers off, lay on my bed, curled onto his side, and stuck his hands in the pockets of his green sweatshirt. I stood at the foot of the bed, just watching him, scared, confused, having no idea what to do or say. The rain started up again outside the window, beating on the pane like it was trying to break in or get our attention. I lay down next to him, spooned him from behind, and rested my chin on his damp shoulder.

"Thanks for coming, Alex," he said. Drew never called me Alex. Coming out of his mouth, it sounded like someone else's name.

I kissed his cheek, and he turned over onto his back. He

stared up at the ceiling, tears forming and falling from the corners of his eyes.

"Do you want to watch a movie or something?" I asked.

"Can we just lie here?"

"Sure," I said, and rolled over and lay on my back to stare at the same blue ceiling.

We lay there for I don't know how long, minutes, hours maybe. Not talking, just listening to the rain and each other breathe and staring at the ceiling. I waited for him to talk first, not wanting to say the wrong thing, or anything at all, if he didn't want me to. I closed my eyes tight, trying to stifle my own tears, because they seemed selfish and unfair.

"It's weird," he said finally, eyes still fixed on the ceiling, "that people can actually die, because of nothing—because of an accident. As stupidly and easily as someone spills a drink or stubs their toe, a whole life can just end."

I stayed quiet.

"It's not like he really added much to our lives," he went on. "I often thought about how different life would be if he left, and I usually came to the conclusion that it wouldn't change that much at all."

I stayed quiet, but I rolled over onto my side and propped my head up with my hand.

"Life without a dad is different," I said.

He turned to me. "God, I'm an asshole. I didn't mean…"

"No, no, it's totally not the same thing. I can't even imagine what must be going on in your head right now." I paused. "Have you called Veronica?"

"No," he replied, then rolled over and looked straight into my puffy eyes. "I can't deal with her or that dumbass fucking party right now."

He pushed my hair back behind my ear.

"You're my best friend," he said.

I smiled and told him that I felt the same.

"No, I mean it. You're not just *my* best friend, you're *the* best friend I could conceivably imagine to exist, and I can't believe I'm lucky enough to have found you. I don't deserve you. I'm sorry to put all this on you...."

I sat up. "You're not allowed to worry about me right now."

"I never worry about you," he said. "I worry about me, losing you."

"I'm not going anywhere," I said.

He scooted closer toward me and put his hand on the back of my head.

"Yes, you are," he said. "It's only a matter of time. Some guy'll scoop you up, whisk you away. You'll finally realize that you don't need to be wasting your time hanging around with a pathetic loser like me."

"Yeah, right," I said. "Please, I'm not going anywhere. We'll be fifty, and I'll be single and living in a smelly apartment over your and Veronica's garage, babysitting your beautiful, long-legged children, while you two go out with all the other happy couples on Saturday nights."

He laughed. "There's no way that will happen."

Thunder split outside and we both jumped a little, but he turned back to me. He possessed an eerie focus. My heart raced, and a familiar lump formed in my throat. I looked down at the decorative blue and purple pillows on my bed and twirled one of the loose ribbons around my forefinger.

When I finally looked up at him, fighting tears, fighting everything, I shrugged. He took my head in his palms, pulled my quivering face close, and kissed me, our lips wet and salty from the tears.

I smiled, leaned in, and kissed him quickly again, wanting to get another one in before we both just smiled and lay back down, and I filed the event as an extra intimate expression of gratitude and affection in a time of crisis.

"What was that for?" he asked.

"What was yours for?"

"I just wanted to kiss you right then." He sat up. "I want to all the time, but I just had to right then."

Pressure in my chest returned. "You want to all the time?"

I had to maintain perspective on this situation, keep my grasp on reality and remind myself what had just happened, what was going on, that Drew was not in his right mind at the moment. His right mind didn't want to kiss me all the time; his right mind kissed Veronica all the time. His PTSD mind kissed me, not his right one. Not his right one...

He ran his wide hands over his face and head and rubbed his bloodshot eyes. "I want to all the time!" he said, throwing his palms in the air. "I know I'm not supposed to. I know this is probably the worst thing I could possibly ever do, at the worst possible time, but I just can't fake it right now."

The rain distracted me. It slapped against the windows, and the wind shook the house.

I looked at him, teary-eyed, shaking from my core.

"Really?" was all I could muster to say, fighting a smile, knowing the inappropriateness of such an expression at such a time.

"Really." Then he kissed me again.

We kissed longer that time, got lost in it. My head turned quiet, and I lost track of his hands, my hands, the rain, the thunder, the minutes, and everything that had gone on that day, that week, that year.

"I never slept with Fernando," I said.

A smile spread across his face. "Really?"

"Really."

"Then why..."

"Because you slept with Veronica!"

I started to cry again. I felt less bad about it this time.

He didn't say anything, just took my face in his hands and kissed me again. We wrapped ourselves around each other and fell into the bed.

"You waited for me," he said, smiling. "I wish I waited for you. I'm sorry I didn't wait for you. I just got confused and turned around. It was always you. I always thought it would be you."

He lay on top of me, his wet blue eyes slicing mine. He looked different at this close range, like someone I hadn't known my whole life. Someone younger, less sure. He leaned down, and we kissed again, longer, harder, his hands moving over me with abandon and mine taking the same reckless initiative. He slid my shirt over my head, and I realized that this was happening. I couldn't stop it; I didn't want to. I wanted every part of him, every part of all of it. Whatever it was.

His hands and lips were soft and slow. He kissed my neck and stomach and legs and arms and ears before he did it. It felt strange and good, but strange. I wondered if this was how it was supposed to feel, how it always would. I couldn't help but laugh every time I looked up and saw that it was Drew's face there over mine. I couldn't believe this was him; we were us, doing this. Together.

Afterward, he fell asleep. I lay with my head on his bare chest, listening to the relentless rain. I remembered that no one had called Veronica.

MOLLIE FINN

Veronica's idea to have a day-drinking St. Patrick's Day party was annoying and pathetic. How many goddamn parties did she need to have in one year? She was so desperate to let everyone know on the highest possible volume that she was *so happy* and *so popular* and had *so many* friends. Some of us had better things to do than waste calories and pretend to be enjoying it on a rainy Saturday afternoon. St. Patrick's Day? Really? She wasn't even fucking Irish. I considered not even going.

I'd successfully managed to keep the Sam/me/Veronica interactions to a bare minimum, so fuck her for forcing the three of us to be in the same place again. I wondered if she hoped it might happen again, if she was trying to orchestrate some sort of St. Patrick's Day ménage à sabotage. She called the party for noon, but who's going to set an alarm to get up and start drinking? By the time I got to Sam's, it was almost three.

The dog barked as I approached the front door. His mom answered and told me to go right downstairs as she always did. That stupid mangy mutt yapped and gnawed at my ankles as

I made my way down toward the familiar stale, musky smell of Sam's basement. He sat shirtless on the couch, watching basketball, with his hand down his pants.

I hadn't been there in a while; he looked surprised to see me.

"What're you doing here?" he asked.

"Veronica's party? St. Patrick's Day? Remember? We said last night that I'd come here when I was ready and we'd go together. Any bells ringing?" I paused. "You got a girl back there or something?"

"No, I just didn't remember. What if I wasn't home?"

"It's a Saturday in March. You're watching basketball. You're not exactly an international man of mystery."

I sat down next to him on the couch. His eyes stayed planted on the TV. I kissed him on the cheek and curled up under his arm. A huge bong sat in the middle of his coffee table, like his parents didn't even live upstairs.

"I guess," he said. I wiggled around until I found a comfortable place.

Something purple stuck out from behind the couch cushion. I reached over Sam's lap and pulled it out—a baby-size J.Crew cardigan. I recognized it; it was Veronica's. It was one of her favorites—I hadn't seen her wear it in months.

"Is this Veronica's?" I asked Sam as coolly and rationally as I possibly could, trying with every inch of my being to sound as if (and truly myself believe) I hadn't jumped to any conclusions.

Sam stayed focused on the TV, but I felt his skin tighten. "I guess so. She must have left it here sometime."

"When was she here?"

Sam took his hand out of his pants. "I don't know," he said. "Maybe that time we all came here after the game a few weeks ago. Calm down, Inspector Gadget, Jesus."

Another hard swallow.

He pulled me in closer to him and rubbed my shoulder. I relaxed for a minute, but it started to rise again: the goose bumps, the headache, chunks in my throat.

"Veronica was not wearing this that night. She was wearing that heinous black sweaterdress thing." My heart started to race and my throat closed in. Thoughts, images, occasions ran through my head and crawled over my skin.

"Babe, stop. You're being psycho," Sam said, squeezing my shoulders, eyes still glued to the TV.

I wanted to believe that I was crazy. More than anything. And I'd almost talked myself into believing I was, as I'd done the last time I'd had this feeling and the time before that. I tried to find a place where I could believe that maybe I just hadn't noticed that she had that sweater that night, or some night, but I couldn't. Not now, not after what had happened. It all made too much sense.

"No, I'm not!" I stood up. I looked down at him sitting on the couch and pointed my finger. "Did you fuck Veronica? Here? Did Veronica fucking come here and did you fuck her? Just fucking tell me."

He grabbed my wrist and pulled me back down to the couch, but I sprang to the opposite end so that I could see his face. So that he couldn't touch me. Comfort me. Diffuse me, like he always could.

"No!" he said, but there was this smile, this half smirk, a lack of focus in his left eye, and I knew he was lying.

"Just fucking tell me!"

He rested his forearms on his knees and shook his head.

"Just fucking tell me!"

"Fine!" he said. "I fucked Veronica. Are you happy now?"

I immediately regretted asking. I wished I never knew. I couldn't take it back and pretend I didn't know now.

"Oh my god" was all I could say. "Oh my god."

I looked down at my shaking hands in my lap.

He went to put his hand on my back, and I slapped it away.

"When?" I asked.

"Do you really want to know?"

"After New Year's?"

"No," he said. "We stopped fucking after New Year's."

I couldn't swallow anymore; the tears burst. I couldn't breathe, couldn't talk. I didn't know what I was even feeling. Anger. Humiliation. Devastation. Destruction. I didn't know who I was maddest at. I was going to throw up. I noticed everything: when Veronica changed her highlights from honey to caramel, when the bitches at Starbucks used 2% milk instead of skim, when Sam changed the blade on his razor. How could I have missed this? Maybe there was a lot I missed. Maybe I didn't know anything. Maybe everything I ever believed to be true was a lie. This whole time, I'd been the butt of this whole joke. Did anyone else know?

"Why did you tell me?" I asked through sobs, bleary eyes still focused on my lap.

"You fucking begged me to tell you!" he yelled back.

"Fuck you," I said. And I got up.

"Babe, don't leave. I didn't mean…" He reached out for my wrist, but I snapped it away.

"What the fuck did you mean, then?"

"I'm an idiot. I'm just a dumbass, animal guy who can't help it sometimes. But, I love you. Don't go." He looked at me with sincere regret in his eyes, but not enough.

"She's my best friend…."

"I thought Alex was your best friend?"

I swallowed one last time, picked up the bong, and smashed it on the ground. "Fuck you, Sam! Seriously, fuck you." I was wheezing, and my chest hurt too much to even get the words out.

"What the hell?!" he yelled. "You bitch!"

I turned my back to him and started for the door. The basketball announcers cheered for something behind me.

"You should have just denied it," I said. "I would have believed you eventually."

"Now you tell me…."

I stomped up the stairs and slammed his front door with no concern for what his parents might think.

He didn't even follow me.

I DROVE AROUND FOR a few hours thinking about driving off a cliff. I thought about how guilty Sam and Veronica would feel if I just died, right then. I thought about how the only appropriate revenge would be the eternal guilt they would both be burdened with if I just died that afternoon.

I thought about driving over to Veronica's and confronting her at her party, in front of everyone. Causing a huge scene, throwing something in her face, maybe slapping her. But I didn't have the strength yet, I needed to rebuild, be organized, fuck her in as premeditated and calculated a way as she'd fucked me. If I went over there an emotional wreck, I'd just humiliate myself even more than I already had.

When it started to get dark, my blind rage took me over to Alex's. I banged on the door, and Josh opened it to find me shaking, hysterical and red-faced, keeled over as if I were about to faint or vomit.

"Holy shit," he said. "What the hell happened to you? None of you guys came to Veronica's; Alex won't come out of her room. What the hell is going on?"

"I need Alex."

He hugged my wet convulsing body and led me upstairs.

"Wait," he said, and he ducked into his room. He gave me a big sweatshirt. "Don't freeze. I'm sure all Alex's clothes are dirty on the floor."

"Thanks, Josh." I looked up at his sad face and hugged him. Wondered what he could possibly think was happening to me, and if I should just tell him, or if, oh my god, he already knew. I turned away and crossed the hall to Alex's room.

"Holy shit," she said when I walked in her door. Her room was a mess as usual; clothes, books, CDs strewn all over her floor and unmade bed.

"Sam," I sobbed, "has been fucking Veronica." The words tasted bitter in my mouth.

Her face went green, as I suspected it would, but her eyes shifted to the wall. Please fucking god, tell me that she didn't know about this. . . . There was no way.

Could there be a way? Could she have known and not told me? Was this yet another thing she hadn't told me? Could I trust no one? Did I truly have no one in the world to count on? I panicked, thinking about who else might possibly know. The lacrosse team? Underclassmen? I hated everything. Violence bubbled inside me.

Her eyes refocused. "No fucking way!"

I realized I'd have to tell her about New Year's, about all of it. I suddenly wished I hadn't told her anything, but at the same time I had never been more grateful to have her to tell. I wanted her to tell me that she'd fix it, kill Veronica, kill Sam, defend me and my honor. As I sobbed in her lap in her messy room and she pet my head and called Veronica an evil cunt, I realized how much I'd missed her, missed the truth and having someone understand and be on my side the way she always did and always was.

"What are you thinking right now?" I asked through sobs as she glared out the window at the unyielding rain.

"So much," she said. "I am thinking so much."

VERONICA COLLINS

I went to school that Monday anxious—anxious to talk to Alex about Drew, anxious to see if everyone was talking about how I'd been guzzling green beer and playing beirut while my boyfriend's dad was dying in the hospital, and none of my friends showed up to my party. I hadn't seen Drew yet. He told me that he didn't want to see anyone, and I wondered if that had applied to Alex, too. Somehow, I doubted it did. He called me that night, after he just hadn't shown up to my party, after he hadn't called or returned my calls all day. I was drunk when I answered the phone. I picked up and said, "Oh good, so you're not lying in a ditch somewhere." I actually said that. And he said, "No, but my dad is." It took a few exchanges before I understood that he wasn't joking, before I grasped what was actually going on. I tried to will myself out of being drunk. I told him I'd come over, that I didn't care if I was drunk, I'd drive there, anyway. He told me not to, that he was okay, that he needed to be alone and with his family and that I shouldn't worry.

The rain had finally stopped, and it was the first warmish day of spring. That day when everyone gets excited and overzealous and breaks out short sleeves and bare legs, even though it's not *quite* warm enough. I walked into school and saw Mollie and Alex huddled by Alex's locker.

I said something like, "Hey, guys," trying to sound appropriately solemn.

Mollie just whipped her shiny ponytail and marched down the hall, completely ignoring me. I knew that I was going to pay for the way I'd handled everything. That everyone was now running around talking about what a shallow party girl I was again. I *knew* that I was wrong to have given him space when he asked for it, that I should have not listened and gone to his house with flowers or cookies or a mix CD of sad songs. I should have known that that's what I was supposed to do, that that's what a good girlfriend would have done. I figured Mollie, as the ultimate professional girlfriend, was appalled at how I, the raging slut dressed in girlfriend's clothing, totally screwed the one responsibility I had in a time of crisis: showing up.

Alex slung her backpack over her shoulder and shifted her weight. Hallway chatter was beginning to drain around us.

"I really messed up, didn't I?" I asked.

"You think?" I detected sarcasm.

"Is Drew pissed?"

I played with my rings and wondered why Mollie would care so much that I was a shitty girlfriend. Why wasn't Alex the mad one?

She shook her head and made her way toward homeroom, leaving me dumbfounded, standing cross-armed like an asshole in front of her locker.

"Lex!" I screamed down the hall, but hearing her name only quickened her step.

IN HOMEROOM, SHE SAT in the back between Kelly Sanders and Nikki Clayman. She glanced at her untied shoelaces, her chewed-up pen, out the window, at the back of Kim Frasier's head, everywhere but at me. I gazed at the maps on the walls, wondered if I could go live on that Greek guy's boat until someone else did something selfish and stupid and no one cared about this anymore. Crying in homeroom wasn't an option, but tears were fighting their way out. I couldn't believe that they were so mad at me, that they were taking this so personally. How was I supposed to have known the right thing to do? How did they know the right way to act in these situations? It's not like I found out his dad died and threw a party. It's not even like anyone called me and told me when it happened so I could even know to stop the party and go to where I was supposed to be. No one tells you how you're supposed to act in these situations—Drew's dad freakin' *died*. He said he wanted to be alone! I wasn't going to argue with him, tell him that I knew better, because I didn't. How did they? I called him again and again, tried to get him to talk to me, be with me, let me be a part of what was happening, but he wouldn't. He wouldn't let me in. What was I missing that everyone else seemed to get? Why was I so disconnected from Drew, from everyone? No matter how physically together Drew and I were, we were miles apart. I felt like I was slipping through the cracks, with Mollie and Alex, with my parents, with Drew. No matter how loud I screamed or how close I physically was, I just kept disappearing. My head swelled with everything I could have done differently.

"Miss Collins," Mr. Boardman said.

I looked over at him, chunks rising in my throat, panic setting in that I'd just lost my boyfriend and two best friends forever, for no reason other than that I was dumb, ignorant of the unwritten social understandings that everyone else seemed to instinctively know. Maybe more stuff they learned in the books I'd never read and movies I'd never watched.

"Miss Collins, you look distraught today. Is something wrong?" Tears welled in my eyes. I wondered how many people already knew, were already gossiping about what an insensitive, self-involved flake I was.

"Nope, I'm good." I feigned a smile. I looked over at Alex, sitting between Nikki and Kelly with her arms crossed, sneering at her lap. I looked around at the other girls, who all seemed to be whispering and staring with accusatory eyes. Normally, I got a rush out of people talking about me, but this was different. The swarming eyes weren't the usual shade of jealous and intrigued, they were angry, thirsty for blood. The blue walls, the maps, the posters of smug old Shakespeare, closed in, and I asked to be excused.

I went to the bathroom, sat in a stall, and let the tears fall. I told myself I could fix it. I'd go home and call Drew and do the supportive girlfriend thing and everything would be fine. Christ, it had been only two days. How had everything changed, my whole life been ruined? In two days? I truly believed that I could fix it—that I'd get them all to love me again. They'd been mad at me before. Mollie and Alex didn't talk to me for a week in eighth grade because Mollie'd heard that I'd told Max Fischer she had an eating disorder. Which she did. She got over it and started loving me again when she got mad at Vanessa Cooper for making out with Brad Burns, who she'd declared she had a crush on like two weeks before. That's all this was. She and Alex needed to be mad at me for a while, but it would pass; it always did. I started to calm down.

Sitting in the stall, I noticed the lilac paint chipping around the door hinges. Why did the bathroom always smell like the monkey house at the zoo? I did my yoga breathing and told myself not to panic. That this was a bad day—I'd had them before.

I was about to reemerge, when the bathroom door swung open. I didn't recognize the voices. The girls were talking about a *Macbeth* paper that neither of them had written yet. *Macbeth*. Sophomores. I didn't want to deal with them asking if I'd been crying or why, or them seeing that I had and then making up why and spreading rumors about it, so I decided to wait in the stall until they left.

"So, did you hear the big gossip?" one said.

"Which big gossip?"

Sadly, I found myself excited at the thought that I was going to get to overhear some big juicy piece of sophomore drama. The first one hopped into the stall next to mine, and I tried to place the purple Doc Martens. Who in tenth grade wore purple Doc Martens? Mollie would know.

"Apparently," the one in the stall started, and then paused as her pee stream splashed the toilet water. The other ran the sink. "Apparently, Veronica Collins fucked Mollie Finn's boyfriend."

First, I got dizzy—saw flecks of white and felt the blood slowly drain from my head. Then everything faded to black, like when you stand up too fast, except I was still sitting down.

The water stopped running, and I heard the slam of a palm on the wet counter.

"Shut up!"

The other one flushed and left the stall.

"I know."

"What a whore! She's really fucked everyone now, hasn't she?"

"I know."

Their voices echoed around the empty bathroom. My head started pounding; I still felt dizzy. I couldn't remember the last time I had breathed.

"This is going to be bad," the one with the Doc Martens said. "I would not fuck with Mollie Finn. She's kind of insane." Their voices faded out of the bathroom behind another rusty swing of the heavy door.

I turned around and threw up.

How had she found out? Had Sam told her? Had Sam told someone else who told her? Why would Sam tell her? Why would Sam tell anyone? And now, of all times—why now? I threw up again.

By the time I finally willed myself out of the bathroom, the halls were empty; first period had started fifteen minutes ago. Mr. Boardman stood by his classroom door. He skulked over to me and put his pudgy hand on my shoulder, which caught me off guard.

"Veronica, are you okay? You had me worried in homeroom. You're not your usual vivacious self." He looked at me through his thick black glasses with sincerity in his eyes. I thought maybe he might be a really nice guy to the people in his real life.

"I'm not feeling well," I said. "I think it's a stomach bug. I'm going to go to the nurse."

He nodded and told me to feel better, and the look in his eyes made me think that maybe he knew it wasn't really a stomach bug, but he didn't say anything. I knew that he wouldn't.

ALEXANDRA HOLBROOK

The funeral was on a Thursday; we all missed school. Drew's whole Crawford class was excused to be there. The service was graveside, and it was unseasonably warm, had been the whole week. Drew's dad was buried toward the back of the cemetery, away from the road, in the hills where the newer graves were. The blossoms had begun to pop on all the trees; it seemed unfair that this was the first time we'd all had an excuse to do something outside.

Veronica sat next to Drew and held his hand through the entire service. Mollie sat next to me and held mine. Seeing Veronica touch him made me itch and seethe and want to chew the hair off my own head. I felt her hand on his back in my lungs, her lips on his ear in my legs. I hated that he seemed even more intoxicating to me now, that the sex and the sadness were only making him more attractive to me, as if I weren't obsessed before. All these years I'd been afraid that the reality of actual sex with actual Drew would ruin the fantasy of dreamy sex with fantasy Drew, but the officially documented memory only made the reveries worse. Before, all I thought about was what it would be like to touch him, kiss him, bury my nose in the nape of his neck and smell his skin. I'd run different scenarios in my mind, imagined him feeling, tasting, being different every time. I imagined scenes in his room, my room, his car, abandoned log cabins, but now, now that I had touched him, kissed him, felt my cheek on his naked chest, I just kept playing that one, the real one, over and over again in a morbid loop—wondering if he enjoyed it, wondering if I did something wrong or I smelled bad or tasted weird and if that was the reason we hadn't talked about it, and the reason he hadn't tried to do it again. Or the reason he hadn't broken up with Veronica yet.

AFTER THE SERVICE, WE went back to the Carsons' and sat around the deli spread making uninspiring small talk. The house smelled like wet wood and boiling spaghetti sauce, like it always did. The family pictures that crawled down the moss-colored walls above the wooden stairs that had once seemed cliché and embarrassing were now tragic. An old aunt I'd never met sat in Drew's dad's chair. I'm sure she didn't know that was where he'd sat, where he'd drunk, read the paper, and was waited on by his doting wife, where his daughters sat on his lap before they were thrust off to make room for a new paper or a new glass of Johnnie Walker. I wondered if Marcia was upset to see the aunt in the chair, if I should maybe ask her to get up.

Per Mollie's orders, I hadn't spoken to Veronica all week, which was fine by me, because I couldn't look her in the eye, anyway. It was clear she hadn't told Drew about the Sam thing, as much as it was clear that Drew hadn't told her about us. As much as I didn't know how she lived with herself, sitting there, comforting him under a blanket of deceit and lies, I understood why she didn't tell him. Because I hadn't, either. How do you tell a guy whose dad just died that his girlfriend cheated on him? How could I tell the guy whose dad just died and who I'd just lost my virginity to that his girlfriend, my best friend, had fucked our other best friend's boyfriend? When is an appropriate time to bring that up? What is a tasteful phrasing?

I also hadn't told Mollie about me and Drew yet, which was actually the worst burden of all. I hadn't told her partially because nothing felt real until I told Mollie about it. If I told her, I'd have to acknowledge that it had happened and deal with it, rather than just pretend it didn't, which seemed much easier. And partially, because a small part of me was worried that she'd be mad at me. Technically, I had done the same thing to Veronica that Veronica had done to Mollie. I was the other woman in this scenario, and with everything going on, and so much up in the air, everything changing at such a frenetic pace, I couldn't risk losing Mollie.

I was somewhat proud of V's attempt at funeral-appropriate modesty. Yes, her skirt was too short for an event with a priest in attendance, and yes, I would have buttoned one more button, but there was no body glitter or underbutt or sideboob, which was a small but important gesture on her part. Mollie kicked my calf and rolled her eyes every time V touched Drew or talked to him or kissed him or offered to help his mother. Every twenty minutes or so, I'd tear up or wonder if this was a nightmare and then remember that I was at my best friend's father's funeral, and feel even worse for having the gall to feel sorry for myself.

Mollie left after about an hour, and I walked her to her car.

"It took every bone in my body not to punch her shiny little bird face and cause a scene right in the middle of the cemetery," she said as she pulled a Marlboro Light from the pack I'd extended to her.

I made a short exhale that resembled a chuckle.

I lit my cigarette and looked out at all the dew-covered cars lined along the leafy street.

"Drew, six o'clock," she said, and gestured behind me.

I nodded and tapped the hood of her Audi as she pulled away. I choked back another wave of tears as Drew's gravity closed in. I stomped out my cigarette, turned around, and saw him standing about a foot behind me in the driveway. He looked morbidly handsome in his dark suit—taller, older, like he was beginning to look like what he'd look like when he became a man.

"Can I have one?" he asked.

I handed him my pack, still choking on words and tears.

"Let's walk down the block," he said. "I don't want any relatives to see me smoking."

"They'll all smell it when they kiss you," I said.

There were no sidewalks, so we walked down the middle of the road. I stayed about a foot away, because even so much as an accidental brush of his jacket on my elbow would have destroyed me.

He said something about not knowing anyone there. I said something about what a good job he was doing being strong for his mom and sisters. He shrugged and thanked me for helping so much. We got to the end of the cul-de-sac and sat down on the curb.

"You don't have any weed, do you?" he asked.

I laughed and told him I was sorry I didn't.

He took a deep breath and put his hand on my back. My cotton cardigan was thin; I felt his heat through the material.

He took a long inhale of the cigarette. "So we should talk about the other day," he said.

Tears gathered in my throat, in the emptiness that swelled there since it happened.

"We don't have to," I said.

"Yes, we do. This can't ruin us." His eyes stayed fixed on his dusty black wing tips and mine on my bare knees. He regretted it, I could tell. We were going to go back to being best friends and pretend like it never happened—it'd be something we'd laugh about in our twenties over beers, a quip for an embarrassing speech at his wedding... to someone else.

"It doesn't have to," I said. "It was an extenuating circumstance. I understand."

The late-afternoon sun tried desperately to hide behind some clouds, but it peeped through the holes and stung our eyes anyway. Birds, bugs, fresh-cut grass, lawnmower exhaust, fertilizer, pale legs under floral dresses: there was no hiding from the awkwardness of early spring. I ran my hands through my hair for lack of a better idea of what to do with them.

"I just…" He paused and leaned back into the grass on his elbows. "I'm going to tell Veronica. I don't want you to think…"

"I don't."

I wiped a tear away with my knuckle.

I looked over my shoulder at him lying in the grass, perched on his elbows. He sat up and hugged me from the side, laying his head on my shoulder. His hair smelled of the sun, and his jacket was wool, itchy and stiff, too thick for the warmness of the day.

"I'm not going to tell Veronica. I haven't even told Mollie. I understand. I understand everything. Please don't worry."

"Then why are you crying?"

His head was still on my shoulder, and his long arms were still wrapped around me.

"Because this is sad!" I began to sob. "It's a sad day. I'm sad for you and your family. I hate to think that you're sad, about your dad, about me, about anything."

He kissed my slimy cheek.

"I just didn't want you to think I haven't been thinking about it, because I have. A lot."

"I know," I said, and slipped out of his grasp.

"Did you tell Fernando?"

I had barely even thought about Fernando or the band or music or the fact that we were playing at the prom since it all happened. I'd barely thought about the songs I'd written that I'd have to perform or the fact that I now had a million more songs in my head but couldn't write them, because then it'd be written and I'd have to actually look at the truth of it.

"I was sort of waiting to see if you'd tell Veronica," I said.

He rubbed his eyes with the palms of his hands.

"Yeah," he said.

"Yeah," I replied.

A sharp breeze shook the leaves on the trees. I hoped he'd offer me his jacket. But instead, he reached into it and pulled something out of his inside pocket.

"I want to give you something," he said. And he handed me a stack of white paper folded over itself. I opened it and read the top: "Women and Boys," by Andrew Carson.

I skimmed the first paragraph. It started: "Without the man, she became the best version of herself..."

"What is this?" I asked.

"It's what I've been working on. It's about you. Sort of."

I flipped through the pages to see how many of them there were: forty-seven.

"You wrote a forty-seven-page story about me?" I started to choke up again. And panic. Wondering what Drew knew, or thought he knew, about me that could be worth forty-seven pages.

"It's not just one long story; it's a collection of a few of them. I started it with one I wrote when your dad left, which led to another, and then another. It's a little embarrassing, which is why I never told you that this is what I was doing. I just started thinking a lot about you and your dad, what him leaving meant about him as a man, how you handled it, and what that meant about you as a girl, as a woman."

A woman? I wasn't a woman; I was just a kid. A girl, a chick.

I had never thought of myself as a woman, and was certainly shocked by the notion that anyone else, let alone Drew, had. I started to cry. Again.

"You don't have to read it," he said. "But in light of, I don't know, everything, I wanted you to have it. I wanted you to know what you mean to me, because, for the first time, it occurred to me that you might not."

I felt exposed. "I can't believe all this time, you've been sitting up in your room, writing . . . about me."

"I love you, Alex," he said. Just like that. In such a breezy way that I was sure that he didn't mean it the way I would have meant it if I'd said it. But in a way that I understood what he meant.

And for the first time in a long time, I looked at him, really at him, not at his neck or at his nose or over his shoulder, but into his welling blue eyes, at his crumbling face, and locked my eyes on his, even though it made me nervous and self-conscious and every muscle in my face was programmed to look away. And he looked right back at me, seemingly not nervous at all, like he was totally at home there, warm, safe, and cozy, just melting in my gaze.

I fell into him, and we wrapped our arms around each other and wept on each other's shoulders and stayed there, on each other's shoulders, until the sun fell behind the clouds and the sky once and for all succumbed to gray.

I folded his story back up, put it in my pocket, and handed him another cigarette. He stood up, took my hand, and pulled me off the curb. He didn't let go of it until we walked back inside.

MOLLIE FINN

That Veronica could just go on breathing, eating, and dating fucking Drew and holding his fucking hand at his father's fucking funeral was totally ludicrous. She had done the unthinkable. She wasn't a human; she was a goddamn monster. I wanted her caged and poked and electrocuted and studied by scientists.

A month after D-day, and the Wednesday before prom, Alex and I sat at my kitchen counter after school and ate grapes from a glass bowl, which soothed me because knowing that one grape equals exactly one carb makes tracking intake and the subsequent necessary burn off extremely simple. If only all equations could be so simple. If only every action could be undone with an equal and opposite reaction.

Lately, though, my rage had been satiating my typically insatiable hunger. I didn't crave food anymore—just revenge. I was going to be in fighting form by prom. I wasn't going to let Sam think that I'd been at home wallowing and sobbing into Ben and Jerry's; fuck that and fuck him and Veronica and whatever skintight boobtastic trash can she'd be wearing that night. I hadn't eaten a real meal in two weeks. I was going to make Sam hate himself.

Alex, however, looked like shit. She sat across the black granite counter, her hair even more unbrushed and disheveled than usual, wearing her smudged, crooked glasses and a gray hooded sweatshirt with coffee stains on the sleeves. She stared blankly into the bowl of grapes, picked them off the vine one by one, and chewed with the vigor of a sedated cow.

"Alex!" I screamed at her. "What is with you lately? Snap out of it!"

"Sorry," she said. "Just thinking about stuff."

It seemed strange that she'd be so distraught about the Veronica/Sam thing, but my guess was she was more upset about what Veronica had done to Drew. I couldn't believe she hadn't told him—it took every bone in my body not to blurt it out at the funeral, but even I knew that it wasn't my call, and even if I decided I didn't give a shit, his dad's funeral was clearly not an appropriate forum. I couldn't believe he hadn't gotten wind of it, though. *Everyone* knew. Even the teachers had been talking about *why Mollie and Alex weren't sitting with Veronica anymore.*

"We need to come up with a plan. Figure out how to publicly humiliate and disgrace Veronica the way she did to me."

Alex took off her glasses and rubbed them with the bottom of her sweatshirt.

"What could we possibly do that would rectify what she's done?" she said. "We'd need to physically harm her—do something illegal."

"We could beat her up?"

Alex giggled a little. "You're going to risk a black eye before prom?"

"Good point."

"We could frame her for something?"

"Like what, like a crime? Like a murder?" My wheels started to spin.

"That would mean we'd actually have to murder someone and make it look like she did it. Are you willing to murder someone? Who would we murder?" Alex posed as she popped some more grapes in her mouth. "What if we drugged her? Slipped her some acid so she'd be tweaking out and tripping balls at prom and not know why?"

"Not mean enough," I said. "She'd take it as an excuse to get naked and dance in public."

We laughed, picturing that.

"We could roofie her," Alex said between giggles.

"We could roofie her!"

I stopped laughing.

"Yes!" she said. "We'll roofie her at the prom, and when she passes out, we'll strip her naked and plant booze and drugs and shit on her and leave her for everyone to see what a dumb, drunk whore she is."

The wheels ground to a halt.

"Alex, that's a brilliant idea...."

She crossed and uncrossed her legs and went back to picking grapes. "Veronica probably eats fucking roofies for breakfast...."

"I'll be right back," I said.

I ran upstairs and rustled through my sock drawer. In the back left corner was an antique embroidered change purse that some dumb aunt gave me for some dumb graduation from something dumb. I kept drugs in it mostly. I grabbed it and ran back downstairs, adrenaline pumping like during the slow climb of a roller coaster before the first big drop.

When I got back to the kitchen, I opened the change purse and dumped two round white pills out into my palm and showed them to Alex.

"Painkillers?" she asked. A grape skin was stuck to her front tooth.

"Roofies," I said.

And the lights behind her eyes switched back on.

"Are you kidding? Why do you have roofies?"

I popped a grape in my mouth, brushed off my kilt, re-adjusted my ponytail, and stood up straight. I debated lying to her but realized there was no point in continuing to defend Sam anymore. The jig was up. I had to be honest about what a truly vile douche he was now, which still somehow felt embar-rassing. Even though his douchiness was no longer technically my problem. I thought if I covered for him, made it look like we were the couple I knew we could look like, that everyone would see us as that perfect couple—the couple that I knew we could actually be if he would have just tried a little harder to be the guy I needed him to be instead of the guy he actually was. I'd spent so long trying to hide what a truly mean and selfish and foul person he was that I'd become a part of it; I was no better.

He'd sucked me in and down with him, and I'd legitimately forgotten that I could get out and remove myself from it at any time, that I had a choice, and I didn't have to be with him if I didn't want to be. . . . It was strange, like a Stockholm syndrome thing. I had to snap out of it; I had to stop thinking of him as a reflection upon me. But I still wasn't quite there yet.

"Apparently, a bunch of guys on the lacrosse team got them. Sam said it was a joke, but I mean, I'm sure some of them probably used them. I took Sam's, just in case he ever thought to try them on me."

Alex dropped her jaw.

"That's terrifying, Mollie," she said.

"Yeah. . ." I trailed off and brought the conversation back around to a productive place.

"So, I'm serious. We should do this." My eyes thumped with my heart, like the *National Geographic* soundtrack, that throbbing bass they play before an animal pounces, played in the back of my head.

"Mollie! I'm kidding! We're not going to date-rape Veronica."

"We're not going to rape her; we're going to roofie her, at prom, just so she passes out. We'll make sure she does it in the lobby, and we'll take her dress off and spill shit on her, just so she looks like a drunken mess and everyone will walk by and see her all passed out like she's hammered and puked on herself. It'll be hilarious."

"She could get in seriously big trouble!" Alex gnawed on her cuticles.

"Fuck her. She'll have been drinking anyway. It's not like

we're even framing her for something she didn't do. She'll get in trouble for being drunk, which she will actually be! We're just going to add a layer of public humiliation to it."

I had to admit: it was genius. Alex's pink little mouth twisted into a smirk.

"What about Drew? Drew will see that she's out of it and take her home."

"That's where you come in. You're on Drew duty. Distract him while I get her out of the room and into the lobby. He won't know where she went."

She tapped her long fingers on the counter and adjusted her glasses. She squirmed on her stool a little, crossed and uncrossed her legs.

"Alex, come on. This is brilliant. We said we needed a plan, and this is a plan. Plan on? Are you in?"

She looked at me, then out the window, twiddling her thumbs and appearing to be counting something behind her glasses. She took them off and rubbed her eyes.

"Plan on," she said, and put her hand out, her black nail polish half bitten off and chipped. I laid my hand on hers.

"You're my best friend," I told her. "You know I'd do the same for you. If anyone ever fucked you like this, I'd fucking kill them. You know that, right?"

"I know," she said.

She put her other hand on top of mine, and I put my other one on top of that one.

"Go, team."

ALEXANDRA HOLBROOK

I sat at my desk with Drew's stories, swallowing, digesting, and savoring each word for the thousandth time. Pages and pages had been written about this beautiful girl—a girl who took care of everyone she loved, who thought of others before herself, who showed no sadness, weakness, or self-pity. She exhibited strength and creativity after she was abandoned by the only man she'd ever trusted. This girl was not me; I was not like that at all! All I did was second-guess myself and feel unsure and unworthy and selfish—how did Drew not see that?

Drew had made me into this person that I wasn't. For whatever reason, he clearly saw something lacking in himself, so he invented it in me. Maybe I had done the same thing. Maybe we all do that. Maybe I had invented Drew, too....He had become this creature to me, this savior. This thing that if acquired would make me whole and make me happy—but it wasn't playing out that way. The sex that I had had with Drew hadn't changed anything. I was still miserable. He was still with Veronica.

As flattering as they were, the stories made me self-conscious, made me wonder what I was doing that made Drew see me this way. I wondered how other people saw me, where the gap was between how others thought I was and how I thought I was— and who was right and wrong? On the last page of the last story, he wrote:

I knew that one day she'd find a man who'd tell her secrets about the world and the truth about things; things that I didn't know and truths that I didn't understand yet. He'd be able to make her feel safe and taken care of, the way I felt when I was with her. And it broke my heart, because I knew I'd lose her. Because I wasn't a man, not yet, anyway. And I'd never catch up; I'd be too late, because already, she was no longer my girl, but something of a woman.

Again, that word. *Woman.* It made me uncomfortable, like I should be wearing nylon stockings and carrying compacts of pressed powder. I was only sixteen; I clearly was not a woman. Nor did I want to be—yet, anyway.

I folded Drew's stories up again and took them downstairs. I sat at the piano and stared at the keys. I started banging away, a G chord, then a C. I let my fingers walk around and didn't think much about what kind of song I was writing or why. I took the pencil off the mantle and started writing some of the notes.

This is about you, it always was, it always is

I stopped and wrote down the chord progression.

I'm not what you need, I'm just me, and just barely...

I looked at his pages again, and words swirled in my head and rhymes and rhythms, and this idea that rhythms are relations between what you believe and what you believed before, which I'd read in a book.

I kept going. I had all these words in me about how being an adult means knowing who you are, and how being a friend means seeing someone for who they really are, not just who you need them to be.

I lost hours at the piano and wrote the song in one sitting. I called it "Grow Up."

It was a ballsy move, but sometimes a day at the piano will do this to me; I'll fly on this adrenaline of creation and musical transcendence and, if only for a fleeting moment, believe that I am stronger and smarter and capable of more than I really am: I called Pete and told him that I had a new song I wanted us to learn before the prom.

VERONICA COLLINS

Mollie and Alex were a few people in front of me in the cafeteria line, so I tried to keep my eyes straight and not look at them looking at me and feel them whispering and giggling and pointing and everyone else looking and whispering and pointing and knowing that I used to be whispering and giggling and pointing with Mollie and Alex, but I wasn't now, because I was a big fat backstabbing whore. Like I couldn't hear them, like I wasn't a real person with feelings and ears who maybe had a side of the story also.

I sat down at a table by myself and heard Nikki Clayman's shrill voice a few tables over.

"They're still not talking to her," she said loudly enough that I could hear it over the clang and clatter of the cafeteria.

"Would you?" some other girl asked. I didn't look over to see who.

"Should we invite her to sit with us?" Nikki asked giddily. Like she'd be doing me some great favor. Like I needed her charity.

Then from another corner, I heard Mollie's insane cackle. It echoed through the room and resounded over my head like a thundercloud.

I couldn't take it anymore. I picked up my sandwich and walked out. I tried to appear calm and collected. Look like maybe I forgot something in my locker, or that I had an appointment I forgot about, or maybe was just done eating and was moving on with my day—not like I had lost the cold war of Harwin social scorn, or like the looks and the whispers had gotten to me and I'd been broken and humbled and would accept and acknowledge the disgrace and exile that had been passive-aggressively thrust upon me. I would not cry in the cafeteria; they didn't deserve that. I would not run out in shame and be fodder for even more gossip and conversation—I had given them plenty to work with for one semester.

I choked back the tears and weaved through the tables and out of the glass double doors on the far end of the room so that I wouldn't have to walk past our—or Alex and Mollie's—table. I felt their eyes on the back of my head, but I refused to let them burn through it and push the tears out. *Keep it together, Veronica. Let them talk. This, too, like everything else, will blow over.*

Head down, tears still at bay, I skulked through the halls until I made it outside. I gasped in the fresh air like I'd just freed myself from drowning. It was a beautiful day, a day that Mollie and Alex and I maybe would have gotten our lunches and eaten them on the steps by the art building.

Hums of children laughing and playing resonated from over by the lower school, and I found myself following the sound. Little girls, who looked like they were in second or third grade, ran around the playground in their little tunics and shiny Mary Janes jumping and squealing and smiling. I walked over to the grassy hill behind the swing set and sat down with my half-eaten sandwich, overwhelmed with warm feelings of nostalgia and extreme pangs of longing for simpler, happier times.

Alex and I had first become friends on this very playground. I had just moved from New York, and she was the first person to be even a little bit nice to me. I didn't come to Harwin until fifth grade, so groups were already pretty much solidified and cliques set and locked. Alex and Mollie ran the best one, obviously.

One day at recess, Mollie summoned me over to the seesaw. She looked me up and down and said, "You're tall—you seesaw with Alex. We're too little!" Alex looked at me and looked at Mollie, took my arm, and took me over to the seesaw at the end of the row. Not to the empty one next to Mollie's, on which she and Lily Garrison, who has since failed out of Harwin and been shunned to public school never to be heard from again, were already gleefully popping up and down in all their petite prepubescent glory.

"Mollie is so annoying," Alex said as she threw a knobby knee over her end of the seesaw. "She thinks she and Lily have this bond because they're both sixty-five pounds and don't have boobs yet."

I laughed. I was so excited to know that there was a chink in the Alex Holbrook–Mollie Finn armor, that they weren't an impenetrable force that couldn't be infiltrated. Maybe there was room for me.

"How tall are you?" she asked as we began to see up and saw down.

"I'm not sure," I said.

She said, "Let's go back-to-back."

She jumped off the contraption, sending my end plummeting to the ground. I dusted myself off, and she reached out her hand to help me up. Worn-looking friendship bracelets were stacked three inches thick up her thin arm. We stood ponytail to ponytail. She rested the flat of her hand over the tops of our heads, then spun around, keeping her hand out flat in front of her freckled face like she was saluting me.

"Looks like we're the same height," I said.

She smiled and said, "I need a tall friend! Let's be tall friends."

The young girls sang on the swing set at the bottom of the grassy hill, kicking and pumping their legs in time with one another. Two of them were perfectly in sync, gliding to and fro on beat like pendulums, while the third one, the smallest one, pumped her little legs faster, which was only slowing her down and throwing her rhythm off more.

The two synchronized ones giggled and sang a song that neither I nor the slower one knew. The little one just pumped harder and harder and, finally, caught up! I found myself strangely excited for her, proud. The three of them swung up and back as one unit, perfectly in time, and I took a satisfied bite of my sandwich.

Then the blond one said, "One...two...three!" and the first two flung themselves off the swing and landed hard on their little Mary Janed feet. They linked arms and ran off laughing, ponytails bouncing behind them, leaving the little one on the swing alone, head down, pumping her scrawny legs back and forth, having finally gotten the rhythm down.

Part 6

THE PROM

ALEXANDRA HOLBROOK

I stood in my prom dress and stared at myself in the mirror. I stared so long that I didn't even recognize myself by the time I blinked. I stood there in that black dress with all that eyeliner, hair straight and silky, ready for my drummer quasi-boyfriend to take me where, as I understood it, the plan was to drug my friend and then go on to perform in front of hundreds of my peers, one of whom was Drew, my best friend, life's obsession, and now the holder of my virginity, writer of my memoirs, and intimately invested in a song I was about to sing onstage. If I told the Alex from a year ago that she'd be standing here now, she'd never have believed me.

At this point, I wasn't sure Mollie would actually go through with the roofie thing. I wasn't sure if we had actually worked out the technical physical logistics of this plan or if we'd been kidding, but I went along with it, hoping that she'd decide that we were kidding. And I understood where this twisted plan came from. I understood jealousy and pride and the idea of revenge—the notion that causing someone else pain would somehow soothe your own. Even if I knew it wasn't true, I still understood the impulse. Mostly, I understood that

Mollie needed to feel like she could fix it, take control of what she felt had just happened unfairly to her. So I said okay and went along with it, like I was on board, because even if I wasn't in real actuality, I was in theory. Even though I understood why Veronica'd done what she'd done, too.

And honestly, I had other things on my mind.

And I was mad at Veronica, too—irrationally, but I was. I also wanted to see her suffer. I knew she didn't deserve it, but that didn't matter. I didn't deserve to suffer, either, but I was. I didn't deserve to feel the way I felt every time she and Drew made out in front of me, every time she said his name, every time I thought about the two of them touching or fucking or posing for a prom picture—but I did, and whether she did it on purpose or not, it was her fault.

But, more important than all of that, I was about to get up and sing in front of all of Harwin for the first time. I'd sung in front of many of them before, but there was something different about this concentrated audience. Word had spread about me and the Cunning Runts and word around town was that we were good, that I was good, and I knew Harwin girls and knew that meant that two hundred finely tuned, highly critical ears and eyes would be on high alert, scanning me and my performance for signs of imperfection to exploit. They all desperately wanted me to fail. To believe that no one had anything that they didn't and that this band was just another pathetic cry for attention, from another pathetic, unspecial, insecure girl who was no better than them or a threat to them in any way. And in some ways, I feared it was, and that I'd be exposed.

And I would be, in a way: in a way that I'd fully signed up for. I wondered if they'd know that "Grow Up" was about Drew. If Veronica would know. Drew would definitely know. Would he be mad? Flattered? The song was really a response to his stories, a reaction, not a critique of it, and I was worried he wouldn't take it that way. It was going to be like we were having an actual conversation via our art, and that was kind of cool. I hoped he'd get that. But maybe he wouldn't. Maybe I'd misinterpreted his stories. Maybe he'd hate the song, and hate me, and I'd have to be okay with that. I made this choice to put it all out there, and fuck it, I had to stand behind it now.

I had never been the type to put myself in a position where people had an opportunity to make judgments about me or form opinions. That was Mollie and Veronica's job. They seemed to like their names being on the tips of everyone's tongues, to have eyes on them and buzz and mystique surrounding them. I did not. I stayed neutral, on the sidelines, bit my tongue, and never stirred the pot or made a scene, because I never wanted to give anyone ammo to—god forbid—not like me. Or not think I was cool. But all of a sudden, I'd made all these choices, subjective choices, and it was out there for all the public to judge whether they'd been right or wrong.

What the hell was I thinking? Like one day, just like that, I decided that I didn't care what people thought. Maybe I wanted so badly to be someone who didn't care what people thought, that if I just acted like I was someone who didn't, then maybe eventually I would become said person. Had it worked?

Sort of.

It had to have, because I'd gone too far to turn back now. What was done had been done, what was said had been said. And I was still alive; I was still me. The band, the music, was about making *me* feel good, and if people didn't like it, they could walk away, and it made no difference. Drew or anyone. *You don't do this for them; you do it for you. You do it for you.* I repeated this to myself. Over and over. Fuck everyone.

There was a knock on my door, and I told whoever it was to come in.

"You wanna go in five?" Josh said. He was all squeaky fresh in his new tux and haircut.

"Yeah, five minutes," I said.

"Nice dress, Morticia," he said.

I gave him the finger.

"So, are you guys gonna be bitches to Veronica tonight, or are you going to cut her a break?"

"Cut her a break! She slept with Mollie's boyfriend!"

He plopped down on my bed and cracked his knuckles. "Like you didn't do the same thing to her."

He knew?

"How did you..."

"I didn't really," he said. "I came home from Veronica's that day and heard him in your room, and I've seen how you've been acting lately, and I put two and two together...."

"Am I a horrible person?" I asked, and I sat down next to him.

"You're all horrible," he said. "Girls are horrible. I think that's normal. I think that's why you're all friends."

I laughed a little.

"So what now?" he said. "Is this a huge secret that we're never to speak of again, or are you going to tell Veronica?"

I dropped my shoulders and exhaled in complete and utter relief. "I don't know!" I said. "It feels so weird now. Everything is different, yet nothing is . . . I'm so confused."

It felt so good to talk about it out loud. I wanted to unload everything on him, give him every gory detail, know what he thought. If what happened was normal, if sex was always going to be this complicated. Figure out if he still thought I was his cool, complicated big sister, or if he all of a sudden felt sorry for me. . . .

"He's probably pretty confused, too," he said. "He's been through a lot in the last few weeks, maybe give the kid a minute to catch his breath."

"Yeah . . . ," I said. "But, Josh, you don't understand. It was so intense. . . ."

"Yeah, I don't really need the details," he said. "I'm your brother, gross."

I laughed a little again. "Sorry," I said, catching his eye in the mirror.

"But you're okay, right?" he asked, holding my gaze.

"I'm okay," I said. And I went back to fidgeting with my dress.

He got up and brushed off his pants. "You almost ready to go?"

"Two minutes."

He looked handsome in his tux, all grown-up-like. I felt better going into the night knowing that he would be there. So much had changed—there were so many things up in the air and different than they used to be, that were complicated and shady and that had gotten lost or forgotten or out of control. But not Josh; he was still there, and our relationship was the same, no matter how horrible or different I allowed myself to become.

I slapped my cheeks and straightened the dress. I told the strange-looking girl in the mirror to have fun, to fuck it all, to focus on the music and her cute date, the fact that she even had a date, and ignore her pounding chest and the uncertainty of her relationships and the looming threat of public humiliation. I told her not to worry about her psychotic best friend and her demonic plans. I even told her she looked beautiful, and I never tell her that.

MOLLIE FINN

The night of the prom was gray and windy and annoyingly cold. Even though I hated Sam, even though he was the amoeba on the scum of the bottom of the shower drain, I couldn't believe we weren't going to the prom together. I'd been excited about the prom with Sam for two years. Since the moment we started dating—before that even. We were always our best us at these events. He looked great in a tux, and we always looked good together in the pictures, the right height difference, complementary coloring, and all that. His prom the year before was probably the best night of our entire relationship. We got drunk in the limo with his friends and all their cute blond girlfriends and got a room at the hotel and stayed awake all night hooking up and taking bubble baths. I remembered thinking how lucky I was, that this was my life, that out of all the girls in all the schools, I got to take bubble baths and prom pictures with Sam Fuchs. But it was all gone now, the pictures, the bubble baths, the envious eyes. I was going to the prom with Josh Holbrook. Fucking kill me. Alex's overgrown little brother offered to take me to the prom at the last minute, and I said yes, because I had to go and couldn't go alone. How the mighty had fallen...

But I kept my eye on the prize. This prom wasn't just a dance: it was a mission. I pictured myself in a James Bond montage, carefully zipping my red dress, clasping my bracelets just so, and strategically placing the pills in my bra. I fixed my hair in a slick low bun, in a way that made me look severe and dangerous. If I'd had a gun, I'd have strapped it to the inside of my garter. If I'd had a garter, which I sincerely wished I did. I stood in front of the mirror and slid my red nails over my red dress and felt hot and tight and not fat or anxious, for the first time maybe in my life. I felt sexy and powerful—like I'd want to fuck me if I were Sam.

I heard that Stephanie Black had asked Sam to the prom at the last minute. What a whore. She hated me, because she was the *hot senior* and she and Sam dated in eighth grade. She always flirted with him and gave me dirty looks but kissed my ass while we were dating. I wondered if they'd been fucking behind my back, too. My stomach twisted again, but I was determined to stay focused and ardent. I was not going to fall apart at this prom. I started out on top, and I was going to come out on top, too, goddamn it. I had Alex and Jesus on my side.

The pre-party was at my house and awkward as all hell. Alex and Josh came first. She looked awesome, and thin, like she hadn't eaten in weeks, either. Bitch. Her dress was really simple, long, black, strapless, typical neutral, don't-look-at-me Alex, but with a new feminine, sexier kick. I could tell she thought she looked good, even though she told me she felt like *an obese Morticia Addams* when I told her she looked hot. It was like she went out of her way to make you forget or talk you out of how pretty she really is. Josh handed me a corsage. I smiled and put the box in the kitchen. A corsage. Seriously? Sam would have known better.

Fernando came shortly after her, looking cute and Latin, and then our B-list friends. I wondered why he hadn't picked Alex up. He handed her white lilies, and I wondered if that was a lucky guess or if he really knew her well enough to know that she had a thing with white flowers. They kissed, and he stood with his arm around her. She looked uncomfortable having it there, but they looked cute together. Drew showed up next, looking nice, but like he was wearing his dad's tux.

Veronica, of course, was the last to arrive. I wasn't sure she even would at all, but the limo was on her credit card, and if she decided not to share a limo with us, she would have had to tell Drew why, so bully for her for throwing herself willingly into the lion's den. And I guess she knew what time to show up, because no one had taken her off the e-mail chain. She rolled up busting out of some corseted animal-print hooker nonsense. It was probably expensive, but with her South Philly fucking updo and tits hanging out, she looked like she could have been working Las Vegas Boulevard, per usual.

She gave me a hug and told me she loved my dress. I accepted the hug with limp arms, gave her a toothless smile, and walked away. We hadn't spoken since I found out. Not a word. Just dirty looks in the hallway. I even asked Nikki Clayman to switch lab partners with me. I knew Veronica knew I knew, and I couldn't believe she hadn't at least tried to apologize. I would have told her to go fuck herself, but she could have tried.

The moms were all running around taking pictures. All the girls, all the boys. Alex and Drew, me and Josh, Alex and Fernando, Fernando and Drew and Josh, Drew and Veronica, other rando girls and their rando dates in various combinations, and so on and so on. I wanted to rip my teeth out. I heaved at the thought of Sam posing with Stephanie, at the thought of her college dorm room next year plastered with pictures of him holding her and smiling with her like she'd been the one sucking his smelly balls for the last two years.

The limo was comically quiet. We just passed around the bottles of vodka and champagne and took long, self-loathing chugs. Fernando held Alex's hand and Drew put his arm around Veronica, who attempted to make jokes about getting wasted and occasionally did a little tit shake to whatever Kesha song was playing on the radio. Josh gave up trying to talk to me or make me laugh after the pre-party, which I appreciated. He just leaned to his left and talked to Drew about video games or rap music or something. Clearly, I wasn't listening. I didn't care.

Alex and I exchanged one more conspiratorial glance before we exited the limo. We walked into the hotel and the chaperones were all lined up to shake our hands and smell our breath for alcohol. Morons.

"Hello, Mollie," Mr. Boardman said, shaking my hand with his clammy paw. "And who is your escort this evening?"

"This is Josh Holbrook of the Crawford School for Boys," I said, pulse ticking like a time bomb.

"Pleasure to meet you, sir," Josh said.

"Are you perchance related to Miss Alexandra Holbrook?" Mr. Boardman asked. I wanted to die. He now knew I couldn't get a real prom date, fucking perfect.

I pretended like I hadn't heard him and yanked Josh's arm onward.

We made our way through the hotel lobby, which was mauve and corporate and filled with dusty pink flowers, into the elevator, and up to the ballroom. The room didn't look half bad, hats off to the decoration committee, which I think I was technically on, despite having never been to a meeting. The theme was some sort of Japanese Garden/Orient Express something, so there were chintzy lanterns and fans and kimonos and bamboo shoots strewn about the room. The tablecloths were red, and the centerpieces were fake orchids with fake dragonflies swarming them. Cute. Cheap, but cute. Kinda like Veronica.

The DJ was already playing, and people were on the dance floor. It's always strange to see your classmates, who you're used to seeing in kilts and ratty sweaters, all dressed up. Some of the girls really looked surprisingly beautiful, and some I just wanted to tell to go home, put on sweatpants, and get back to playing field hockey.

I spotted Sam sitting next to Steph. I could see from across the room that he was already drunk. I wondered if he'd try to talk to me, if I'd try to talk to him. If he'd be sweet, ask me to dance, and apologize or if he'd be an asshole, totally ignore me, and be all over Steph the whole night. You never knew with Sam; it could always go either way.

We sat down at a table, and everyone threw in their two cents about the decor or someone's dress or who was here with whom or how dense the teachers must be to think that no one was drinking. Alex and Fernando were getting psyched to meet the ginger hobbit twins and set up with the band.

Veronica and Drew were close-talking, and I needed her to get up so I could slip the pill in her punch, which she'd already spiked with vodka. Perfect.

Good old Alex asked Drew if he'd help with the equipment. Obviously, he obliged. Obviously, Veronica said she'd help, too, because obviously she wasn't going to be left alone at the table with me. I told Josh to go with them.

And that was it. It was time.

I stared at her glass of punch and wondered if maybe this was a stupid idea. If maybe she could really get sick from these drugs or if she could somehow end up in the hospital and it could all end up being traced back to me. If maybe I should try to talk to her first, see what she could possibly have to say in her own defense. If I could really do this to someone, really physically hurt someone, even though she really emotionally hurt me. Maybe it wasn't the same. Maybe this was going too far....

The night I lost my virginity, I ran right over to Veronica's afterward. We ate cookies and drank champagne, and I told her that I felt different. That I felt this raw little pinch inside me, and I asked her if that would always be there now. She said it would go away, and that she was really proud of me and excited for me. She asked if it hurt, and I told her that it did. She said her first time didn't hurt at all, that she felt like there was something wrong with her, because she barely felt anything. I told her she was lucky. That was the thing about her, that she didn't feel anything—nothing ever affected her, she maintained an even keel all the time. No matter what was going on around her, her parents, boys, rumors, trouble, whatever. She never got mad and she never got depressed or hurt. Never got down on herself. She didn't care what people thought or said. She was made fun of, rejected constantly, but it didn't matter. She still walked around like she was the shit, and I'm pretty sure she genuinely believed that she was...thus actually making it sort of true. How did she pull that off? How could a person and her entire sense of self-esteem be completely isolated like that? I was like a ripe peach, eternally bruised by a stiff breeze. It wasn't fair, and it was frustrating, but it was impressive. And made me sort of understand how the Sam thing could have happened— because she just didn't think. She just didn't understand how something like that could affect someone else because she was never affected by anything. It didn't excuse it, but it somehow made me take it slightly less personally. It wasn't a move to hurt me, like the move I was about to make. Maybe this wasn't an eye for an eye, maybe I was taking this too far....

I looked over at Sam. He was ripping leaves off the centerpieces and throwing them at people at his table. He grabbed Steph and spun her around, and I watched as the two of them giggled and convulsed. And then he kissed her. A wet, sloppy one. Just for a minute. No tongue. He may as well have punched me in the throat.

Fuck him.

And fuck Veronica.

I reached into my cleavage and pulled out the small sack of pills. I slid Veronica's plastic punch cup toward me and dropped in one pill. It fizzed and bubbled and disintegrated immediately. I stirred it with my finger. I pushed the glass back toward her seat and made sure to put it right next to her purse so that there was no confusion as to which drink was hers.

VERONICA COLLINS

I found myself wishing Mollie would just be mean to me. Not that she was being nice, but a dig, an insult, or a punch in the face would have at least showed me that she still felt something toward me, even if it was anger. I could work with anger—anger meant she still cared. When we were friends, she was mean and I couldn't stand it. I resented her, was hurt by her stupid comments, and fucked her boyfriend to show her that she could make as many backhanded remarks as she wanted and she still had nothing on me. But now that she wasn't speaking to me, I ached for a snide comment about my hair, a loaded question about who made my shoes, how much they cost, or if I knew that some D-list celebrity had been put on a worst-dressed list for wearing them. Anything of this nature would have let me know that she was still Mollie, I was still Veronica, and there was still something between us. But nothing. Her wilted hug and *you look pretty* was like a poisoned arrow through my chest.

I think I thought that going to the prom with them would somehow jolt us back into being us again. Even though we weren't talking right now, it was the *PROM*, and this was bigger and more important than any little squabble we'd had, and we'd all know that and things would snap back into perspective. Also, not going to the prom with them would have required me to tell Drew why we weren't going to the prom with our best friends, and I wasn't ready to do that yet. I needed to smooth things over with the girls (and also get a little distance behind the whole dad dying thing) before I could let Drew go. Because then I'd really be all alone. Even though being with Drew like this, under this web of lies, made me feel lonelier than I'd ever felt in a lifetime of feeling alone.

The hotel looked amazing. The whole thing was set up like a Japanese tea garden. Cute little Asian stuff everywhere. I hoped Harwin was classy enough to spring for sushi. I couldn't believe this was actually our prom. We'd actually made it. We'd been looking forward to it for so long. And it could have been so beautiful.

As soon as Drew got up to help Alex and Fernando with the band stuff, I followed, because there was no way I'd be left sitting at that table alone with Mollie. I did want to talk to her, but not there, not then, not like that, and not while she looked so intense with her devil eyes in her scary red dress. We went back through some secret service hallway behind where the stage was set up, which I thought was pretty badass. In all the hotels I'd been to, I never knew hotels had secret passageways like that. There were laundry bins and kitchen supplies and millions of housekeeping carts filled with soap and shower caps and all sorts of fun hotel stuff. We got to a loading dock. The twins stood there by the van straightening each other's ties.

"You're all too late. Everything is done."

"Fuck," Alex said. "I'm sorry. I'm a shitty bandmate."

"We set up everything this afternoon while you were busy primping. You look very pretty, by the way," Ned said, to her, I presumed.

She blushed. "I'm going to throw up, I'm so nervous," she said.

"Oh, stop," Drew chimed in, patting her back. "You're practically a pro now."

I smiled and took Drew's arm, not sure why I was there or what I was supposed to do to help, but trying not to look as awkwardly useless as I felt.

"Veronica, you look hot, too."

I smiled and said thanks.

"Nando, I got the guitar, just grab the set list and I think we're good to go," Pete said. I think it was Pete, the taller one who talked less.

"Can I help?" Drew asked, cracking his knuckles, trying, it seemed, to act cool in front of these guys.

"We're all good, bro, gonna have a quick band meeting before we go in," Fernando said, patting him on the shoulder. "See you out there."

I held the crux of Drew's elbow as we made our way back through the service hallway to the lobby.

"God, it's cool back here," I said. "Who knew hotels had all these secret back hallways and rooms and stuff?"

"I know. We should steal bellhop and maid uniforms and sneak into someone's room, pretend we're Russian spies, and take pictures with our tiny pen-phones." He squeezed my arm into his side.

"I was thinking more we'd just sneak back here and fuck later."

He laughed, a throaty laugh, and said, "That works, too."

Drew and I hadn't had sex since his dad died. I was hoping tonight would be just the fun, fancy occasion to snap him back into the mood, snap everything back, really. Mollie was still sitting at the table by herself, prodding her cell phone, when we got back.

Drew and I sat down, and he asked her what we missed; without looking up from her phone, she said, "Drunk seniors being assholes."

"Wanna dance, baby?" I asked Drew.

"I don't think I'm drunk enough," he said.

The band came out and introduced themselves. Everyone cheered. It was still strange seeing Alex up there with a mic in her hand. So poised, so comfortable, so much older than she was standing on the ground next to me. God, what I wouldn't give to have a voice like hers and to be able to get up in front of all these people and make them love me for it. Love me for actually being good at something, something special, something particularly mine, and not just something anyone could be good at, like throwing parties or having big boobs.

Maybe one day someone would, though. In all the time I'd spent being alone and trying to distract myself from the fact that I was alone, I realized that I wasn't such bad company. That I did just fine entertaining myself, and one day, maybe there'd be someone who'd find me entertaining, too. And as hard as I tried to make it true, that person just didn't seem to be Drew.

He sat next to me, with his hand on my thigh, staring at Alex onstage, and I just wanted to tell him that it was fine. He didn't have to keep his hand on me, that he could let go and I'd be fine. Drew and I were never really supposed to be together, I could feel it. It was a nice thought that someone like him would be into someone like me, whatever *someone like me* even meant anymore, because I felt that definition rapidly changing. Whatever it was, I knew it had to be a more important factor in deciding who I dated than it had been. I'd been so caught up in making sure that he was into me that I forgot to think about whether I was even into him, or if that was even something I was allowed to consider. I'd tried so hard to make it work with him, but it was never really about me or about him, it was just about being with someone, noticed, loved by someone—anyone. And he had noticed me, and stuck around, and that was something, right? It just wasn't everything. Clearly.

That distance that I thought I could fill with sex, with watching his movies and listening to his music, and just being next to him, was never going to go away. He was never going to look at me the way he looked at Alex, and I was never going to care as much as I knew I was supposed to. I looked at Mollie seething across the table, her face tight and skin on fire, and I just wanted to reach out and hug her and tell her that I was sorry, and that I was wrong. About everything.

I accidentally made eye contact with Sam, who winked at

me. I quickly turned away, nudged Drew, and poured some vodka from my flask into his punch. He gave me a wink and hooted and hollered for the band. I poured some more into my own, too, and gulped it down. I knew I had to get drunker faster if there was any hope of me having any fun at all at this prom.

Alex started singing the song I liked, the one about not always being able to get what you want.

And that's the last thing I remember.

MOLLIE FINN

watched her guzzle the punch. I couldn't believe we'd—
I'd—really done this. Up until that exact moment, I'd maybe
thought we were half-joking. I started to get that I-know-I-
just-did-something-really-wrong-I'm-fucked-if-I-get-caught
pressure in my chest.

Josh asked if I wanted to dance when Alex's band started,
and I said sure, because at this point, all I had to do was wait
and not look like I was waiting. I went up to the dance floor and
bobbed my head and watched Alex, eyes closed, singing and
swaying like no one was watching—but everyone was. Onstage
Alex and offstage Alex were slowly meshing into the same person; I could see it in the way she stood and hear it in her voice.
No costume, no character anymore. It occurred to me that I was
proud of her, an emotion I was not entirely familiar with. Raging envy, yes. But pride? The stuff of fairy tales. But I really was
excited for her; she seemed happy. And I was excited that I got
to be this girl's best friend, and that I finally felt like that again
for the first time in a while. Finally, I felt like we were back
on the same team. Maybe she'd be famous one day. Maybe I
seemed cooler because I was friends with the girl in the band.

"Alex has gotten so good!" Josh screamed to me between awkward shuffles of his feet.

"I know!" I screamed back. "They all have!"

We both laughed, and I gave in to his silly shuffles and danced around with him. I even let him take my hands and twirl me once or twice.

"Thanks for taking me to the prom, Josh. You're always saving me, it seems."

He smiled and twirled me again.

"Thanks for letting me," he said.

I glanced back at the table; Drew and Veronica were making out. I rolled my eyes and looked up at Alex, who also seemed to notice and seemed to be singing angrily at them as if to tell them to knock it off and fucking pay attention to their fucking friend singing her fucking heart out onstage.

Sam was three feet behind me on the dance floor; I felt him in my orbit—his body mass created waves of pressure that dented everything within a ten-foot radius. We'd been there maybe an hour, and already his shirt was untucked and his tie was around his head. He caught me looking at him.

He smiled and waved. I waved back and gave him the finger.

He bopped over to me and Josh smiling his shit-eating smile and hugged me from the side. His dress shirt was moist with sweat, and I tried not to let the smell of Jack Daniel's, cigarettes, and Hugo Boss evoke any kind of warm emotion.

"So you're still mad at me?" He slurred his words.

"Go away."

"Ouch" was his response.

"You came with Steph Black, huh? Feeling nostalgic for middle school?"

"She asked me. You know I can't turn down a party. And I knew I'd see you. I hoped maybe you'd talk to me."

The music and the kids pounded around us, circled and knocked us, jarring our conversation. I looked into his sweaty face, into those electric blue eyes I'd melted for so many times. I so easily could have said fuck it, hugged him, kissed him, started dancing our little dance, enjoyed the rest of the night, and forgotten everything. Then I looked at Alex up there by herself singing in front of everyone. I touched his clammy face and that familiar *make him love you, don't let him leave you* panic feeling started to set in, that feeling that I had previously called love.

"Fuck you," I said.

"Whatever. Have fun with Josh Holbrook. You two look cute together...."

Josh waved at Sam, a small, polite acknowledging wave that also dismissed him and implied a *good-bye, you're leaving.*

"You like my sloppy seconds, Little Holbrook? How's my dick taste?"

Josh just laughed and shook his head. He went to take a step toward Sam, but I put my arm out as a barricade and he halted. I wasn't going to let Josh get involved—he didn't deserve this. He didn't deserve Sam. He was a good person.

I said, "Your dick tastes like the shit you stick it in, Sam. Leave us the fuck alone."

"Well, if my dick tastes like shit, it's because it was in your ass, Mollie," he said.

I wanted to punch him, but I just blew a kiss in the air and flipped him off as Steph Black yanked him back to their table.

"Are you okay?" Josh asked, putting a comforting hand lightly on my back.

The tears clumped in the back of my throat, but I was okay. I nodded, and then the music stopped.

"Thanks, everyone! We're gonna take five!" Alex looked right at me and jerked her head toward Drew and Veronica.

It was time.

Alex and I beelined for the table. Drew stood up to hug her when we got there.

"You..." He paused. And then he said nothing. He just hugged her again, she smiled and mouthed *thank you*, and he held her shoulders for a little longer than normal.

"Come outside for a smoke?" she said.

"Veronica is really hammered," he said. "I hate to say this, but I think we may need to get her out of here."

Veronica sat in her chair, but barely. Her eyes were practically crossed and filled with water, and her mouth gaped open. She rested the weight of her bobblehead on her hand, which seemed to be slowly crumbling under the pressure.

My heart rate sped up again. I had a line; what was my line...?

"Oh, she's fine. It's Veronica—when is she not inappropriately hammered? I'll take her to the bathroom, and we'll get her shit together."

Drew shrugged, and they scurried out to the terrace, where people were smoking. I looked at Veronica, glaring at me with empty glassy eyes.

I bent down, put her arm over my shoulder, and hoisted her up to a standing position. She was heavier than I thought she'd be, like a bony sandbag. She could barely walk, and her breath was shallow. Had I given her too much? Was she too thin to handle this? How bad were these drugs? I started to panic a little, wondering why I didn't do more research. But it was too late. I'd committed to this and was going to follow through. I always followed through.

I looked around. Mr. Boardman was the only chaperone in eyesight and, obviously, he was hovering by the food, so I went out the side door by the stage, which meant I had to get by the dance floor. There were some whispers from the people we passed, but nothing any more suspicious than *Oh, there's ol' drunken Veronica again.*

"Whurrwehgoin?" Her tongue was thick. I knew she'd be out in a minute. I had to get her to the lobby while she could still (sort of) walk.

"Outside," I said, and got her out the side door and into the hallway. There was no one there, thank god. I got her to an elevator. We got in, and I looked at us in the mirror, her arm around me, her face contorted into a sheepish, oblivious smile. There were about a thousand pictures of the two of us like this: she, a mess, tits out, drunkenly smiling, me, eyes wide, trying to stand up straight, smile too big, trying to look together for the camera.

The doors opened to the lobby, which was empty. I dropped her onto a sofa, and she did the embarrassing tits out/crotch flash thing all on her own. I took one shoe off, just for effect, and mussed up her hair a little more. I'd forgotten the drink to spill on her and looked around for something to dirty her with. There was a plant. I picked up some dirt and smudged it on her face and dress. I debated turning her over and rubbing it in her ass to make it look like she shat herself, but for some reason decided *that* would be going too far.

I heard people coming, brushed off my hands, stood back, and admired my work. She just lay there on her back, mouth open, legs apart, covered in dirt. I started to wonder if maybe this trick wasn't even mean enough. I'd seen her in this condition on any rowdy Saturday night. This wasn't extreme. This wasn't her demise. This was just fucking hilarious.

ALEXANDRA HOLBROOK

Everything, all of it, Mollie, Drew, Fernando, roofies, sex, it all went quiet when we got onstage. I'd been so nervous, so worried about what people would think, what would happen with Drew and Veronica and Mollie and Fernando, been so prepared to throw up on someone's face, cry in public, spontaneously combust before I even got to the hotel, but once I got onstage, I felt better. Singing, playing, felt better than sitting, thinking. All that unfocused anxiety became one noise, a noise that once I made, I realized I really didn't care if anyone liked. I sang the songs, watched everyone dance, and gave in. Finally.

And Drew smiled when I sang "Grow Up." He knew. He understood.

And then Veronica's limbs went limp, and her eyes went dark. I saw it happen from the stage halfway across the room, and I got scared again.

We were actually going through with this. I was in awe of Mollie's strength. This is why she got boyfriends and I didn't. When she decided she wanted something, she threw caution to the wind to make it happen. No fear. She'd see this through to the end; she always did. I should have known. But now, everything had to go exactly as planned or we'd be royally fucked. I wanted to run, but I checked myself into gear. Mollie was counting on me.

I asked Drew to come smoke with me as planned and wondered if the teachers cared, if we'd all get in trouble because we were smoking at a school event, or if they were just choosing to ignore us and saving their energy prowling for scents of underage drinking.

"Do you want my jacket?" he asked as we made our way to the ledge of the balcony.

We were on the top floor of the hotel, and the terrace outside the ballroom was windy. The bridges, buildings, and Boathouse Row were lit up across the river, and glowing Matchbox cars puttered around hundreds of feet below. Being up so high, I felt wobbly, like we could tip over and crash like a Jenga tower.

People told me how good the band was, how great I sounded, and I smiled politely and thanked them and wondered what they *really* thought, what the whispers were saying out of earshot. The wind cut through the silk lining of Drew's jacket and sent sharp goose bumps up my bare back. I reached into the pocket and took out a pack of Camels and a lighter. I lit one and handed it to him, then lit the other for myself.

"So, we did okay?" I asked. My heart sprinted thinking about what in god's name Mollie could be doing with Veronica's flaccid body and how she was managing to get her to the lobby without anyone noticing. I tried to stay cool and calm and be normal in front of Drew. Normal with Drew, like I even knew what that meant anymore.

"You're awesome. Get over it," he said. "Every girl in here wants to be you right now."

That was hard to imagine.

"Did you like the song?" I asked.

"I loved the song—" he started.

"Holbrook!" a familiar, slobbering voice hollered from somewhere noisy behind me. It was Sam, pummeling through the band of smokers in my direction.

"Dude, can I have a smoke?" he asked, his face about an inch from mine, reeking of sweat and whiskey.

"They're Drew's," I said, and turned my back to him.

"Hey, homo," he said, turning to Drew, backhanding him in the chest, "can I have a fucking stog?"

Drew coughed up the air that Sam had knocked out of him and nodded.

I furrowed my eyebrows in disgust.

"How about you ask fucking nicely?" I couldn't believe I'd actually talked to Sam, talked to anyone, like that. I never talked to anyone like that. It's like I was drunk, but I wasn't.

"What, Holbrook? You think you're tough, because you're a fucking rock star now?" Sam said, snatching the pack from my hand. "Better watch out. You're next, ya know. Gotta complete the trifecta."

He smiled, reached around me into Drew's coat pocket,

and rummaged around for a lighter, touching my leg, which, even through the silk coat lining, turned my stomach. I pushed him back, but he lunged at me, thrusting both hands into both pockets this time.

Drew grabbed his thick shoulder and pulled him off.

"Chill," he said.

He stood in front of me and faced Sam, then pushed him back one more time and stood like a tower between us. I prayed Sam would walk away before he said anything else. I begged, pleaded with every god I didn't believe in, to let this be the end of this conversation; but we didn't deserve that.

"Or what?" Sam snapped back, and poked Drew in the shoulder. He fell back into me, and I lost my balance in my heels and almost fell over the railing. "I already fucked one of your girlfriends. Now you're not gonna let me take a crack at the other one?"

"What the fuck are you talking about?"

Drew stood up straight against Sam. He was much taller, which was easy to forget. He hovered over Sam's head and peered down his long nose into Sam's wet, spiteful eyes.

Sam cackled. "Dude, tell me you know."

"Know what?"

I lost my breath and swallowed hard; an already bad night was about to get a lot worse.

Sam stepped back and bent over laughing, his thick sandy hair shaking as he convulsed and his eyes glowing brighter with each burst.

"She didn't tell you?" He pointed at me. "She didn't tell

you I fucked Veronica? Dude, why did you think Mollie and I broke up?"

Drew spun around and glared at me. I hid my face in my hands and shook my head.

"Is that true?" he asked.

I just stood there with my face in my hands, squeezing my eyes closed, hoping that when I opened them I would have traveled through time and not be here right now.

"Where the fuck is Veronica?" It was a tone I'd never heard Drew use with me, or anyone.

"I don't know," I said, eyes still closed.

He pushed Sam, grabbed my wrist, and pulled me back inside. He said nothing, just weaved through the people into the ballroom, dragging me along like a short-legged, disobedient child.

He spotted Mollie.

"Where is Veronica?" he asked her. Mollie's face lit up, not knowing the turn this quest had taken, thinking our plan was still on course and that we were all about to boil over laughing about silly, drunken, passed-out Veronica. I stood an arm's length behind Drew, trying desperately to tell her with just my eyes that this situation had suffered an unforeseen complication.

She looked at me, confused. I looked at her and mouthed SAM, gesturing outside, and her face darkened and she bit her thumbnail.

"Maybe she's in the lobby?" She gulped.

Drew marched past the elevator and galloped down the stairs, the two of us tailing behind, trying to keep his pace.

The lobby was empty when we got there.

I looked at Mollie, confused. The pink drained from her face and the white from her eyes. She looked around, and I sensed panic growing in her, that something was not right.

"Sh-she," she stammered, "she was right here, on this couch, when I left her."

She looked at me, shaking her head, throwing her palms to the sky, mouthing *I LEFT HER HERE* between frantic shakes of her head.

"Check the bathroom," Drew ordered me.

Mollie and I ran into the bathroom by the lobby, disoriented by the overwhelming stench of lavender and Windex. We screamed Veronica's name and looked under all the stalls, but she wasn't there.

"I left her right there! Oh my god." Her shoulders, then her head, then her whole body, started to shake.

"She can't have gone too far," I said, feeling the water rise in my own eyes. "She could barely walk."

Tears started to roll down Mollie's cheeks, drawing black lines down her flushed face. I grabbed her wrist, the way Drew'd grabbed mine, and led her out of the bathroom. I marched up to the bellhop desk and asked if they'd seen a girl in a leopard dress.

"Yes," the girl behind the desk said in a Southern drawl. "A man came and got her." Desiree. Her name tag said Desiree, and she was round and blond, pretty, but with sharp snaggleteeth.

"A man?" Mollie asked through sniffles.

"Yes, a man. He took her that way. She seemed pretty out of it. Don't let your teachers catch her like that."

We thanked her, grabbed Drew, and went in the direction she had pointed, toward the service entrance where we'd come in with the band equipment.

I felt a brief wave of relief. I was sure that Ned or Pete or Fernando had seen her and taken her out to the van to get her out of public view.

"Let's go in here," I said.

Drew pushed open the heavy door, and the bright, sterile service hallway stung my eyes. We walked briskly toward the van, past the maids' carts and room service trays.

"Veronica!" I screamed. "Veronica?"

I heard a knocking sound coming from down the hall. We all heard it and started toward it; it seemed to be coming from behind one of the metal doors. Drew pushed one open. It was a janitor's closet. Mollie opened one across the hall, which just upped the volume on the dull hum of washing machines.

I pushed open the next one. And there she was with Mr. Boardman.

MOLLIE FINN

"What the fuck?" Alex gasped.

Mr. Boardman dropped Veronica and looked panicked, but then composed himself. Veronica fell over and squealed.

"Getttoffff!" she yelled, and she crawled over to and curled up on a pile of dirty sheets on the ground.

Mr. Boardman just stood there, red-faced and dumbfounded. "What are you girls doing down here?" he yelled.

"What are you doing with her?" I couldn't breathe or think. My heart was racing, and my face was getting hot, like when I found out about Veronica and Sam—when something so big is happening right in front of you that you just can't even process it, it's more like watching a movie than an actual moment in your actual life. I just wanted to sit down and see what was going to happen, see the girl run or the guy get arrested. I couldn't interject myself into the scene, that would have ruined it, it was outside of what I was qualified to handle. But I had to, this wasn't a movie, this was happening, and it was largely my fault that it was happening...and what could have happened had we walked in five minutes later.

"You sick fuck," Drew said, and he lunged toward him, but Alex grabbed his wrist.

"Now hold on just a minute," Mr. Boardman said in his teacher voice. "She was passed out in the hallway. I brought her here to keep her out of trouble." He coughed and wiped his mouth. "Look, I know you girls have been drinking. I am fond of Miss Collins, and I didn't want her to get into trouble." He looked down at his belt buckle.

I couldn't tell if I was just so deranged and oversexualized that I was creating this lecherous scenario in my head. Reading into his stutters and crotch glances, when really maybe he was just being a nice guy. Or maybe my gut was telling me what was really happening here, like it told me with Sam and Veronica. If I was going to learn anything from any of this, though, it was to trust myself. I couldn't prove it, but I could feel what was about to happen, what definitely would have happened, if we hadn't burst in at the exact moment that we did. And it was fucking horrific.

He saw me look at him looking at his belt. He looked at me, looked at Drew, and just stood there steadfast, holding his ground that he had done nothing wrong. Drew stood there in a standoff with him, but Alex and I ran over to Veronica, who was sprawled out on the floor, half asleep, half awake, half dressed, half alive and half...well, barely alive.

"Girls, I'm not going to tell anyone about this, but you need to get her out of here before another less understanding member of the faculty finds you." He started for the door.

"Thank you?" Alex said, emphasizing the form of the question.

"You're welcome," he replied. Then he turned to Drew and said, "Make sure they get home okay." We all stood there befuddled, but we'd have to ask those questions later.

Alex slapped Veronica's cheeks and pulled down her dress. "What did we do, Mollie?"

Tears started to well in the back of my throat, but there was no time for that. I swallowed them. We had to get her, and ourselves, out of there, fast.

"I don't know, Lex. Let's just get her out of here. Let's get her in the band van...." My mind was working in overdrive now. I was running logistics and plans, playing out different scenarios of how we'd get her out of the building, who we'd see, and what damage we could control, and if we could trust Mr. Boardman to help us or if he was really the villain here. There was no time to panic. This was not a disaster yet, and we could prevent it from becoming one if we just worked together.

"Veronica!" she screamed. "Are you awake? Can you walk?"

Veronica batted her milky eyes and sloshed around on the ground. "Gone?" she asked. "Messter Boardman," she slurred.

We both laughed a little, despite the fact that this really wasn't funny at all. We hoisted her up.

All of a sudden, the door swung open and there stood Headmistress Cottswald, with her hands on her hips.

"Ladies," she said in her signature quasi-British accent, even though she was from Massachusetts.

We gulped but stayed frozen there, the three of us in arms.

VERONICA COLLINS

Monday morning, we sat on the old couch in Headmistress Cottswald's office awaiting our sentence. Me in the middle, Mollie to my left, and Alex to my right. None of us said anything. We just sat there, tapping our feet, Mollie biting her thumbnails, and Alex picking at her split ends.

I hadn't spoken to either of them since prom night, because we'd all been grounded and banned from our phones and computers. Well, they had. I woke up the morning after prom with the worst hangover of my life and no recollection of what had happened the night before. Like, zero. My only clue that we were in trouble was the note my mother had left on the fridge saying, *I had to change my flight to Palm Beach because you and your friends were drunk at the prom. Get it together, Veronica. Be back next week.*

When both Mollie's and Alex's phones went straight to voice mail, I'd assumed they'd been grounded, and that something happened at the end of the night where parents were called and that we were all in trouble. When Drew didn't pick up my calls, I was almost relieved, because I was too hungover to deal with him anyway. I was too hungover to sit up, to open my eyes, or to even lift a remote control, let alone have *that* conversation. I wonder if maybe I'd broken up with him in my blackout. I had no idea what I drank or took or ate that night, but that morning, it felt like nothing but knives and battery acid in my veins. My headache was eons beyond the powers of Advil, and I spent all day needing to throw up but unable to even muster the energy to heave. It was horrible, so I could only imagine what kind of trouble we were all in. But, as sad as it was, I couldn't help but be a little bit grateful and relieved that we were all in trouble together, like old times. Like when we all got in trouble for sneaking out the windows of the motel in Williamsburg on our eighth-grade field trip or for writing secret dirty codes underneath desks in the computer lab. We were all on the same side again, and it felt great to be there, on that couch with my sisters in crime.

At the beginning of the night, Mollie wasn't even talking to me, and by the end, clearly, we were all having enough fun together to feel as shitty as I did on Sunday and get us to Headmistress Cottswald's office on Monday morning. Despite being in trouble and on the doom couch, a place most girls dread and fear, there was nowhere else I'd rather have been.

Headmistress Cottswald strolled in, in her Talbots pantsuit and smudged glasses, and sat down in the antique rocking chair positioned kitty-corner from the couch. The office was still dusty gray and green like it was the last time we were all there, with the window incident, and Headmistress Cottswald still had gray roots and smudged glasses just as she'd had then.

"Girls, you know why you're here."

We all nodded. Even though I didn't.

"And you all know that the penalty for drinking at a school function is expulsion?"

We all nodded again. Or so I thought. Mollie raised her hand.

"Headmistress Cottswald?" she posed ever so meekly.

"Yes, Miss Finn?"

Tears had started to form in the corners of her eyes.

"I was not drinking." Alex snapped her head and looked at her in disbelief.

"Is that so, Miss Finn?" I sensed the sarcasm in her voice.

"No, ma'am," she said, tears freely falling now. Mollie and her goddamn crocodile tears.

"Mollie, do you think I was born yesterday?" Headmistress Cottswald asked. "I've been chaperoning this prom for eighteen years, do you really expect me to believe—"

The phone rang, and she excused herself. She greeted whoever was on the other end of the phone emphatically, looked up, and said, "I'm sorry, girls. I have to take this. Please sit quietly across the hall in Mr. Boardman's classroom, and I'll come get you in a few minutes."

The three of us filed out of her office and into Mr. Boardman's empty classroom. I sat on one of the desks, and Mollie stood across from me with her arms crossed. Alex pulled up a chair and crossed her legs.

We all sat there in silence for a moment. Alex was the first to speak.

"Molls, I'm not going to let you do this," she said.

"What do you mean you're not going to *let* me do this? You're not my mom. You don't *let* me do anything!"

"Guys," I said. I was scared to speak, and I didn't want to admit that I had no idea what was happening or where we all stood. If we were even friends again or not. I was hoping to just play along until it became obvious, but they were being so cryptic. So I spoke. "Can someone please tell me what happened on Saturday night? Clearly, we all had fun together and made up, right? Are you guys fighting now? I'm sorry, blackout city..."

Mollie looked at Alex and said, "Don't."

Alex looked at her and said, "I'm going to."

"Alex!" she screamed. "We weren't even drinking! Why should we get kicked out of school for something we didn't do?"

"What about Veronica?" she yelled back. "Should she get kicked out of school for something we did?"

"Something you did?" I asked. Now I was really confused.

"Alex, if you do this, if you fuck me on this, our friendship is over."

"Whoa!" I said. "Whatever it is can't be that big a deal, guys! If we've made it through what happened these last few months, we can make it through anything. No one's friendship is over, okay?" My eyes bounced back and forth between the two of them, trying to gauge their expressions. Alex was stern and focused, and Mollie was panicked. Alex sat up tall, and Mollie had her arms crossed over her chest. They both looked mean, tearing each other apart with their eyes, and neither one of them seemed even remotely interested or aware of me or my part in any of this, which I didn't even know at this point.

"Mollie, I'm here because of you, and I'm not doing this to Veronica anymore," Alex said.

"Don't be a cunt," Mollie said, eyes red, her voice cracking on the *unt*.

Doing this to Veronica. I took a breath. I braced myself for one of those occasional, *Oh my god, you're such an idiot, Veronica* moments that I knew was about to wash over me.

"V." Alex took a breath. "The reason you don't remember anything from Saturday..."

"Is because we fucking roofied you," Mollie wailed. She sat on the desk across from mine, snot running down her nose and her shoulders shaking.

"You what?" I laughed a little, because I honestly thought they were joking.

"We put roofies in your drink at the prom," Mollie said, calming down, catching her breath.

I said nothing. My mind was just blank; I was in a state of shock. Roofies? Those were real?

"We thought it would be a funny prank...," Alex started.

"No, we thought it would be fucking revenge, because you fucked my fucking boyfriend," Mollie finished, her hysteria slowly congealing into anger.

"The plan was to roofie you, and then display you somewhere public, so everyone would see you drunkenly passed out. Ha. Funny, right? Everything was going great, until we couldn't find you where we left you..." Alex trailed off and looked to Mollie, who sat knocking her knees together, wiping her tears.

I felt like a rabbit stranded in an open field, just waiting for gunfire from any and every direction, scared to move, scared to stay still.

"And then we found you in a laundry room with Mr. Boardman," Alex continued. Mollie smacked her forehead with her palm.

"Mr. Boardman?" I asked. Now almost laughing, almost thinking that this was a joke, that I was on some sort of hidden-camera show.

"Nothing happened," Mollie said. "He said he was trying to help you, and keep you out of trouble. But it felt sketchy to me."

I couldn't think or feel or see. I racked my brain for a memory of any of it, but it came up blank. I had no recollection of Mr. Boardman or the prom or anything. I felt like I should cry or feel something, anger, fear, disappointment, something, but I felt nothing. I just looked at the two of them sitting there, looking sorry and scared, and I felt like I was looking at two strangers. Any connection I ever felt to either one of them was gone. All this time I'd feared being left alone, but I'd always been alone, and any trust I'd put in either one of them had been a mistake. I was never their friend.

"Also," Alex said, "I had sex with Drew."

And now I laughed.

"Holy shit!" was what Mollie said.

"What the fuck!" was what I think I actually said.

"After his dad died. Right after. It was confusing, it was emotional, it only happened once. But there it is. It's all on the table."

"I can't believe you've been keeping that a secret this whole time!" Mollie screamed. "When I was pouring my heart out to you! You shady bitch."

I was as lost as ever. This was a sick joke. All that guilt I felt about Sam and Mollie, and Alex had been doing the same thing? And yet she'd still sided with Mollie and frozen me out? Drugged me? This wasn't real. These people were not real. I wanted to get out of there, to wash my hands of these two girls, this whole thing, rip my skin off, purge. And I was supposed to be the bad one? I was supposed to be the loose one and the party girl and the irresponsible one. What a joke! Finally, the tears started to come. The anger, the sadness, the disappointment. It all started to kick in. Why did it seem that my whole life operated on a ten-second delay?

All of a sudden, I remembered that we had to go back into Headmistress Cottswald's office. That somehow, after all this, we were going to have to be in trouble together, possibly get kicked out of school together. Was I going to tell on them? Was I going to turn them in? Somehow, that still felt wrong. I didn't want to deal with this that way. I didn't want to send them to jail or get them expelled. Even though I was so mad at both of them and so hurt by them, I still didn't like the idea of them being together and me being on the other side—that felt like giving them exactly what they wanted. I didn't know what I wanted to do, but I knew it involved keeping this between us, whatever *us* even meant anymore.

I tried to process, to ask the questions on my mind. Maybe there were answers.

"So you and Mollie froze me out, made me feel like shit,

like the scum of the sluttiest universe, for what happened with Sam, all the while you did the exact same thing to me?"

"I guess I never really thought of it that way. Drew was my best friend first...."

"I thought I was your best friend," said Mollie.

"We can have this all out later," Alex said. "Right now, we need to present a united front to Cottswald. Mollie, we should all just admit to being drunk."

"But I wasn't even drunk!" I yelled. The emotions were starting to stir. "You guys freakin' drugged me!"

"Please," said Mollie. "Who brought a fucking flask into the prom? You're hardly completely innocent here."

She had a point.

"I say we go in and we all admit to drinking. We all took at least one drink that night. We take responsibility for our actions and accept the consequences for once. We all fucked up. At the very least, we'll all go down together," Alex said.

"You guys don't understand," said Mollie. "My mom will kill me."

"We all have parents," Alex said. "And they'll all be pissed. At least we'll have each other in public school?"

"Oh great," I said. "Thank god I'll have you two watching my back...."

We all laughed a little, through the tears, through the settling mania. We were fucked, but it was starting to feel like us again, an us that hadn't existed all year. I almost felt like I was having fun. But we were about to get kicked out of school, and these two girls almost killed me, so I couldn't feel that. That was completely ridiculous.

"Mollie," Alex said. "Are you with us? United front?"

"Do I have a choice? Let's all go down like the depraved little bitches we are," she said.

They both looked at me. "Well, V," Alex said. "I guess our fate is in your hands now...."

It was. And I was uncomfortable holding that much power. I didn't want it. I wanted fate decided for me. If left in my hands, I would surely make some sort of mistake with it.

"I can't believe you whores drugged me," I said. "And what the hell? Mr. Boardman? What if I'd gotten raped by Mr. Boardman? Gross! And where is he in all of this? Can't we blackmail him or something to get us out of trouble?" I realized how absurd it sounded coming out of my mouth, but I was half serious.

"He's standing by the story that he was trying to get you out of trouble," Alex said. "He's not in school today. Do we hedge our bets and tell the truth about it? We can't prove anything. It's his word against ours...who are they gonna believe?"

Mollie bit her nails and wiped her eyes. "Your call, Veronica," she said.

Deep down, I knew they'd never believe me over him. Everyone knew I flirted with him, everyone saw us drinking, this story, the real story, was too crazy for anyone to believe and would just make things worse. Maybe he was just trying to do me a favor? Maybe Alex's and Mollie's dark twisted imaginations were making this more sinister than it had to be. How could *they* understand a selfless favor, right?

"I can't believe you guys roofied me," I said again.

"Honestly, I can't believe we did, either," Alex said. "I can't believe a lot of things that happened this year."

"I don't forgive you," I said.

"I don't forgive *you*, either," said Mollie.

"But we all made this mess together...." I ran my fingers through my hair and played it all out. "And it's not like I wasn't drinking...." I stood up, straightened my skirt, and fixed my bra. "And I guess we all deserve what we get. I'm in."

Alex went to give me a hug, but I brushed her aside.

I looked at Mollie, who shook her head at me, and Headmistress Cottswald knocked on the door and motioned for us to come back in. We all filed out of Mr. Boardman's room, ready to accept whatever punishment she had in store. And oddly, I was a little excited about it.

MOLLIE FINN

We didn't get kicked out of school. We got suspended for a week and banned from all school activities for the rest of the year, which was only a month, but still. No bonfires, no pep rallies, and no annual Harwin-Crawford Six Flags trip. We were sentenced to hours of community service. Literally cleaning up the school, walking around picking up trash, scrubbing windows, and scraping gum from under desks. I actually thought that Cottswald was joking when she doled this out. I could see the fucking glimmer in her eye when she came up with this plan. *Ha*, she was thinking. *I'm gonna make these spoiled little brats work.*

My parents were hysterical. My mom didn't stop crying for a week. She made me go to church *every day* after school. *Every fucking day.* Said she prayed for my soul, and that Jesus would forgive my sins. Made me say Hail Marys, in front of her, before bed. It was hell. But at least I wasn't expelled. Cottswald said that we were pillars of the Harwin community and she believed in second chances. The truth was that between V's family and mine, we paid for half the school's endowment, and there was no way that they were going to throw that out on the tiny technicality of us breaking a rule that everyone breaks. She said she respected the fact that we all came forward and accepted responsibility for our actions. But fuck that. I couldn't believe that Alex sold us out. All of a sudden she was Little Miss Righteous? After months of lying to her best friend? About something as *huge* as the fact that she and Drew had sex? I couldn't believe it. Why did she hate me so much? What had I done?

We were all on pretty serious lockdown, so it was hard to talk. We had no phones, no computers, no free time. I wanted to talk to her, but I was pissed. Alex had agreed to a plan, and then decided my fate and my future and what I was and was not obligated to accept responsibility for with no warning. She took the power away from me and gave it to Veronica. Veronica held our futures in her hands now. She could blackmail us, extort us at any moment. Didn't Alex see that? Information is power, and you never give up the power. Maybe she did understand that, though. Maybe that was why she'd kept the Drew secret. Maybe that was why she kept so many secrets, because she was playing the same game I was. And winning, at that.

Our first day back in school after the suspension was tense. We all kept our heads down and went to class. Sat in the back, didn't make much noise, and avoided one another like we'd just had a one-night stand...or a threesome on New Year's Eve. At lunch I sat at our table, but neither Alex nor Veronica showed up. Where were they? Were they not eating? Were they eating together? Were they friends now? How had this turned into everyone being mad at me? Of all of us, I was the only one who hadn't fucked someone else's boyfriend. How was I the bad guy here?

At the end of the day, I sat on the hood of Alex's car and waited for her. I saw her come out of school and slip her sunglasses on. She saw me sitting there and proceeded toward me.

"So, you wanna talk?" she asked.

"I do," I said.

"I need to get home," she said. "I'm on a serious leash."

"We all are," I said.

"Maybe tomorrow," she said. "I really can't deal with you yelling at me right now."

"Alex, I'm not going to yell at you."

She fiddled with her car keys and looked at the ground, at her untied green Converse that were still not in uniform.

"I just want to know why you decided you hate me so much. I want to know what I did to you," I said.

"Jesus Christ, I don't hate you," she said.

"You just decide to screw me over with this whole Veronica thing, and also decide not to share the biggest news in your life with me? What the fuck? I'm your best friend."

She took her sunglasses off, cleaned the lenses with the stretched-out sleeves of her sweater, and put them back on. "Mollie, the fact that you see it that way is the reason I can't deal with talking to you right now."

"That I see it what way?!" I started to choke up a little. "Tell me how I'm supposed to see it! I thought we told each other everything. We used to tell each other everything. I thought we always had each other's backs." I lost my breath, because maybe this was really the end of Mollie and Alex. Maybe it had ended a long time ago and, like with Sam, I was holding on to the illusion that as long as I made it look like everything was okay on the outside, everything would eventually, actually be okay. Was this like that? Was it the same thing?

"We do," she said, staring off onto the lacrosse field. "Well, we did. I had just fallen too deep into your hole of deceit and denial, and I needed to get out. The Veronica shit was wrong. It felt wrong for us to let her get in trouble. I'm sorry I brought you into my moral meltdown," she said. "But I think some consequences could do us all some good."

"I wish you'd talked to me about it first. We could have gotten away with it. . . . We could have had a plan."

"I guess I just decided I was done with your plans," she said.

That was a dig. I'd always thought she looked up to me, took her cues from me, but this whole band thing, her keeping the Drew thing from me, it was because she saw through me after all. She knew I was a sham. Alex, the one person I thought would always see me as the Mollie I wanted everyone to see, no longer trusted or revered me. I didn't know where to go from here. I sniffled and tried to catch her eye.

"I'm sorry," I said. I wasn't sure exactly what I was apologizing for, but I knew I needed to apologize. "I miss you," I said.

"I missed you, too," she said.

"I never went anywhere!"

"Mollie, you have not thought or talked about anything but Sam or how many calories you ate in the last three years. . . . It's always about your boyfriend, your sex life, your parents, your fat ass. Eventually, I just stopped trying to get your attention...."

I looked down at my nail polish and let what she said sink in. And tried to ignore the fact that she'd just called me fat. Had it been that bad? I searched my stomach for an argument, but I knew I didn't have one.

"So, that's what this band thing has been about?" I asked. "It wasn't about you being mad at me, more about...you just doing something for you?"

She laughed. "Yes, Mollie. As shocking as it is, not everything I do is about you."

I fought a little bit of a smile. I could feel the genuine warmth returning to the space between us. My shoulders dropped and my knuckles unclenched. Release. Finally.

"So, you boned Drew?" I asked, and knocked her on the shoulder.

She smiled a little, crossed and uncrossed her arms, and said, "It's really complicated."

"Isn't everything?" I wanted to hug her.

"I guess we'll see...."

"Does he know everything? About Veronica, the prom, everything?"

"I don't know," she said. "But I'm going to tell him if he doesn't."

The girls squealed from the fields, running and laughing. We'd all been kicked off the tennis team.

"What do you think he's going to do?"

"I think that he'll hate me," she said definitively.

"And you're okay with that?" I asked.

"I have to be," she said. "I've gotta get home." She motioned toward her car.

"Okay," I said. "See you at manual labor camp?"

She smirked, got in her car, and drove off. I stood there, watching the girls play lacrosse, running around, ponytails bouncing, a distinct odor of shit from the grass fertilizer wafting over the parking lot. I thought about what Alex said, about the toxicity of secrets and lies and self-absorption. For the last three years, my life had been entirely dedicated to creating the illusion that I was somebody I clearly was just not. And after all that, clearly, it hadn't even worked.

I was still angry—angry at Sam, at Veronica, even at Alex a little now. But I was angry at myself, too, which I guess I hadn't admitted yet. I'd let my anger at myself, my frustration with Sam and Alex, my jealousy of Veronica, and my fear of exposure completely misdirect my emotions, and I got myself here. Everything I did explicitly to prevent all this from happening explicitly led to all this exactly happening. Fuck. It was all my fault.

VERONICA COLLINS

V eronica! It's been ages!"

"I know, Mrs. Finn. How are you?" I asked.

"Frankly, somewhat disappointed in you girls."

I bowed my head but smiled a little, enjoying the sentimental feeling I had being at Mollie's house, talking to her mother, and being made to feel like a child.

"I know, Mrs. Finn," I said. "Is Mollie home?"

"She's not supposed to have friends over right now," she said, when Mollie emerged behind her.

"Mom, she doesn't have to come in. Can I just talk to her quickly on the porch? Please? It's about school."

Mrs. Finn looked at Mollie and rolled her eyes. "Okay, quickly!" she said. "You're still in trouble!" She scooted Mollie along with a hand on her back. "Veronica, can I get you something to drink, sweetheart?"

I smiled. "No, thank you," I said. "I promise, this will only take a minute."

Mollie nudged me outside, and the two of us sat on the steps to her front porch. We sat side by side and looked out onto her yard where our whole childhood, sleepovers in tents, snowmen,

Slip 'N Slides, played out like a movie in front of us. Her porch wrapped around her house, and as kids we'd run around it like banshees and swing on her porch swing, paint Easter eggs, and watch thunderstorms. Mollie's house was the best.

"I'm glad you came over," she said. I just looked down at her little legs knocking into each other. She was so small; I wanted to take her under my arm and hold her on my lap like a little baby. She was so mean, and her presence and domain so large—it had been a while since I'd sat this close to her and remembered that really, she was a very little person.

"I just want to talk," I said. "I want to understand. Was it just the Sam thing? Was it always Sam? Because..."

"It wasn't just the Sam thing," she said. "The Sam thing just gave me an excuse."

I was quiet for a minute. "Why do you hate me, Mollie? Because I thought about it a lot, and I think the only reason that I ever even hooked up with Sam in the first place was because I was pretty sure that you hated me anyway...."

She sighed and twirled a piece of hair around her finger.

"You just made me so mad," she said. "You're so pretty. You eat whatever you want. Boys love you. Girls love you. You're always having a good time. You never worry about anything. Sam always had this thing with you, and it made me crazy. It wasn't fair. I admit it. It wasn't even about you; it was about me and my bullshit. Apparently, everything has been—"

"So you roofied me? Your bullshit led you to drug me?"

"I guess so," she said. "And the Alex thing. The Alex thing pushed me over the edge."

I scooted over and looked at her. "What Alex thing? What did Alex have to do with it?"

She rolled her eyes and looked at me like I was a moron. "Come on! Like you didn't know that it killed her to see you going out with Drew?"

"It was her idea!" I said.

"Veronica...come on. She's been in love with him forever. How could you have done that to her?"

I leaned back on my elbows and looked out over Mollie's front yard. It was warm, hot almost. Like summer was really just around the corner, like we'd officially made it back through to the other side.

"I really didn't know," I said. And I meant it. Alex had said she wanted us to go out. I would never even have thought about Drew if she hadn't mentioned it. If Alex had told me to stay away, I would have. Why would she have told me to go out with him? Why didn't people just *say* what they *meant*?

"Well," she said. "Now you know."

I could have stopped there, but as long as Mollie was having such an honest moment, I was going to take advantage of it. We might never be able to talk like this again. I felt like we were sitting in some alternate universe, where we actually spoke real words and told real truths to each other, and that the portal to the next dimension would close any minute and we'd go back to doublespeak, secret code, and roofie-ing each other, so I better ask questions now while her answers might still be in English.

"So, at that party freshman year...Sam really did like me?"

"Oh, get over it!" she said. "Yes, he did. But look at it this way, you lucked out. He could have been your problem all these years...."

"So, you really did tell people I had chlamydia!"

"You did!"

We both laughed. "It was a yeast infection!"

"Sure," she said. She put her hair up in a ponytail. "So, what're you gonna do now?"

"Break up with Drew," I said. "Start clean."

She just nodded, and had a satisfied look about her. "I should probably go back inside. My mom's probably got a stopwatch."

"So, now what?" I asked. "Are we friends? Were we ever?"

"Sure, we were," she said. "Now? I don't know. Would you even want to be friends with a maniac like me?"

"I probably shouldn't," I said. "You're a pretty evil bitch, now that I really think about it."

"I know," she said. "But I'm gonna try to work on it. You're a good person, V. I really am sorry."

"Okay," I said, and I got up and stretched out my back. "I appreciate hearing that. And I'm sorry I slept with Sam. Not cool."

"Yeah, but I'm still really glad you didn't get raped by Mr. Boardman," she said as she headed back inside.

"Gee, me too!" I replied. She smiled a small but sincere smile and closed the door.

I WAITED A FEW days before talking to Drew. I needed to process how I felt, physically feel better, and really think about what I was going to say to him before I said anything, which was sort of a new thing for me. Because Drew was a good guy. In all of this, between me, Mollie, and Alex, he was probably the most innocent and oblivious. He meant well, and I needed him to understand that nothing anyone had done in all of this really had anything to do with him at all, which was probably slightly emasculating and offensive.

I drove to his house and asked him to come for a ride with me. We never went for drives. It was his and Alex's thing, but it felt appropriate. We were pretty silent in the car. I wasn't sure exactly where I was going to start or how I was going to phrase what I needed to say. I pulled into a park and suggested we sit on a bench.

"Weird," he said. "I've never been to this park."

"I have," I said. I had with Jon Glick, freshman year. We shotgunned beers, and I gave him a blow job right on the very bench we were sitting on.

Drew cracked his knuckles and looked forward out onto the meadow, where there were girls sunning on blankets and groups sitting around with beers and guitars.

"So, you fucked Sam," he said, with a crick of his neck.

"So, you fucked Alex," I said, with a swivel of mine.

His pool-blue eyes swelled and widened. He hadn't expected me to say that.

"She told you?" he asked.

"Not exactly," I said.

"I'm sorry, Veronica..." He trailed off. "It was right after my dad..."

"Drew, honestly, you don't need to explain."

"I don't?" He looked out at the girls tanning, then at my legs and feet. I tried to bend around to catch his eye, but I couldn't.

"We were never really supposed to be together," I said. "You're a great guy, but let's face it...you were never my guy."

"I really wanted to be," he said.

"That's nice to hear," I said.

"I was so mad at you that night," he said. "When I found out about Sam, and when I saw you so drunk."

"Right, well...the drunk thing wasn't exactly my fault," I said.

"Whose fault was it?"

"Alex didn't tell you? They drugged me." It was funny how that just rolled off my tongue now, like it was already becoming a funny story or wacky shenanigan from our youth. My crazy friends and that time they slipped me a mickey...

"They what?!" His eyes pulsed.

"They found out about the Sam thing and decided to exact revenge by roofie-ing me at the prom and having me pass out and publicly humiliate myself."

He rubbed his temples. "Are you joking? They drugged you? And then you almost were legitimately assaulted by your teacher?"

I hadn't really even put it in that exact an equation yet. "Yeah, I guess so. But it's not like they planned that part, and whether he intended molestation is still up for debate."

"Do you have any idea how fucked up that is?"

"I suppose I do," I said. But then it all played out, Sam, the threesome, the fact that I was dating Drew, Alex and Fernando, it all began to roll out in front of me, and I was beginning to understand how it all worked. "But no more fucked up than anything else that we've done to each other this year," I said. "A tangled web we've weaved…" I didn't really know what that meant, but I'd heard it said and it seemed appropriate.

"I can't believe Alex would do something like that… intentionally hurt someone like that. Mollie maybe, but not Alex…"

"People do crazy things for love," I said.

He finally looked up, smiled a little, and put his arm around me. He laid his head on my shoulder, and I felt almost a motherly affection toward him.

"You'll always be my first," he said.

"I'm honored," I replied.

We got up and went back to the car and rode home in complete silence. I dropped him back at his house and kissed him good-bye. He asked if I wanted to come in and hang out, just as friends, watch a movie or play a video game or something, but I said no, because for the first time in my whole life I realized that I just wanted to be alone.

ALEXANDRA HOLBROOK

More than a week had passed since the prom, and I still hadn't gathered the nerve to talk to Drew. I did talk to Fernando. I told him that I needed space and that I thought we should just be friends. He didn't seem too broken up about it. I told him that I still wanted to play in the band, and that I hoped things wouldn't be weird. He just laughed and asked, Why would they be? And I realized that they wouldn't, because in the end, neither one of us ever really cared about the other one like that anyway.... Only when real feelings are involved do things get weird. Like how they were with Drew. *Weird* wasn't even a strong enough word to describe what was going on between the two of us, or even what was going on between me and Mollie or me and Veronica. It was like everything that had lived under the surface and allowed us to be friends had been blasted onto a 3-D HD screen, and now we didn't know how to relate to one another anymore. Honesty. The ultimate destroyer of comfort. Everything was out on the table now, and I didn't know if that would ultimately lead to us all being closer or us all never being able to look one another in the eye or trust one another again. All I knew was that the floodgates had been opened, and everything had to bleed out before we could close them again. I had to talk to Drew, but I was still grounded.

Mr. Boardman was back in school. I couldn't look him in the eye, either. I just kept seeing that caught expression on his face when we found him in the laundry room. I couldn't believe he had the balls to continue teaching us, and I wondered if he really thought that any of us bought his story. I wondered if Veronica was the first, or if there were other girls at Harwin or other schools he'd taken advantage of, and I thought about how horrible a man he really was, and who else in our lives that we saw every day, and trusted with things, were capable of such ultimate betrayal and sickness. I was mad at everyone. Disgusted with humanity. I didn't know how to get back to feeling like a worthwhile human being again, or believing that any human wasn't a lying, evil sociopath.

So I decided to start with myself. If I could become someone I respected again, maybe there were other people out there like me.

About ten days after the prom, Drew's Pathfinder was waiting for me in my driveway. My heart jumped into my throat, and the pressure mounted between my eyes. I walked up to his window like I was walking the plank. Drew and I hadn't gone this long without talking since we were eight years old. It's like ten days had set us back eight years.

"Hey," I said.

"Hey," he replied. "Can you go for a drive?"

"Probably not. Warden will be home any minute."

"Can you just get in the car?"

I looked up at my house, and it looked like the lights were out. Josh's car was in the driveway, but he wouldn't sell me out. "Okay, just for a minute."

I hopped up into his car and was immersed in that same familiar smell of pot and Polo Sport that had once made my heart flutter and my soul melt. I avoided eye contact and vacillated back and forth about what I was going to say, how this was going to go. He looked incredibly serious, his hands firmly planted on the wheel at ten and two. Ice-blue eyes locked on the horizon.

"So, Veronica and I ended things," he said, "obviously."

"Oh," I said. "I guess I didn't realize that was that obvious."

"But she told me what happened that night. Not that it changes what she did with Sam, but she told me what you guys did to her."

"It was Mollie's idea...." I knew that was the wrong thing to say. That that was a statement in the opposite direction of the mature, moral cleansing that I'd planned on embarking upon.

"Please, Alex." Again, my name sounded so foreign in Drew's mouth.

I sat in silence with my head down, ready to take my berating like a woman.

"I think I just need a break from all you girls...," he started.

"What?" I said. "Even me?"

"Especially you," he said. "I don't even know you! You drugged your friend? Who are you? Who does that?"

"It was just supposed to be a joke! Drew, I know things got messed up, but—"

He cut me off before I could finish. "Well, it's not funny. None of this is funny. You guys are all insane, and I really just don't want to be involved anymore." His eyes stayed planted on the horizon over the steering wheel. I tried to catch his eye, get him to look at me, fall into the comfort he used to find there, but I couldn't.

"Drew..." A tear rolled down my cheek, and I felt gut-punched. I slapped my hands on my thighs, then hid my wet, blotchy face in them. The bleeding had begun.

"Things got complicated with us, and I think it's best for everyone if we all just take a break...."

I didn't know what to say. It's not like I could defend myself or talk him into wanting to be my friend. Or more than that. "Is that what you came here to say?" I asked.

"Yes," he said.

"Okay." And I opened the door to his car. "I just want you to know..." I knew I should stop myself, but I couldn't. I was in full purge mode, and I couldn't leave anything unsaid. "I really do love you. I always have. I still do. And I'm sorry."

"Me too, Holbrook," he said, and ran his hands over his head, as he often did. "And I probably always will. But everything is just too fucked up."

"Okay," I said. And I turned to grab the door handle.

"Wait," he said, and he grabbed my arm.

I looked at him, and he at me, for the first time in the course of this conversation. I had that same feeling I did the day of his father's funeral, of wanting to run away, but forcing my eyes to stay on his, because I knew if I locked them there long enough they'd settle, calm down, feel at home there, and fall into his the way I'd seen his fall into mine. He put his hand on the back of my neck, pulled my face in, and kissed me, just a soft press of his lips on mine. He pulled away and said, "Bye."

MOLLIE, VERONICA, AND I all had to report to Harwin for community service at eight AM. It was a Saturday, the day all the girls and Crawford guys were supposed to go to Six Flags. Last year, Veronica had given Austin Markel a hand job on the back of the bus on that trip; it had been the talk of the Harwin halls for weeks.

Our first assignment was to clean up the lower school playground. We each had a bucket, a sponge, and a giant trash bag and were told to get to work. It was a gray day, but warm and a little muggy. Veronica's hair was frizzing, and Mollie had hers back in a bandanna. Veronica avoided eye contact with both of us, and we all dispersed to separate corners of the playground when Cottswald told us to get scrubbing. I went to the swings, Mollie to the sandbox, and Veronica to the seesaw.

I started scrubbing, making a game for myself of picking off the rust, and wished that we had music and that this wasn't actually what we had to do, but that we were in some sort of cleanup montage and we were sprucing up the park for the big fund-raiser that we were putting on to raise money to get to the finals in LA for the big sing-off that no one thought we'd win, but that we totally would with some trick number at the last minute. But there was no music. No sing-off. Just birds chirping, cars zipping by, and the awkward silence that festers between three girls who used to be best friends, but didn't know how to be anymore.

All of a sudden, I felt something hit me in the back of the knee. I looked behind me, and Mollie was smirking. I looked down to find the headless Barbie doll that had hit my leg. I picked it up and threw it back at her. She put it in her bucket upside down, split the doll's legs open, and placed the bucket in the middle of the sandbox. She took a Ken doll and bent him over so that his face was planted in headless Barbie's crotch. I started to laugh.

I picked up a tennis ball and threw it at Veronica by the see-saw. It hit her in the back of the head.

"What the hell?" she said.

Both Mollie and I fell over laughing as she rubbed her head. She threw a soapy sponge at Mollie and missed. Mollie ran to pick it up, and then squeezed it over Veronica's head.

"You whore!" she yelled, and Mollie laughed and threw the sponge at me.

I grabbed my bucket and tossed the whole thing on Mollie, who was then fully soaked from neck to knees.

"Oh my god!" she said. "I can't believe you just did that!"

"Don't mess with me," I said, and then sat down on the see-saw as she wrung her shirt out.

"You guys, my hair smells like dishwater," Veronica said.

"An improvement from booze and jizz?" Mollie retorted, and we all lost it.

"Too soon!" Veronica yelled back, and she hopped on the

other end of my seesaw. Instinctively, we began bopping up and down.

"What the fuck, guys," Mollie said. "I wanna saw!" and she sat in the middle and swayed back and forth as we bopped up and down.

"Girls!" Headmistress Cottswald yelled from over the hill. "What are you doing? No seesawing! Cleaning!"

We all got off and went back to our corners, fighting the smiles breaking through our cheeks.

Mollie took the porno Barbie bucket from the sandbox and put it smack in the middle of the teachers' bench.

I swallowed my gum I laughed so hard.

ACKNOWLEDGMENTS

Many, many people played a part in the inception, formation, and publication of this book. First, I'd like to thank my parents, brother, and grandfather for being my biggest supporters and cheerleaders, as well as for being better publicists than money could ever buy. Thank you, Maggie, Laura, and Liz, for being my best friends, the coolest and smartest girls I know, and for entertaining me, challenging me, and providing me with enough material over the course of the last twenty-five years to fill up this book. I'd like to thank everyone at the University of San Francisco Masters of Fine Arts program for providing me with a safe and productive creative environment, and for giving me the motivation and support to write the best story I could. In particular, I'd like to thank Lewis Buzbee, Nina Schuyler, and Karl Soehnlein for the appropriate balance of encouragement and critique I needed to build the foundation of this novel. Thank you to Brian Gilton and Nino Urisote for being my friends, readers, therapists, teachers, sounding boards, and drinking buddies. Thank you for getting me through the blocks, the doubts, and the performance anxiety, and for conceiving some of the best parts of this book. I truly could not have done it without you two, and you continue to keep me moving, writing, and believing that other people think I'm funny and care what I have to say. Thank you to my editor, Farrin Jacobs, and my agent, Kirby Kim, for taking a risk and allowing me to tell the story I wanted to tell, the way I wanted to tell it, and standing behind it and me, when many would not. Thank you for making my dream a reality.

And last, but really most of all, I'd like to thank Josh Mohr. Thank you, Josh, for being the first person to take this seriously as a book and me seriously as a writer. Thank you for being my friend, my mentor, my inspiration, and my barometer of sanity and perspective. Thank you for every genius piece of advice that you've given me; for deep talks in Dolores Park; for telling me to kill Rachel; for understanding my characters; for understanding me; for having a sense of humor; for being the best, coolest, most talented, and kindest guy I know. This book would truly not exist without you; I would probably not have finished it without you. Thank you for taking me under your wing. Thank you for being the prolific adviser, the wealth of knowledge, and the exceptional soul that you are. Thank you for being you, and also, thanks for being really, really good-looking—that really helps.